SCALPEL'S PLUNGE

[illegible]
A pleasure to
see you
Hope you
enjoy the book!!
Best
[illegible]

SCALPEL'S PLUNGE

END OF THE PARTY

RICHARD A. BROWN, M.D.

This book is a work of fiction. The names, places, organizations, and incidents herein are either the author's creations or are used fictitiously. Any other resemblance to actual persons, living or dead, or to actual events is entirely coincidental.

www.scalpelscut.com

Published by Sharp Knife Publishing

Cataloguing-in-Publication Data is on file with the Library of Congress
TXu 2-258-168
U.S. Trademark SN 88871790
ISBN 978-1-7341394-0-2

Cover design by Emily Mahon
Cover photos: Shutterstock

Printed in the United States of America

SCALPEL'S PLUNGE

PART I

THE TRUTH

PRESENT DAY—BOSTON, MASSACHUSETTS

I LAY QUIETLY in my narrow, state-approved bed, unable to focus. Maybe it was the drugs they were endlessly feeding me. I remained awake, groggy, my reality too harsh to allow sleep. The door opened and in walked the nurse, cradling still more medications he intended to force down my throat.

"Dr. Brio, take these. Do it, or you can forget getting out of here."

I remained motionless, contemplating my next move. His pockmarked, wicked face drew close to mine. He whispered malevolently, "Take them now!" The straps on my wrists prevented me from strangling the man.

I was frazzled. What the *hell* am I doing on a psych ward?? Why don't they believe me? They told me there was no such thing as the Cooperative. How could they deny the undeniable? The Cooperative *had* stolen tens of millions of insurance dollars, murdering anyone who got in the way. Petra, their leader, *had* sent assassins to shoot me. Together, Leila, Harvard medical students Tess and Axel, and I *had* taken the Cooperative down. These facts were indisputable! Yet they told me it was all just an elaborate delusion. They wanted me to believe I was completely out of my mind. I closed my eyes, hoping it would all magically go away.

When I opened them again, I expected to see the sadistic sneer of the nurse. Instead, it was Petra who stood glaring at me. She started to laugh, an awful, terrifying cackle.

I shouted, "How did you survive?" The knife in her hand began to move toward my chest. Then the Dark Angel's face blurred, and the room began to spin. I struggled to leave but couldn't. My legs felt like they were shackled in irons. The panic was overwhelming; my despair absolute. Could this really be happening?

GRAND CAYMAN SURPRISE

EARLIER, GRAND CAYMAN ISLANDS

A BOLT OF LIGHTNING signaled the beginning of a Caribbean squall. Rain pummeled the sand and water. I was mesmerized by the majestic sea turtle I was following oblivious to the happenings above. Leila circled behind me and grabbed my fin to get my attention. She signaled that it was time to go. Reluctantly I followed. The water created such a beautiful, serene world.

Juggling our gear, we made our way out of the surf and onto the sand, aiming for a nearby lean-to. Fresh raindrops washed the salt off our skin. Dramatic claps of thunder punctuated the air. We cuddled together, watching the violent ocean theater as the heavens continued to empty. Being away from Boston for this vacation felt almost like escaping from prison. I was completely content. Even in the tumult of a storm, Cemetery Pointe on Grand Cayman Island was the place to be.

PEERING THROUGH A SET of small binoculars a hundred yards away, another set of eyes took in the scene. Sporting a floral-patterned tropical shirt over his huge torso, Rick observed the couple with great interest. They were like so many others he saw near his beach house. Joyous, in love. But there was one difference. He knew this man—the Swedish doctor, Eric "VJ" Brio. Brio had brought down the Cooperative, the hospital-based crime syndicate Rick had run with Petra at MRMC—Massachusetts Regional Medical Center.

It was ironic that Brio was here now, literally in his backyard. There was no way the man's surprise appearance was anything but a coincidence. If Rick had been so inclined, he could snuff out Brio's life in an instant. But it wasn't necessary. Not a stranger to violence, Rick still preferred negotiation as long as he had the tactical advantage. Though he had had broken every law that could be broken in the billing and collections side of medicine, he did not share Petra's impetuous, homicidal personality. He had not been a party to the "disappearances" of malcontents. Ultimately, that's why Petra had failed and he had survived.

Business, both illicit and legitimate, was thriving. Cuba was an added financial bonanza for his enterprises. Rick harbored no ill will. Brio had done what he had to do to survive. He didn't recognize the toned, radiant woman with him but assumed it was Brio's new wife, Leila. Rick had done his research. She had been the mole in the medical intensive care unit at MRMC, identifying patients the Cooperative had targeted for its scam. She was no innocent. That her long, curly black hair and skin color were so similar to Petra's struck him as somehow funny. She was every bit as dazzling, and likely every bit as dangerous. Brio clearly was drawn to a certain type of woman.

Rick did not see the third member of the Brio troika, Tess. She was no doubt back in Cambridge, continuing her medical studies at Harvard. Apparently, she had inherited both of her parents' smarts while seemingly avoiding her mother's sociopathic personality. Rick had only recently discovered, like everyone else, that Petra was Tess's birth mother, and Brio her father. Neither he nor Petra had anticipated the damage Brio, Leila, and Tess would inflict on the Cooperative. This peculiar family group reminded him of the German submarines hunting in wolf packs during World War Two—stealthy and lethal.

The question now was what to do, given that Brio and Leila were here. What if he were seen? How long would it take for them to alert the police? That would be messy. Rick decided to take a beach stroll. The rain had abated, and although thick with humidity, the air had that perfect fresh smell.

LEILA KEPT HER EYES CLOSED while I sat up to survey the landscape. An extremely large, surprisingly familiar man drifted into my view. Familiar in the way that the skeleton with a black cape and scythe is familiar. Not happy familiar. My adrenaline surged. I knew Rick had escaped, but until that moment I'd had no idea where. The irony was overwhelming. My first instinct was to run, but I stayed, knowing I had to protect Leila.

Rick held up both hands to show he meant no harm and said, "Nature's work is amazing, isn't it?" Leila's eyes were now open and trained on his face. Rick gestured to her. "You must be Leila. A pleasure to finally meet you. The work you did in the ICU was very impressive." She remained silent, but nodded.

I disregarded his overture to my wife. "Yes, nature is absolutely spectacular. Unpredictable in its fury—like people. What can I do for you, Rick?"

His body language and voice conveyed only a businesslike calm, but his hulking presence was intimidating. "Oh, my name here is Daniel, but since we already know each other so well, let's keep it at Rick. I like my real name better anyway." His voice was measured, self-assured.

"Once I left Boston for this paradise, I thought a couple of other changes would be a good idea." He gestured toward the large house at Cemetery Pointe. "That's my place. I've grown to love it."

After a moment's pause, he continued, "It's funny, I'm glad you came to visit me. I've wanted to talk to you for a long time. You may not believe me, but Petra was responsible for everything that happened to you and your friend Nick. Pity about his fingers, but I know you successfully reattached all four of them. Lucky for him you're a pretty decent surgeon. I think you understand this: If it was me who wanted you dead, this conversation wouldn't be happening."

I gripped Leila's hand. There was no obvious escape route. True, Petra was the one who'd shot me. She'd also admitted that she had ordered the hit on me. Still, those facts hardly exonerated Rick. He was her partner in crime, plain and simple, and a menacing one at that.

"No one's going to hurt you or this lovely lady as long as we reach an understanding," Rick continued. "For years the Russians and the U.S. government maintained the principle of mutually assured destruction. That understanding worked. I think we can agree on something similar. I still have a lot of friends in your town and all over the country. You're easy to reach. Same problem for me. You could tell any number of people I'm here. Checkmate, either way." The words, though dark and certainly threatening, seemed appropriate and the analysis shrewd. I felt only slightly less anxious.

"You're a reasonable person, Brio. And from what I've heard, Leila, you are too. You might think that I should go to jail for bilking those insurance assholes out of all that money. You're right, I probably should. I just don't want to. Take my advice; forget our past. Make sure Tess does the same. Do you think you all can do that?"

After a long pause, letting his words sink in, he added, "I want you to be able to come here and enjoy this splendid island any time you want. I don't think we'll be friends, but I believe you're intriguing people. From a business perspective, I'd like to know how you pulled everything off. It would be nice to avoid those mistakes in the future. I'd also like to hear how you neutralized those two hitters in Sierra Lakes. Petra went berserk when that plan went south."

His assurances had the intended effect. I thought about the implications of everything on the table. "Rick, I may be completely insane, but I believe you. I don't doubt for a second that you could have us eliminated. That's not the best feeling I've ever experienced, but somehow it gives me confidence in you. As curious as you seem to be about us, we also have a number of unanswered questions about you and Petra. At some point, maybe we'll talk about it over a drink. But not *this* trip."

Rick stuck out an enormous paw, which after a moment of reflection I decided to take in my grasp. We shook awkwardly, his powerful grip sending a curdle of dread down my spine. "Deal," I said.

He started to walk away, but suddenly swung around, holding something small in his hand. "Here, VJ. Take this card. It has my cell number on it. You can reach me anytime. I'm looking forward to getting that drink. See you when I see you." He turned his head toward Leila, gave her a wink, and left.

Both of us watched Rick trudge up the beach on the way back to his fortress. I turned and looked straight in my wife's magnificent eyes. "Well?"

Leila nestled her arm around my waist, saying, "I don't think we're going to find the answer to this situation in one of our medical journals. He knows we'll keep our guard up. He's right, though; we're still a threat to him as long as we're breathing. Yet here we are, still breathing. That's something."

I fingered the card in my hand, wondering if I'd ever use the number written in bold red letters. I was hoping I'd never need it.

KANZULINZULI

NORTH KIMU PROVINCE, DEMOCRATIC REPUBLIC OF THE CONGO

AN OCEAN AWAY, an awful killer was on the rampage again, one that was all too familiar to the people of the Democratic Republic of Congo, or DRC. The baseline poverty and violence in this ethnically diverse region were bad enough, but this latest outbreak of Ebola was devastating. The Tutsis and Banyamulenges, frequently persecuted groups, were being scapegoated again. Attacks against both were on the rise.

Despite the country's rich natural resources, the DRC's medical system was seriously challenged, even before Ebola struck. The majority of people could neither afford nor access care, and frequently gravitated toward herbal or spiritual healing as a substitute for no care at all. Radio news, the primary source of information for almost everyone, was dominated with pleas to adhere to safeguards. But most people still chose to ignore the public health directives. Like many other places in the world, science was eschewed for magic. Ebola marched on.

The medical tent stood on the outskirts of town by a stand of imported eucalyptus trees. Nearby, peddlers of fruits and vegetables, sitting under an array of brightly colored umbrellas, hawked their prized foods. A group of Roman Catholic nuns walked hurriedly on their way to Mass. Small cars going nowhere slowly clogged the adjacent dirt road, pushed away by a large, light-blue flatbed truck filled with rebel troops. Likely they were members of the Allied Democratic Front, which was anything but democratic. Given the plethora of rebel groups in the country, they could have easily represented a different self-interested militia.

The country's oppressed, embattled citizens were caught in the middle—entirely dissatisfied with the government leaders in Kinshasa, but equally weary of the almost daily bloodshed. Multiple factions were in conflict. The only constant was that these battles, large and small, never really benefitted the inhabitants. Just maintaining was a challenge for even the hardiest people. Life expectancy stood somewhere between horrible and abysmal. Within this context, huge efforts were still being made to save those who could be saved.

Inside the tent, a tall, wiry physician with strong, calloused hands uncharacteristic of his profession donned blue gloves, a yellow plastic suit, white head and shoulder coverings, and a thick rubber apron. He was battle ready. The nurse led him to the ward. The patients in the ward had volunteered for the study that would pay them handsomely if they survived, or their families if they did not. None of these men and women had received the vaccine they'd previously been offered on the outside. Fear was a powerful deterrent, distrust trumping opportunity.

Now each of them had contracted the killer virus. The medicine provided in this tent represented a rare second chance at survival. Many previous volunteers had arrived sick, then returned to their homes cured. The growing presence of these study patients in the community sent a strong positive message.

Unfortunately for the current treatment group, altruism was not this particular physician's chief priority. Vials from a special box marked "Yonaker-Wood Pharmaceuticals Ebola Study Drug X-1975645" were pulled. The doctor moved from patient to patient, administering the medication that each hoped would save their lives. A select group received an additional, separate medication.

South African infectious disease specialist Harrison Sherako arrived just as the man completed his task. Sherako, a ruggedly handsome man with dark curly hair, was originally tasked for neurosurgery, but a ski injury cost him one of his fingers. The world was a better place for his contributions in the domain of bacteriology, virology, and parasitology. Sherako wanted an update on the trial he was running. It would have significant implications for the patients being treated here in the DRC along with those he was managing in South Africa.

Sherako didn't know the doctor who'd administered the meds; he just knew that he was connected with Yonaker-Wood somehow. The layers of outer garb made it impossible to glean anything about his appearance other than that he was quite tall, like Sherako himself, who stood six foot seven. Before Sherako had a chance to introduce himself, the interloper decontaminated and left.

BACK FOR A TIME

BOSTON, MASSACHUSETTS

LEILA AND I RETURNED from Grand Cayman to Boston and the world of MRMC. The Cooperative no longer ruled, but the institution still didn't feel hospitable. A new routine was established. And that's the way things went for months. Life without the drama of being pursued by people trying to kill me had its benefits. The biggest issue was my daughter, Tess, deciding to change the spelling of her last name from Risdall to Ryssdal—the original Norwegian version. Her pain from her adoptive parents' death at the hands of a drunk driver was still very fresh. She'd researched her adoptive father's heritage and decided the name alteration was exactly the right thing to do.

Despite the bliss of a new marriage and a stable work environment, I still couldn't escape certain painful challenges. The electronic medical record system remained my ever-present nemesis.

A patient of mine who also happened to work in Health Information gave me a call one morning. She was one of my few allies in that particular house of horrors.

"Hi, VJ, I just saw a list with your name on it. Apparently, you are about to be fined two thousand dollars for records you haven't signed on the computer. Were you aware of that?"

I was literally speechless. For the first time in my career I had actually been going out of my way to do what I was supposed to do. Finally, words formed. "Are you fucking kidding me? At what point was someone going to tell me about this? Has anyone else there ever heard of this marvelous invention called the telephone? Would that have been the hardest thing to do?"

My spy told me what she'd found out. "VJ, according to the data I'm looking at, you've been getting e-mail notifications once a week. They're being sent to EBrio@duke.edu. Remember, to the Health Information Department, you're just another number. They neither know you nor care about you. Don't take it personally."

I was struggling to maintain composure. "That was my e-mail address twenty-five years ago. I haven't used it since then. How they got it or thought it would reach me defies logic. I'll get this sorted out."

So often I've felt powerless against the nameless, faceless, arbitrary forces that govern our lives—random determinations creating angst and frustration. Not this time. Agitated and resolved, I made the necessary phone call. No e-mail or texting fingerprints could be left behind for this task.

Axel Syndergaard was a brilliant hacker. He had easily found a way into the hospital system once when my life was on the line. I thought he might be willing to help me navigate this small set of rapids. He answered on the first ring.

"Axel, it's VJ. Long time no speak. How's it going?"

"Good, VJ, good. I'm doing my psychiatry rotation. It's really interesting, and I don't have to stay up all night. Works for me." He seemed relaxed, compared to the standard intense baseline of most medical students. "What's up with you?"

I answered directly, "Axel, I'm doing fine, but I've got a little problem that I think you can assist me with . . ."

The next day, my Health Information connection found me on my way to get a coffee. "Hey, VJ, we had a surprise staff meeting this morning. Remember that hit list I told you about yesterday? Somehow every name on it disappeared. The director was miffed. I think he'd already mentally spent that money. Just curious, might you know anything about it?"

I smiled broadly. "No, after last year I decided not to let the trivial things bother me. After all, life is about perspective, isn't it? How's your hand doing? Is the scar sensitivity gone?"

She laughed. "Why, yes, it is [illegible] as you promised it would. Thank you so much! You have a good day, VJ. But you'd better keep up with those records. You might not be so fortunate next time."

I didn't mention that coupled with the spontaneous evaporation of the doctor penalty data, her boss was going to find out in thirty days that he'd donated a month's salary to the local food bank. That would be gloating, plus, as it is said, "Revenge is a dish best served cold." I loved the taste of victory, however small. Unfortunately, my sense of triumph was short-lived. The office was awaiting.

THE NEEDLE PENETRATED the patient's skin as I began the routine injection. The task was one I performed at least ten times a day, but this time an ear-splitting scream reverberated throughout the office. Foolish doctor—I'd failed to close the door before starting. I should have believed the woman when she told me she hated injections and had no pain tolerance. A normal person would learn such an easy lesson after being burned so many times.

Everyone dropped what they were doing to see if an arm or leg was being amputated Civil War style. Sheepishly I looked around while still grasping the offending weapon. "It's okay, everyone, I was giving a trigger-finger shot. Mrs. Palin was just a little startled. My fault, I apologize. Take us back down to DEFCON Two. Please notify the police and tell them not to come. Order is restored."

Rule number one—if a patient tells you something, listen. Rule number two—if what you are contemplating doing will cause pain, listen harder. The road to office hell is paved with inattention.

Terri, my long-time admin, approached me at the end of office hours with a devilish smile. "Mrs. Palin called to say that her finger was already much better. Unfortunately, she forgot to mention to you that her elbow is hurting too. She wants to come in tomorrow."

Without flinching I responded, "That's fine. While you're at it, please schedule the coroner. It'll give him great pleasure to see me slit my own throat."

Terri laughed. "I put her on for eight. Enjoy your afternoon surgery." With that she walked out. Before I left the office to head over to the OR, my cell rang. The clerk from the OR said that my first patient had an unexpected family emergency and had to cancel. It was a long case, so the second patient wasn't expected to arrive for at least forty-five minutes.

I decided to have a relaxed lunch at the new hospital café. While I was working on the gourmet barbecue chicken pizza I'd ordered, an extremely tall, sinewy man wearing a freshly starched white coat approached and asked if he could join me. I recognized his face but had no idea who he was. Our paths had never formally crossed.

"Good afternoon," he said as he stuck out his hand to shake, continuing in heavily accented broken English. "Hi, Vijay. That your name, right? My name Slobodan Marjanovic. Your hand fellow told me I find you here. I hear you have patient with problem infection you want consult for. I here doing research. Working with Myron Tribolsi on Ebola drug trial. He head of Infectious Disease here, so he let me be attending one day per week. What I do you for?"

I studied him between bites. His approach was classically Eastern European—very direct. Adorning his small finger was a distinctive diamond pinky ring with scorpions etched on each side. His hands had characteristic cuts and calluses, and his grip had been quite strong.

"Let me guess," I said. "You're a rock climber."

He smiled. "Very perceptive for orthopaedic surgeon. How you know?"

It was my turn to smile. "Classic build, classic hands. I work part-time in Sierra Lakes, California. Climbers are everywhere. I'm there every six weeks doing my thing. I'll tell you more about that gig another time over a beer. But after I talk to you about my patient, I want to hear about this drug study of yours. I'm sure the people at Doctors Without Borders will be interested too, if your results are good. They'll take any help they can get. This new Ebola breakout in the DRC is awful."

Dr. Marjanovic studied me with probing eyes. "You know much for orthopaedic surgeon. You sure that all you do?"

I could almost see him making a mental note of the DRC comment and wondering how much this Swedish doctor with the odd name knew.

I continued, "The guy I want your team to see has *Mycobacteria marinum*. Sort of a typical case—stabbed himself with a fishing hook about six months ago. The infection has been percolating, and no one recognized what it was until he came into the

ED with a florid tenosynovitis in his hands and wrists. We took him to the OR, washed him out, and debrided his flexor tendons. They were pretty chewed up. I don't know how well he's going to be able to bend his fingers when all this is done. No matter what, though, we have to get rid of this damn *Mycobacteria*. I'm hoping your team can come up with a plan to get him definitively treated. He lives on his boat with a dog and a cooler full of six-packs. Probably not the most reliable guy on the planet."

Slobodan helped himself to the remaining pizza slice on my plate, took a bite, set it down, and laughed. "My new friend, food quite tasty. I order one next time we dine together over that beer. I tell you about my drug then. No worries. I already know about Doctor Without Border in DRC. Just got back. They good people. Too bad can't save everyone. Why your name Vijay? You not look like Indian person to me."

I grinned. "I picked it up during my residency. There aren't that many Swedish Jews. They started calling me the Viking Jew. 'VJ' just stuck."

Slobodan returned the smile. "Now I get it. V then J, not Vijay. Funny name, you funny guy. Administration here also tell me you not to be trusted." With that remark he gave me a knowing wink. "Right now, many things to do. I very tired. Still, I go solve patient's infection problem. I very talented at that. See many thing like this in Russian fisherman when training there."

I was a little taken aback by the entire exchange, but thoroughly entertained. He clapped me hard on the shoulder and started to leave the dining area.

I stopped him with a shout. "Hey, Slobodan. You've got my computer bag." They were not identical, but looked similar enough. I reminded myself for the thousandth time to put something bold like red duct tape on the sides so it would be more distinctive. Slobodan returned, obviously embarrassed. "VJ, I so sorry. I told you I tired."

I shook off the mistake easily. "Slobodan, it's the curse of our business. We're constantly rushing *and* tired."

While still digesting lunch, I thought about his comment from someone in administration that I was not to be trusted. Clearly someone had filled him in on the events of the past. The notoriety was something I didn't like, but couldn't escape. It was obvious that Slobodan had his ear to the ground. Fortunately, the past really wasn't an issue between us. Putting my musings aside, I wandered up to the locker room, changed my scrubs, and visited the pre-op holding area at the Main—the affectionate name for the forty-suite operating room complex at MRMC.

One of the nurses called out, "Hey, is that really VJ? The man himself? Here during daylight hours?"

I just shook my head. "Yeah, it's me. Get used to it. I'm going to be doing my cases here for a while."

Unfortunately, my primary work location, the Ambulatory Surgical Center, was no longer a happy place for me. Once, the ASC had stood as the shining beacon of the hospital. Efficiency at its best. But the professional time wasters had moved in stealthily and wrestled away control. The patient became the last priority, while data entry now ranked first. Two-hundred-and-fifty-page documents for a single outpatient procedure were being demanded and produced. To management, the ideal patient was the one that got cancelled. That way, awesome numbers of perfect computer documents could be generated without actual surgery occurring. The avoidance of legal exposure was a spectacular win for the MRMC risk-management team.

So, in protest, I decided to do all my outpatient cases at the Main. This collection of operating rooms had its own issues. Their dysfunction, however, was too massive to permit a speck like me from altering it. I could do my thing and likely no one would even have an idea I was there at all.

But sometimes, miracles do occur. Four of the most qualified

ASC employees were mistakenly written up for illegal installation and use of a toaster oven in the outpatient lounge. The reality was that an anesthesiologist smuggled in the noncertified offending device in the middle of the night. He was forced to act because the microwave was not doing an adequate job of making his grilled cheese sandwiches. His crime was exposed, but it was too late. Displeased with the environment, the innocents left the ASC and formed the new OR hand team with me at the Main. Alyssa, Hayley, Chloe, and Kelly were *da bomb*. The whole episode reminded me of a quotation from the irrepressible, irascible father of the American nuclear navy, Admiral Hyman Rickover: "More than ambition, more than ability, it is rules that limit contribution; rules are the lowest common denominator of human behavior. They are a substitute for rational thought." In its infinite wisdom, the ASC chased away high-quality, efficient personnel, I was the beneficiary, and now, back on track.

Today there was a problem with my patient's cardiac clearance. This was an actual problem, not a manufactured hospital delay tactic. The man was yelling at the admissions nurse. That's always a bad sign. I decided to be a coward and leave the vicinity while the issue was sorted out. The first case cancelled, and now this.

The depressing news feed on my cell was wearing me out. Democracy was on the ropes again, with direct attacks on voting rights being mounted. Yet another international leader was tacking right. The Swedish national football team had lost. While considering leaving on a slow boat to Antarctica, I took the easier path and tossed my phone into the locker. I opted to find an interesting case to watch while waiting for the cardiac storm to clear. One of my colleagues was doing a dusted proximal phalanx fracture on one of the faculty nephrologists. I found out that the doctor took a spill off a ladder while rooting around for a box of baseball cards he wanted to sell. Bad business decision. I decided to grace his room with my presence.

After watching for a few minutes, I couldn't contain my need to bestow orthopaedic wisdom. "What do you think about using the 1.3 locking plate instead of the 1.5? It's lower profile, and it's strong enough. The extensor tendon will glide better if you put it on the radial side instead of dorsally."

My friend did not look up from the OR table. It was obvious to everyone but me that he was already extraordinarily frustrated. "VJ, go fuck yourself with a swastika-tattooed circus clown on a trapeze. This plate is fine, and where I have it is fine." I took that suggestion as my cue to leave. Sometimes I am extremely intuitive. People admire that about me.

I returned to the pre-op area to find out if my belligerent patient was ready yet. Apparently, the cardiac issue was resolved. But I did encounter something unexpected. Tess was sitting there, casually talking to the gentleman. I interrupted the pleasant conversation. "Well, Ms. Ryssdal, nice to see you here. What do you think I should do? A fusion or a joint replacement?"

She rolled her eyes in a way that only I could see. "Dr. Brio, that depends on what this fine man plans to do. My understanding is that he enjoys woodwork. Since it's his index finger, I think from a stability standpoint it would be better if you fuse the joint."

I nodded in agreement. "Thoughtful and correct. I think that *is* what I'll do." Winking, I added, "When I see your father, I'll tell him that you are preparing well for your cases."

Tess's surgery rotation had brought her to us. She'd mentioned what she was doing, but I didn't realize she'd be there on my day. It was pure coincidence. Once I got over the surprise of having her in my OR workspace, I fell back into normal teaching mode.

"So, Ms. Ryssdal. What can you tell me about the anatomy of the extensor tendon to the index finger?" She started to recite what I'd taught her. Quite precisely, I might add.

Sadly, her answer was interrupted by a phone call into the

room from the Emergency Department. Apparently, they'd tried my cell multiple times. Given the fact that the bloody thing was ensconced in my locker, their attempts had been unsuccessful. A short-lived triumph. They tracked me down in my Main OR hiding place—resourceful bastards.

I was scrubbed, so everything was being relayed through Alyssa, the circulating nurse. "VJ, they say they have a three-digit replant on one of the hospital construction guys. Special request from administration for you to do it."

My blood pressure rose. I struggled to maintain decorum, since Tess was in the room. I wasn't entirely successful. "Are you kidding me? Can't Doctor-Not-Me do it?"

Alyssa shook her head. "She says *only you*."

I was dying inside, overwhelmed with replant anxiety. I handed the needle driver to the resident and said, "Just close the extensor; I need to talk to the ED doc." Practically snatching the phone out of Alyssa's hand, I pleaded, "Can you tell the man that I'm tied up and just can't do the case—please?"

I was surprised to hear a Cantonese-accented response. "Gotcha, VJ. Two can play this game." There was a perfectly wicked laugh, then the line went dead.

It was Chi, my gifted former hand fellow. She had exacted revenge for the prank call I'd engineered when she worked with me. I'd had one of my surgery friends phone the room and suggest that she was implicated in a medical equipment-smuggling scheme. Her own ruse was 100 percent successful. She had me thoroughly convinced that I was doomed to a night of extreme pain. I loved her for it. Talented, scheming, and sly—a dangerous combination. The decision to keep her on as an attending was a good one. But now that the ice was broken, no one was safe.

After I recovered from my panic attack, I felt like I had just won the lottery. In my state of euphoria, I said, "Drinks for everyone when we're done, unofficially of course. I'll deny covering the bill if asked. Where do you all want to go?" The consensus was a raucous new place on Charles Street.

Alyssa interjected, "You're buying food too. You still owe us for that stunt you pulled last year. You know, the part where it looked like we killed you? The cases of wine were nice, but frankly, just a down payment on your debt to us. By the way, VJ, before we go you should probably do a wardrobe adjustment." Apparently, my leopard-print boxers were on display, more than peeking out the back of my scrub pants. During a previous case I'd told the team about Leila's birthday gift. I had a whole variety of underwear prints ranging from space aliens to pink flamingos to dancing red llamas.

Tess couldn't resist the opportunity for a dig. "She's right, Dr. Brio, you really should try to look more professional around staff and students. I might have to file a claim against you for creating a hostile working environment." I chose not to respond.

When we finally did finish hours later, the crew made its merry way to Hackford-Regan's. We walked in together. Two drinks and a plate of hot wings later, I scanned the crowd for any patients of mine. Life in the bubble can be awkward that way. I watched as the lithe young server with short curly brown hair moved effortlessly through her patrons. She had the grace of a dancer as she meted out the alcohol and food. She could have been a model or really anything she wanted. She was that stunning. The young woman approached a patron in a sharp black suit.

The well-appointed late-twenties man flashed a brilliant smile. He whispered something in her ear. There was a conspiratorial nature to the moment. She responded with a big grin of her own and playfully pinched his waist. I often engaged in the game of trying to divine what unrelated people were discussing. For this pair, I imagined a late-night rendezvous at a smoky jazz club.

Another, louder man vied for her attention. It was none other than my new acquaintance, Slobodan. His interface was much briefer. He restarted what seemed to be a spirited conversation with a person I didn't recognize. She was an attractive mid-forties woman with a serious corporate executive look. Her blond hair was pulled back tightly, her clothing impeccable. She appeared completely out of place in this establishment. As I wandered over to greet him, Slobodan caught sight of me and shifted gears.

"Hi, VJ, we meet again so soon. I not expect see you here. VJ, I introduce my associate, Mikalyn de Grom. She donate lot of money to research. She also know owner this place. Say it a lot of fun." As he winked and took a long pull on his beer, he said, "I here strictly on hospital business."

I noticed her giving him a puzzled look, but she said nothing. Slobodan went on. "VJ, I been thinking about you all day. We fix your *Mycobacterium* patient. I look up Eastern Sierra. Many say one of best place for rock climbing in United State. I have meeting in San Francisco soon. Maybe we connect?"

"Of course," I said, not quite sure what to make of his comments. Just as I was about to leave their table, de Grom spoke up. In a distinctive South African accent she said, "So Dr. VJ, I understand you are a hand surgeon with a special set of skills. One day, perhaps, you can guide me through the parts of the hospital we normal people don't get to see."

Now I was really perplexed. What special skills? I just answered positively, "Sounds like a plan."

The man in the black suit from the other table approached. He too spoke in a clipped, cultured South African accent. "Ms. de Grom. I have to take care of that issue we discussed. I will see you in the morning." He turned on a dime and left.

After more brief pleasantries, I retreated back to the surgery group. I walked into a conversation about ridiculous things that happen in the Emergency Department. Hayley, a former ED nurse, was speaking. "This guy from Waltham comes in with his girlfriend. She's seizing. We ask how long it's been going on.

He says since the night before. We ask him why he waited so long. He says, 'We were having sex and I thought her comer was stuck.'"

Tess, devouring sushi, reacted incredulously. "Yet again, I am reminded that in Boston, ignorance and stupidity have no limit."

I chimed in, "Daughter, I am afraid that paradigm is true everywhere. By the way, what you're eating looks like some of the muscle Dr. Shoemaker debrided from the forearm shotgun blast yesterday."

Tess was not amused. "VJ, every day you say something that makes me wish I wasn't related to you. Remember, there are people in the world who don't necessarily share all of your opinions—shocking as that might be."

I feigned being wounded. "Easy, killer, you love me and you know it.

She changed the subject. "Who were those people you were talking with?"

I glanced back at the pair. "He's a new ID attending—Slobodan Marjanovic. We just met today. He seems like a character, also very sharp. We might go rock climbing together in Sierra Lakes the next time I have to work there. The woman is some big-shot donor. I definitely had no interest in talking to her."

Tess, stuck on the middle part of what I said, practically choked. "You—rock climb? You're terrified of heights!"

With a smile I said, "Go ahead. Make fun of me. I've been working on that problem. I'm in the midst of becoming the new, improved VJ."

Tess looked unconvinced. "Believe it when I see it."

WATCHING VJ across the room, de Grom said, "He doesn't know anything about us—right?"

Slobodan answered, "No, he know nothing. I keep eye on him, though. He smart guy."

De Grom remarked dryly, "I was thinking the same thing. What is it people say? 'Keep your friends close and your enemies closer.' He intrigues me. But I still have no intention of being deported or going to jail. What do you imagine he would do if he knew our Russian allies are really in charge here?"

Slobodan looked toward the bar where the hand surgeon was now encamped. "I believe he think not a good idea to be here. Maybe he think that already after he talk to you."

De Grom glared daggers at Slobodan.

LATER, TESS AND I strolled back to the town house together. The crisp night air was pleasant, with a slight, bracing chill. Sirens blared, horns honked, dogs barked, the city was doing its thing. It was invigorating. Tess was staying the night so she could get to the hospital early for a seminar. She said, "VJ, it was nice of you to treat the staff. I know they appreciated it. I don't think people give them the recognition they deserve often enough. It's really good that you do that.

"I've been watching you. When I've come to the office, you dance from room to room. This person gets an x-ray; while that person is out, you pop into another room and give an injection. You go into another room and go over a study, come back to the original room and go over the x-ray. Everything seems orchestrated. The only thing missing is the music. Now I realize the OR is the same way. Everyone is moving to an invisible conductor."

"Tess, first of all, you're right about the OR staff. They work their butts off and really do a great job for the patients. But you've seen me when all the parts are working in synchrony. It would be nice if it was that way all the time. It isn't. Imagine that the lead ballet dancer drops the prima ballerina and she breaks her ankle. Too often, that's what it's like. We have to scramble."

Tess cracked, "VJ, don't tell me that. You're going to ruin my image of perfection in the world."

I shook my head. "Always the cynic. I'll give you this; you seemed to fit right in. What did you think?"

"It was great. But there's a big difference between watching something and doing it. Let's see what happens when I actually have some responsibility."

She thought for a minute. "There's something else I wanted to ask you about. I remember what you told me about doing that four-digit replant on your old partner, Nick. Today, when Alyssa told you that you had another one, I thought you were going to have a complete meltdown. I haven't seen that before. It's not like you've forgotten how to do them."

I answered with the truth. "Tess, I think it's like most things. If you're used to doing replants on a regular basis, it's much easier. Now that I've been out of the loop for a while, I'm not as emotionally protected from the stress they cause me. I can still handle it if I need to, but I've lost all my desire to reengage in that aspect of my practice."

Tess looked at me hopefully. "Will you at least show me how to do some vessel repairs in the rat lab?"

With gusto I said, "Now *that* would be my pleasure!"

THE FDA COMETH

BOSTON, MASSACHUSETTS

THE FDA INSPECTION TEAM interviewed the research staff at the MRMC lab and examined the clinical data obtained from the Ebola trials conducted in the DRC and South Africa in great detail. Their evaluation of the trial was standard, but rumors had surfaced about several irregularities. Material disclosure of all trial data was mandatory.

When the investigation was completed, the lead on the team, an articulate, thoughtful man, Dr. Raphael Miralles, sat in principal investigator Myron Tribolsi's office to review the findings. Miralles peered over his reading glasses. "Dr. Tribolsi, the data from the study arm in South Africa are flawless. However, in the treatment group from the Democratic Republic of the Congo, I think you know you have some major issues with drug toxicity. Can you explain the multiple patients with liver failure and sudden death? I'll grant you, these patients all had Ebola virus. Still, I wouldn't anticipate such rapid adverse events."

Rather than the expected lengthy explanation about patient mortality and the multiple variables in play, Tribolsi said only, "Yes, that happened in the DRC group, unfortunately."

Dr. Miralles was taken aback. The implications of those events would stop the trial. Immediate disclosure to Wall Street would occur, and the company value would crater. As chief medical officer of Yonaker-Wood Pharmaceuticals, Dr. Tribolsi had to understand that reality better than anyone. Yet, here he sat, impassive, providing no further insights into the drug morbidity.

Miralles spoke again. "Perhaps we could speak to Dr. Slobodan Marjanovic. We understand he is conducting the trial arm in the DRC."

Tribolsi looked tired and beaten. "He was called to attend an emergency family issue abroad. He is not here."

Miralles thought, *Interesting timing.* He knew what his report would say, that this drug could not be cleared and the trial halted, but chose the diplomatic pathway. "Dr. Tribolsi, we have the necessary data. Our report should be ready for your review next week."

There was the cursory handshake and a quick exit. Miralles viewed the whole analysis experience as odd. In all of his interactions he had found Tribolsi intellectually gifted, but exceedingly squirrelly and opaque. He thought, *This man does not have a long future in the research world. We're about to shut you down and you have nothing to say. Really?*

ROCK-CLIMBING LIAISON

BOSTON, MASSACHUSETTS

AS THE WEEKS PASSED, Slobodan and I ran into each other repeatedly. Often, he was in the middle of a heated exchange with someone on the phone or had his head immersed in his laptop. His enthusiasm for the climbing world was, however, a constant source of discussion. He talked about doing El Capitan and Half Dome in Yosemite. Both of us marveled at Alex Honnold's big-wall free-climbing exploits and shared our passion for the outdoors. Slobodan maintained an air of confidence I admired. If he said he could do it, whatever it was, I believed he would.

One morning he caught me on my way to fix a man with a crushed distal radius and ipsilateral scaphoid nonunion. My mind was on the proper approach and fixation choice. He was very animated and startled me.

"VJ, I do research. I join you in Sierra Lake. We do Incredible Hulk. It fantastic climb. One of best in Sierras. I told you. I have meeting in San Francisco. I think you tell me you be up there around same time. I drive up. We make arrangement to do this thing. You text me later. Got to make talk at grand round."

I was glad he was coming. It was the final push I needed to try to conquer my fear of heights. Leila had an obligation to see her parents in Atlanta and couldn't join me. It would be good to have some company, and Slobodan would definitely be entertaining. Later that day I pressed the send button with the details. The challenge for me to do this rock climb was on. No way I could back out now.

Like most of the people who knew me, Slobodan didn't understand why I would go to such a faraway place to work. I told him about my introduction to the resort town from my Duke friends and the continued draw to return. He definitely connected with the part about being compensated not only spiritually but also financially for time spent.

About a week and a half before we were scheduled to leave, I happened upon Slobodan in the dining area. "Hey, buddy. You ready for this trip? We're going to be using ropes. There is no way I can free-climb. I know you want to. Maybe you can do it with the people I'm going to connect you with. They are one hundred percent badass."

Without a hint of hesitation, he replied, "I show them true badass, VJ. But, my friend, unfortunately I must run to airport. Before I go to San Francisco, must make other quick business trip to London." At that moment one of his residents spied us and cornered his mentor to ask about a consult that had just come in. While Slobodan was distracted, I got a call from the OR telling me they needed me there immediately—apparently there was an issue about the implant I was using for my case. In a rush, I picked up my bag, waved goodbye, and ran up to the OR to resolve the hardware crisis. Fortunately, the equipment issue was settled, and I was able to complete the surgical procedures without incident.

Only much later, when I got home, did I realize that the case I took at lunch wasn't my case at all. Slobodan was also in a rush and likely didn't pay careful attention to the bag left behind before it was too late. The big red letters on the folder inside did catch my attention: "Ebola Trial Data." Slobodan must have printed the data to study on the plane. I pulled the file folder out and set it on my desk, curious. I was nonplussed that my own computer was well on its way to Great Britain by now. I imagined that Slobodan was similarly displeased.

My phone was also AWOL. It was undoubtedly in my OR locker, parked on silent. I routinely do that so people won't call and distract me when I'm speaking to patients or trying to concentrate on a case. I could only guess, however, since no one could hear it ring even if I'd left it somewhere else. I was lacking in energy and couldn't deal with embarking on a search mission until morning.

I was processing this most recent confirmation of my inadequacies when Leila called out from the kitchen, "VJ, glad you're finally home. You got off lucky; it was your turn to grill. I tried to call, but the call went to your always full voice mail. I texted you too. Did you leave it at work again?"

I went in to placate her and admitted guilt. She looked at me with dismissive eyes. "My guess is that you left your phone in your locker and it's now out of juice. If you got an updated phone and didn't have so much data running all the time, your battery wouldn't drain so quickly. When you run out of here in the morning, you'll forget your charger, and no one will be able to reach you. I have this brilliant idea. Why don't you get a spare charger and keep it at the office? Right now, put the one you have in the bedroom where you'll find it so you can take it in tomorrow."

My answer was simple: "I have no words." As directed, I pulled my charger out of the wall and put my car keys on top of it. I also gave my wife a hug and assumed barbecue duties.

A little while later, after I finished cleaning the grill, I walked in and spied Leila in the office poring through the Ebola file I'd unwittingly brought home.

She looked up and said, "VJ, what on earth are you doing with proprietary pharmaceutical data from Yonaker-Wood about this investigational Ebola drug? There's a lot of really detailed information in here. The clinical trials done in South Africa look really good. This triple monoclonal antibody shows superior outcomes. Wow, wouldn't that be wonderful—certainly better than high dose anti-parasitic medicine. That was brilliant. There's another trial arm in the DRC. I didn't get a chance to look at it. Hopefully, the results are the same. There's also something here about Red Mountain Pharmaceuticals. I saw something about them in the news, but I don't remember what it was. How did you get all this information, and more important, why?"

I raised my eyebrows and simultaneously reached for the documents she was holding. "Well, the first answer is simple. It isn't mine. It's Slobodan's. I was in a hurry, and I picked up his bag by mistake today. His looks a lot like mine. Problematic, to say the least. He was headed to London and is probably just getting out of Heathrow. I have no idea where he is. Tomorrow, assuming I find my phone, I'll call him first thing."

Leila sat back in the chair. "Well now, that's a problem, isn't it? Slobodan can't be too happy if he needs to present these data."

Working out what to do, I said, "Slobodan is here working with Myron Tribolsi. I'll try to track Tribolsi down so he can forward information to Slobodan in London." I borrowed her phone and called the answering service. The effort was in vain. Tribolsi wasn't responding.

I sat next to her. "Tribolsi is unreachable. Now that I think about it, I haven't seen him for a few days. He's usually on rounds with the Infectious Disease fellows. My guess is that he's in the DRC, where the outbreak is. I'd be there if I was testing something like this."

I put the documents back in the folder. I still couldn't believe I had done what I had done. If someone did that to me before an important presentation, I probably would have arranged to have something bad happen to that person. I was hoping Slobodan was better than I was.

I was tossing and turning all night. When it came time to get up, I was zonked. I finally got out of bed about five minutes before I was supposed to see my first patient. Just as Leila predicted, I ran out of the town house in a flurry with my hair on fire.

Once in the office, I sent an emissary to my locker to grab my phone. Sure enough, it arrived DOA. I pulled out the charger I'd brought, only to discover that the tiny connector piece that was part of the assembly was not there. Undoubtedly, I would find it stuck in the wall when I got home. Issues like this drive me insane. Overengineering.

Finally, around ten o'clock a Tufts undergraduate came in with a compatible charger leaking out of his backpack. I got his cord while he got his x-rays and a cast change. Once my phone powered up, I saw the multiple calls and texts from Slobodan imploring me to call him.

He picked up on the first ring. "VJ, what is it wrong with you? You take my bag, I stuck with yours; you not answer calls! That bag very important to me. What you do with it?"

I apologized profusely for my screwup. I was responsible and completely in the wrong. I pled my case and eventually he settled down. Innocently I asked if there was anything in the bag he wanted me to fax or e-mail. "Do you need me to overnight your bag?"

"Not necessary, VJ," he responded bluntly. "I returning soon. Do presentation from saved internet copy. Question—why you have so much headphones in your bag? How many ears you have?"

I laughed. One of my habits is to grab throwaway headphones anytime I go to a workout gym at a hotel. Sometimes more than one, sometimes a lot more than one. It's a hedge against the dreaded airline flight when I might have to spend two dollars to buy a pair, or work out at a gym that has none. We all have our idiosyncrasies.

"Slobodan, help yourself to as many as you need."

"In future maybe you not need have all these, I get you special pair. You take them everywhere."

I continued to feel really bad. Before hanging up, we agreed to connect when he returned. He was eager to get back what was his.

ARC OF POWER

LONDON, ENGLAND

SLOBODAN PEERED at the pensive man facing him, another Serb with very serious business interests. He intimately knew this colleague and lifelong adversary—his older brother, Matija. They shared the same physical build and glowing intensity. Many thought they were twins. In reality, they were just a year apart in age. Slobodan knew that Matija would never give him the credit or respect he'd earned.

Their rivalry could easily be traced to the date Slobodan was born. Matija was not someone who played well in the sandbox with others, literally or figuratively. As Slobodan stared at his brother's face, the memory resurfaced of the event that most deeply divided them.

During the Bosnian war in the early nineties, neighbors who shared friends and family found themselves on opposite sides of the conflict. Strong, seemingly unbreakable bonds were destroyed. Horrific events occurred so frequently that almost no day passed without one.

The Marjanovics' experience represented a microcosm of what was happening on a grand scale. The brothers' older sister became intimate with one of the young Bosnian men nearby. The romance was discovered. It was a cliché oft repeated through the centuries, but no less real or problematic. With their father away fighting, Matija viewed it as his personal responsibility to right this perceived wrong. He demanded help from his younger brother, which turned out to be not forthcoming. Slobodan knew this family well and flatly refused to assist Matija in his quest to end the relationship. To prove his point, Matija decided to make a dramatic statement. He torched the Bosnian man's small home, burning everyone inside. Horrified, Slobodan did not reveal Matija's crime to his sister or anyone else. Like it or not, he was an accomplice. From that day forward, Matija held both his failure to help with the executions and his perceived weakness as a cudgel over Slobodan's head.

When their father was killed by an errant mortar, Matija replaced the family leader in battle. The anger that raged inside manifested itself in sadistic acts that even grizzled veterans found disgusting. Matija's journey to the world of crime and subsequent partnership with the Russian Bratva was a natural transition.

At first, Slobodan had resisted his brother's urging to join him. Ultimately, though, he had yielded. The war generated a sense of isolation and detachment that was too powerful a force to overcome. With the help of the Russians and their Boston representative, Mikalyn de Grom, the Marjanovics had managed to form a burgeoning worldwide business. Guns, drugs, prostitution, and now pharmaceuticals were all on the menu. They were poised to exponentially expand. Unless they got sabotaged at the last minute.

Slobodan had just revealed the information about the unintended switch of computer bags.

Standing beside Matija was the other key player in their criminal enterprise, Gwinevere. The brothers conversed in English for her benefit. Matija had found her working in a pub long ago, but Gwinevere had been part of every strategic move for the past few years. Her advice had always been sound and had helped further their objectives, though neither of the brothers fully realized the tiger she'd become.

Matija smiled. "Your plan work. News of failed trial out. Shares of Yonaker-Wood plummet this morning. Acquisition price now only one and half billion. Last week seven billion. That poison you give study subject in DRC best ever." The smile then turned to a frown of obvious disapproval, one Slobodan had seen so many times growing up.

Matija said, "This man who take briefcase. You think he have any idea we sabotage trial? Is he threat to what we doing? We not want problems now. We close to deal. You make sure we still okay—yes?"

Slobodan's eyes narrowed, the hate barely disguised. "Yes, I take care of problem. He hosting me in Sierra Lake, California. I finish job there. Brother, I not like tone in your voice. Of course takeover full go. Leave to me."

Gwinevere spoke up. "What about Tribolsi? Did you get everything you needed from him?"

Seething inside, Slobodan responded, "Yes, I did. He terrified of me. We soon done with him."

The meeting of this dangerous trio adjourned. As Slobodan watched the two leave, he swore and kicked the waste can halfway across the room.

Outside, Matija said quietly said, "I worry. I think big fuckup. Slobodan like that whole life. Do good thing, then do dumb thing next. We not be able to afford mistake now. I think I need to address my way."

"Yes, completely unacceptable," Gwinevere remarked coldly.

"Very sloppy. It's time we took control of this situation. I'll find out everything I can about this Sierra Lake place. I have a contact in Reno—Miro. I've had him do a few projects for me. He is extremely good at making problems disappear. Very professional, very clean. I'll make sure he finds his way there."

TRAVAILS

BOSTON, MASSACHUSETTS

IN THE HOURS before Slobodan returned from London, there was still plenty of work to be done. I'd sweated over this particular case. The woman had the craziest, most unfortunate luck of being in the wrong place at the wrong time. She was on a kayak and had just passed under a railway bridge. A man driving a truck wasn't paying attention and didn't stop before crossing the tracks. A train struck the truck, catapulting it fifty meters squarely into the kayaker's path. (I had never learned to think in inches, yards, miles, and pounds. To my Swedish brain the system was completely nonsensical. I had to remind myself constantly that an inch is 2.54 centimeters, a meter is 39.37 inches or 1.09 yards, a kilometer is 0.62 miles, and there are 2.2 pounds in a kilogram.)

My patient sustained more fractures than could be counted, along with a major head injury. Miraculously, she survived. I now had to tackle a combination of nerve, bone, and tendon problems. The operative technique wasn't the hard part; as usual, the decision-making process was. When the neurologist gave the green light, I made sure my brilliant friend Lige was on board to manage the anesthesia. If the ship was in peril, I wanted him to be in command. I was half surprised the OR staff would let us work together at all. Lige had helped me escape the Cooperative's grasp with a near perfect faked death. The requisite comments were made about whatever mischief we might conjure up together.

Soon after starting, I asked the critical question: "Lige, I've been wondering about something for weeks. I want your opinion. I was in Vegas for a meeting, and there were all these people dressed up in superhero, Disney, and slinky dancer costumes taking pictures with visitors for money. I understand the cash part. I'm asking this—at what point in life does someone decide to pursue street modeling? Do you just wake up and realize your calling is to dress up as Spider-Man and take photos with tourists? Is this a major in college? The whole thing puzzles me. What are your thoughts?"

Lige answered as only he could: "Well, old friend, the answer to that question is complicated. I do lose sleep, but not for the reason you think. It's mainly because I fear for your sanity. For some reason I care about you, and I am concerned that you are not well."

No one could see the broad smile under my mask. "Lige, does that mean that you're not interested in my thoughts on the guy who drives the billboard all day that says GIRLS DIRECTLY TO YOU or the woman who passes out stripper cards even to the people with signs asking us to accept Jesus and repent for our sins? Indeed, what about the lady who tells me in the office, 'I play this game obsessively on my phone so I don't cheat on my husband or eat too much.' Lige, I struggle over their fates. Also, while I'm asking these perplexing life questions, have you noticed that a disproportionate number of OB-GYNs own those electric cars with the symbol on the back that looks like an intrauterine device? Is it subliminal advertising to the female population?"

He chuckled. "No, VJ, I hadn't noticed that. Since you seem to be consumed today with the true problems facing humanity, there is a person you should communicate with. This doctor is from the Psychiatry Department. I called her while you were speaking. She's waiting for you when you finish."

I responded in kind: "Only if you come with me, Lige. Time now for you to stop bothering me. I have to concentrate." I laughed out loud when I saw him rolling his eyes. I'm easily entertained.

Three hours later I was done. The upper extremities of the broken woman were fixed, and fortunately she was still alive. At least by outward appearances we were successful. The family gave me hugs and sang my praises. I've heard a lot worse.

The detailed operative procedures had been refined by the greats in the field. The men and women working in theaters of battle, rehabilitation centers, and even leprosy clinics showed the inspiration and talent to move the field forward. William Mayo once said, "Medicine is the only victor in war." Truer words were never spoken.

I went to the OR lounge to reward myself with a fresh cup of java. There's nothing better than decompressing after a tough case with a mug of hot coffee. Fellow orthopaedic surgeons Chuck Danguerin and Jason Shoemaker were shooting the breeze as I walked through the door. Every day I internally thanked Jason for his amazing work on my femur. I'd avoided any infection from Petra's gunshot wound. Jason had thrown everything at me to get it to heal—platelet-rich plasma, ultrasound, a bone stimulator. The combination of outstanding surgery, extensive physical therapy, and black magic left me almost as good as new.

Jason was freshly back from the Maccabiah Games in Israel, where he'd won gold in basketball. It's the Jewish equivalent of the Olympics for people of all ages. His team had fallen four years earlier when a last-second shot tantalizingly circled the basket then rimmed out. I could relate; I'd seen that show on too many occasions watching NCAA March Madness. The gold this time was particularly gratifying for my friend and colleague.

Before I had the opportunity to congratulate Jason, I caught a snippet of conversation that immediately drew me in. Just as I got inside I heard Chuck say, "The difference is—at least my patient came in with a problem." When he saw me, he turned and said, "VJ, you have to settle this. Whose case was worse?"

Jason and he were having a good-natured discussion about issues that had come up at the monthly morbidity and mortality conference. It's our collective opportunity to talk about what hasn't gone well and brainstorm ways to make an outcome better in the future. Both of them had to present patient cases at the upcoming meeting.

Jason said, "VJ, you have to admit, the construct of the hardware that Chuck put in looked like ass. It took even less time to fail than I thought it would."

I could only see one way to address the situation. "Let's face it. Both of you are walking malpractice. You should take my lead and off yourselves now."

Chuck slugged me in the shoulder and didn't pull it much. "Wrong answer, VJ. After you pulled that shit on me, I had to drink most of that wine you gave me. I'm down to my last bottle. Looks like you need to get another case of Silver Oak ready."

Rebuked, I decided to tell the truth. "Look, guys, both of you did what you thought was the right thing. It didn't work out. Next time it will. Now if you will excuse me, I have to file my police report against Danguerin for assaulting me. Shoemaker, you get his wine restock."

Since my faked death in the PACU just after he did my knee scope, Chuck and I had actually become good friends. He was still a cowboy, but I appreciated his skill set on many levels. While I was recovering from my gunshots, I finally had a chance to explain why he had to be an unwitting dupe in my effort to turn the tables on the Cooperative. The wine gift was a tiny acknowledgment for the stress I'd caused him. His birthday was coming up soon. Ironically, I had already ordered the new case of Silver Oak. He'd earned it.

"You know," Jason said, "it's amazing to me how the littlest things can screw up a business merger. Look at what happened to those orthopaedic companies when it turned out the implants were spontaneously loosening. Those guys were outsourcing with no real quality control—bang, everything goes south.

"Speaking of getting screwed, I saw this article in the paper," he added. "Some multibillion-dollar deal just got scuttled because of bad data from the Ebola study Tribolsi was running. Bad for him."

Chuck kicked in his own wisdom. "Funny you should bring that story up. I talked to my broker last night. I've been keeping track of Yonaker-Wood—Tribolsi's group. I thought I might invest. The market caught wind of what you're talking about, and Tribolsi's company took an absolute dump. He made a special deal with MRMC to let him do the research and still be a part of Yonaker-Wood. That looked like a good situation until the last few weeks. Word on the street is that a group from South Africa, Red Mountain, is about to gobble them up for pennies on the dollar. Assuming the new merger goes through, there'll still probably be some cash to be made. But whoever got in early is going to kill it. Same story as always—the insiders feed at the trough, while we peons grovel for scraps."

The papers in Slobodan's briefcase had mentioned Red Mountain as a competitive suitor for the drug. Tribolsi must have known they were making a play. I kept my mouth shut. Leila had said the data from South Africa were compelling. There must have been something really awful in the DRC trial arm.

I felt bad for Slobodan. He was totally screwed. I hoped his job would last until at least we had a chance to climb together. Nothing like a discouraging job situation to make a trip start off on the wrong foot. I decided what I just found out was the obvious explanation for Slobodan's stressful phone calls. Defusing that tension would be a challenge. Taking his computer was not the best starting place.

CALM BEFORE THE STORM

BOSTON, MASSACHUSETTS

FINALLY, IT WAS TIME TO GO HOME. There were no messages on my phone, so evidently Slobodan had not arrived yet. I was dreading that encounter. Lost in thought, I walked into the town house and spied Tess pounding at her computer on the dining room table with great concentration. She had a dinner date with us.

"Whatcha working on, girl?"

No response. Her intensity never ceased to amaze me. I grabbed a beer, collapsed on the nearby couch, and picked up the latest *Journal of Hand Surgery* to see what surgical standard had changed this month.

About twenty-five minutes later, Tess closed her laptop and stood up. She startled when she saw me. "When did you sneak in?"

I looked around as if to check that no one else was in the room. I answered, "Are you talkin' to me? Are yooouuu talkin' to me?" She didn't laugh like I'd hoped. Clearly, I was a walking, talking anachronism.

"Tess, I've been here for almost a half hour. I said hi, and you didn't respond."

She looked perplexed. "Really, you've been here that long? Sorry, I didn't notice."

I smiled. "Okay, now that we've established I'm a nonentity, will you share what you're slaving over?"

Tess was reticent but finally relented. "You know how you've been bugging me about writing a book? Well—I started it."

I was genuinely impressed. "Wow, that's great! Do you want to tell me anything about it yet?"

She blushed. "You'll find this entertaining. The whole thing takes place in the anatomy lab on Halloween night. A medical student misses a party to come and start a dissection. Then strange things start to happen. Somehow or other, the theme just came to me."

I raised an eyebrow. "Oh, I can't imagine how you got the inspiration for that. Are there any crazy Swedish doctors involved? Perhaps a particular raven-haired administrator? Does the student find out they are her biologic parents?"

Tess sprawled on the couch. "I've been struggling with characters a little. It seems like a copout to write about what we did. I'm thinking of putting more of a sci-fi twist on it. Maybe the cadaver comes back to life, and it ends up being the student's long-lost ancestor or something. Maybe even the student herself in the future. I haven't decided. What do you think?"

Rearranging myself on the couch to give her room, I said, "I suppose it depends on the story you want to tell. Publishing a real-life account of what happened to us is strange enough, and probably interesting to the outside world. Still, I kinda like the idea of having an otherworldly connection between the medical student and her cadaver. It's a good start. I'll let it percolate. We can run it by Leila. She's far more creative than I am."

Tess returned to the computer. I didn't want to limit her, but people write about what they know. She knew I killed those two hit men, and even though technically it was in self-defense, I thought it best we continue to keep that fact under our hats.

I hesitated and then came out with it. "Tess, I've got some news for you. We'll all have to talk about it. I got approached last week by a movie producer. She heard about what happened to us, and she's thinking about putting it on the big screen."

Tess said, "Well, I didn't expect that. But I'm not really surprised. A bunch of people have asked me if it was going to happen. Can we hide who we are?"

I reassured her. "Actually, that's the best part. The offer came from a fellow Swede. They want to play with the story enough to make it fit into their medical system. Sierra Lakes will be Sälen, which is like six ski resorts in one, and Boston will be Stockholm. You're going to become a student at Karolinska—my old stomping grounds. The only people who will recognize us are my own family members, friends, and anyone you want to tell. If you're interested, they said that each of us can do a cameo. Does that sound better?"

Tess pondered my question. "I think I can wrap my brain around it. My involvement made me a known person in the medical school and around the hospital. I see people whispering and pointing to me, mouthing things like 'She's the one.' Randos come up to me and congratulate me or start asking me all kinds of questions. This terrain is completely foreign to me. I used to feel like an insignificant speck, but I liked the anonymity. The life of a celebrity has to be awful. I can't imagine not being able to shop or eat without someone taking a picture or wanting to have some part of you. That's a large price to pay. Do you think the happiness quotient of those people is higher? I doubt it. If we say yes to a movie, what will be the outcome? Even if it is in Swedish?"

I answered frankly, "This is still early stages. Probably won't happen at all. Hold off on mentioning it to your friends. Plus, we still have to get Leila's input. I haven't hashed it out with her yet. She also wants to stay under the radar. Fortunately, even if this movie thing does go, I don't think we'll have those issues. The good or bad thing about medicine, depending on how you look at it, is that physicians almost exclusively rate each other on medical knowledge and performance. You could be the nicest billionaire in the world, but if you're not doing a good job taking care of patients, then you become the subject of derision. Fame and fortune truly mean nothing in the medical world.

"Tess, I've thought a lot about the lives we lead and our situation relative to others. We have the ability to make choices about what we do. In so many places the lot of individuals is no better than that of the animals they keep. They don't have the luxury to worry about self-actualization. They are hoping to get enough to eat, have shelter from the elements, and get clothes for their children. Most jobs are stupefying. We're lucky to engage in a field that challenges and stimulates us every day. So there. By the way, I think the Sox are playing later. Want to go?"

Tess smiled. "VJ, your talent for digression never ceases to amaze me—obviously a function of stream-of-consciousness thinking. Sometimes I think you make schizophrenic patients seem clear of mind. My assumption from what you just said is that at the end of the day, movie or not, we're still blessed, and things will work out for us. Also, you're offering to take me to a game using the Ryssdal family's tickets. Is that about right?"

I nodded in agreement. "On both accounts, you're correct. What do you say?"

Before she could answer, my cell phone rang. When I saw it was Slobodan, my sense of well-being evaporated. I was about to eat a lot of crow. "Yes, hi. Come over now. You can have your bag, and I can get my computer back."

Within minutes he was at the front door, appearing tired and stressed. Rather than have him look at the documents and determine we had examined them, I told him a half-truth. "Slobodan, before I even realized I had your bag, I opened it, it fell over, and everything came out. I'm sorry if anything is out of order."

The admonishment I anticipated didn't happen. He responded with a grin. "No worry, VJ. Nothing too important inside. Same as your computer. I make copy everything. 'SwedishMD10' easy password to remember." He laughed when he saw my grimace. I guessed he had watched me sign in one of the times I was showing him pictures from Sierra Lakes.

"Just kid you, VJ. Don't care what you have on your computer. Not of interest to me. My concerns bigger. I see you soon. Will call you from San Francisco. Look forward to climbing Sierra."

Leila walked in from the office, where she'd been working on a presentation for neonatal nutrition, just as the door closed. She had never met Slobodan, but knew enough about him from my descriptions of his distinct mangled English and strong accent. "Was Slobodan just here?" I nodded yes. "Did you say anything about the study?"

I wasn't happy at all that someone I didn't know well could get into my laptop. "No, I didn't. I was more focused on the fact that he was giving me a hard time about knowing my password. He's a good guy. Obviously, there's no reason for him to access anything. Still, it's a reminder that it's time to change all my passwords. We're supposed to do that every six months anyway. The bank accounts are probably the best place to start." Going to the baseball game that evening was no longer an enticing choice.

I was able to redo everything more quickly than anticipated. By dinner I was feeling a little better. I started downing the outer crispy parts of a Brussels sprout, the only part I can tolerate. Out of the blue, Leila grabbed my hand and snapped at me, "I told you—you can't do that! Either eat the whole thing or don't, but you can't just steal all the outside pieces."

Tess started snickering. "How many times have you two had this argument—a hundred?"

Guiltily, I changed the subject. "Alright, Tess, let's get back to that book of yours. Why don't you tell Leila what you told me?" Tess obliged and launched into her idea.

Leila sequestered the vegetables to guard them from my incursions and presented her own thoughts. "I actually like the concept a lot. I think your idea about having the student and the cadaver be the same person is totally creepy. That's what you should do. If you play the sci-fi angle, there are a million pathways you can explore. If you stick with what happened to us, you'll feel too constrained by the actual events. You definitely don't want any association with Petra. They'd always look at you differently. It's probably difficult enough that they associate you with VJ."

I ignored my wife's comments. "Well, Tess, if nothing else, you should have some free time to indulge yourself. The rotation you're going to do doesn't have any call attached to it, does it?"

"No!" she said emphatically. "As you've said so many times, 'Life without call is the definition of happiness.' I'll have plenty of time to read and study. It'll be amazing. It's hard to imagine what normal will look like."

Normal—what a concept. Nothing about our lives was normal, nor was the path that we were all soon to embark upon.

Leila and I were lying in bed that night doing what neither of us should be doing. I was on my computer reviewing a paper on Ebola treatment. My interest piqued, I was tracking down who was important in the field. Myron Tribolsi was high on the list. He was collaborating with Harrison Sherako, who was based in Cape Town.

Leila glanced at my screen. "I see you're getting into the Ebola world. I'd think that after COVID-19 you'd have had enough of viral threats. Are you worried Ebola could make it here?"

I sighed. "I am. Thank God there are people doing the tough

work, like Tribolsi, Slobodan, and this guy Sherako. Hopefully what they've accomplished won't be crushed by the business power plays." I told her what I'd found out earlier in the day.

Leila snuggled and shut my computer. "I'm just glad we're not involved in any of that."

FANTASTIC FLYING FUN

BOSTON, MASSACHUSETTS

VIKA, OUR TRICOLORED Australian shepherd, was moaning. Something was clearly bothering her. Leila turned over and sleepily asked, "Why are you on your phone?" I didn't respond. She took that as an affront and shook me, this time demanding, "Why are you on your phone?" I wasn't on my phone. I was asleep. When I woke up, I informed her of that fact. She was nonetheless agitated. "Why does your phone keep going off?"

I looked. It was a message that my flight had been delayed, which meant I was going to miss my plane to Sierra Lakes once I got to LAX. Connecting flights and the need to get on them seemed to be a completely novel idea to the airline gods. I cursed and contemplated ways to subject their CEOs to pain. Public caning, Singapore style, had a certain appeal.

I would have to make the five-hour, five-hundred-kilometer drive from LAX to Sierra Lakes. It was one I was well acquainted with, but this time I'd hoped to avoid it. For the rest of the night, I slept poorly. When the alarm went off, I felt wasted.

I rolled into Logan Airport and went to buy snacks, making the mistake of trying to pay for them. I watched the man stare at the cash register screen, doing absolutely nothing. He fiddled with it for a minute. Dark-matter physics would have been an easier puzzle for him to solve. My impatience superseded my hunger; I just put the bag of nuts down on the counter and left.

Despite the day's unpromising start, I reached the delayed plane confident it might actually take off. Mistake. Just when I believe there's not another way to stall the departure of a flying machine, a new one is invented. This time the caterer forgot to load our water bottles. After sitting, and sitting, and three separate announcements from the pilot giving us caterer ineptitude updates, we got the green light to leave the gate. I waited for the tail to fall off, wishing that these problems could all be visited on the cruise ships. I never take those. The COVID virus had put the kibosh on that industry for a long time, so obviously nature decided to mete out their share of travel woes to the airlines. Balance would be maintained.

The challenged flight had one final twist. Just after the captain started to shoot his approach into LAX, we were treated to a touch-and-go non-landing. After five minutes of wondering whether our wheels were functioning, the pilot ruined the suspense by finally getting on the intercom. "Folks, we had to pull up to maintain spacing. We're going to make another pass and be at the gate in about fifteen minutes." Interpretation: We just about smashed into the back of a plane that was taking its sweet-ass time getting off the runway.

Finally, we conquered the task of getting safely on the ground. I called my friend in LA who kept the beater truck for me at his house. It was ready and waiting to take me to Sierra Lakes.

SUNSHINE IN SIERRA LAKES

SIERRA LAKES, CALIFORNIA

SLOBODAN HAD BEAT ME TO TOWN. I picked him up at the Rib Rattler bar and grill. He was chilling with a drink in his hand, surveying the crowd, seeming very much at home. We left, walking the short distance across the street to the cabin. The mountains were framed by hues of orange and pink as evening passed into night.

Slobodan said, "VJ, I now understand. This place beautiful. Why you haven't taken me here before?" I chuckled and directed him up the stairs. He was out of breath by the time he reached the top of my staircase. "What hell this is? I feel like I just climb K-2."

I grabbed some large glasses, filled them with fresh cold water, and placed one in his hand. "Altitude—*eto suka ne tak li?*" I said in Russian, then "Drink this, it'll make you human again."

Slobodan grinned upon hearing the Russian expression. Translated, it means "It's a bitch, isn't it?"

"You surprise me, VJ, man of many talents. How you know Russian?"

"Remember, I'm Swedish," I said. "You don't think I've met my share of Russians? I've picked up some words here and there. I figured you did too during your training."

I settled briefly into the rocking chair and admired the early stars as they winked at me. "Slobodan," I said with authority, "you, sir, are now on vacation." Bearing in mind what I knew about the impending failure of his Ebola research, I added, "If there is a man on the planet who deserves it, it's you. Enjoy a beer after you get hydrated, eat anything you see, make yourself completely at home. I need to run over to the hospital to look over my pre-ops for this week." Thinking it best not to tempt fate—or the password-guessing skills of my houseguest—I did take my computer with me.

When I finished, we returned to the Village, a relatively new section of Sierra Lakes with a concentration of shops and restaurants. It was also conveniently located across the road from my house. The sound of music grabbed our attention.

Lo and behold, we found ourselves in the middle of a beer garden. The crowd was going nuts for the Katie Coltrane Band, led by its sultry, exquisitely talented namesake. We ended up staying for hours and downed a few more beers than we should have. When the gravitational pull of a decidedly attractive woman drew Slobodan, I elected self-preservation. I tattooed the key code of the cabin on my visitor's wrist with a Sharpie. Whatever happened, happened.

I trudged back home and hit the sack, arming myself with my own tall glass of water, the elusive cell phone, and a book. Each of the items would come in handy at some point during the night. About four-thirty I woke up to some rustling downstairs. One of the voices was not accented. *Good for him,* I thought. *He'll have someone to show him around on the days I'm working.* Then

I realized—no. Slobodan was not the type. One-night stand for sure.

After sleeping poorly, with altitude and dehydration the dual culprits, I woke with the morning sunlight. Outside the kitchen window, blue sky, brilliantly green trees, and snowcapped mountains framed a view I never got tired of seeing. We'd had record-setting winter white stuff, great for drought relief, but a challenge for the people in town responsible for plowing, shoveling, and functioning in general. With my femur repaired, I was ready to tackle whatever the Sierras could throw at me.

We were blessed with opportunity. The snow, which had piled high on the roof and set me back six grand to get shoveled during my last visit, was still deep enough on the mountain to provide relatively good skiing. It wasn't without risk, of course. The previous week a skier bought it forever on the Wipeout Chutes. Yet, it was a run I love. The unfortunate death there wasn't going to keep us away. It was a reminder to respect the mountain.

I loaded up our gear in the truck as the femme fatale made her exit. Fortunately, she wasn't a local. That would have made it even more likely people would talk to Leila about women coming and going from our house when she wasn't there. Slobodan borrowed a snowboard and boots. One thing our house has plenty of is extra equipment. It's amazing, the number of items visitors leave behind and never retrieve.

When we got to the lifts at the main lodge, Slobodan looked up with genuine appreciation. "Nice, VJ. Amazing coverage for summer. It look like fun time. We start at top." I couldn't argue. The snow would be firm, but more consistent. Soft spring and summer snow accounted for more than its share of tibial plateau fractures. Skiers would go from fast to slow, and the resultant unanticipated torque was the gremlin. I had no interest in that.

As we made our way up the steep and now rocky face on chair 23, I took note of exposed areas to avoid. We passed through the snorkel at the top. I was juiced to get going, but waited for Slobodan to strap in. Without warning he jumped off the sheer lip and darted ahead. There was no way I was going to let him beat me on my home mountain. I started the chase through the massive bump field. I caught up and made a move to complete a high-speed, in-your-face pass. At that exact moment Slobodan zigged when I was expecting him to zag. I caught an edge and went careening toward the very rocks I had been studiously trying to avoid. As disaster rapidly approached, I regained just enough balance to make a turn into the snow. I crashed big-time but stayed physically intact.

By the time I collected myself and skied back to the chairlift, my mental focus was compromised. I was fully cognizant that what had happened was my fault. Still, I had just the slightest sense that Slobodan knew precisely what he was doing. That was worrisome.

When we met at the bottom, he carried on as if it were just another day at the office. "VJ, you ski out of control. Get you hurt. Must try contain yourself." I resisted the urge to bury my pole in his skull. What hurt the worst was the element of truth in what he said. I decided not to take it personally. I had to do my best to roll with the punches and keep my sense of humor. At least that's what I told myself. The remainder of the morning was incident free.

I did get a tiny measure of retribution. There were still long hours of daylight left when we got back from the slopes. A bike tour of the lakes would satisfy both of our needs to get more exercise. The six-kilometer climb from my house to Lake Marie was always entertaining. At an altitude of 2,733 meters, it was easy to get winded quickly. Seeing Slobodan struggle gave me infinite pleasure. It was even funnier when I saw him try to compete with the less-athletically gifted, morphologically challenged couple that passed him with seeming ease. The look of pain and disbelief on his face was completely entertaining. He didn't realize until later that they were on electric bikes.

ARMAGEDDON BECKONS

SIERRA LAKES, CALIFORNIA

THE NEXT DAY I had to go to the hospital. There was this trifling matter of work. I hated it when being a doctor got in the way of having fun. Typically, I spent two days in the Sierra Lakes office and a similar amount of time in the operating room. The patients came from a 150-kilometer radius for upper-extremity specialty care. When I was taking call, the days frequently stretched to evenings and nights. On those occasions, I would fix any body part that was torn, mangled, or broken. Fortunately, this was my only day on the hook for the emergency department.

Will Burch, one of the four overachieving full-time partners at Sierra Lakes Orthopaedic Institute, had e-mailed me earlier about one of the day's cases. As an orthopaedic team, they could ably handle virtually any problem. The latest addition was Sam Knenirschke, a foot and ankle specialist who was a mountain biking beast. Naturally, his wife was an Olympic-caliber athlete. In Sierra Lakes they were just another run-of-the-mill couple. I was happy the group indulged my presence, and was particularly glad when I could add that extra element of expertise.

The man Burch wanted seen was a prisoner scheduled to be transferred to a state penitentiary. He had lacerations of two tendons in his index and long fingers along with several nerves. If I fixed them, the critical rehabilitation for this injury would be impossible to obtain, and stiffness was a guarantee. Even with a perfect repair, rupture was a distinct possibility without appropriate splinting. If I didn't fix him, the guy was totally hosed. He wouldn't be able to effectively grip with his hand. I hated the idea of performing a repair that had an overwhelming chance of failure. If a second surgery was needed, it would be complicated by scars created from the first. A likely fool's errand. He was first on the schedule.

I pulled into the parking lot thinking about Burch, and sure enough there was his *Mad Max* death vehicle, built to withstand any post-apocalyptic danger. I admired its singular, menacing presence. The spiked bull-bar adorning the grille of the modified Ford 350 cab, along with the flatbed piled with machine carcasses and attached grappling hooks, spoke volumes. Getting in his way was never an option. Burch was the most prepared individual I'd ever met. It was the unifying theme of his professional and personal life. He was on my short list to hang out with in the event of earthquakes or nuclear war.

Before hitting the OR and my appointment with the criminal's severed tendons, I ran into the cafeteria to grab some fuel. Clark Peterson, a rock-climbing fiend, spied me coming in.

"Hey, VJ, I got the word from Lach," he said. "You decided to finally to take the dive and do the Hulk? I guess 'dive' is a poor choice of words. Death spiral, yeah, death spiral—I like that much better."

I started laughing at the jab then answered directly. "Clark, after all that work you've put into training me, not only am I ready to go with you, but I've got someone here who says he'll put you and Lach to shame." Lachlin Jasey was a recovery room nurse, and Clark a family medicine doc. Like so many in Sierra Lakes, their daytime jobs, though expertly performed, in no way defined them. Each was all about pushing the envelope in this huge, backdoor mountain playground. They had the *right stuff.* Easy-going, quick-witted, and generously thoughtful. They almost looked like twins—closely cropped hair, 190 centimeters, 83 kilos. In Millennial lingo, Lach and Clark were definitively "extra," built for speed and strength on the mountains. Each was a virtual Spider-Man at working through the pitches—the sections of the climb between stops at belay stations. When God was giving out life assignments, he touched each of them and said, "climber." They made Burch seem almost human, a virtually impossible task from my perspective. Neither had completely escaped the knife—an ACL reconstruction here, a fixed clavicle there. But they remained largely intact.

The pair had been harassing me for several years to join them on a big wall. My fear of heights had always held me back. But I was sick of myself. It took six months to heal my femur. After that I quietly enrolled in a virtual reality desensitization program. I tested myself in a number of places around the Boston area that once would have totally freaked me out. I was encouraged enough to tackle real climbs.

Lachlin and Clark were going to take care of me. I started working like a madman in the gym. I'd busted my ass strengthening my legs and crimp-training my hands. The last thing I needed was to blow out my finger pulleys. I'd practiced handholds, footholds, arm bars, knee bars, stemming, laybacks, and every other technique that would help me on the wall. I had no intention of being defeated by lack of preparation. The gym is at best a weak substitute for outdoor climbing. Still, it was a good place for me to test my grit. I was never going to be truly *ready,* but like it or not, go time had arrived.

Clark appeared puzzled as he questioned me. "Is this the same VJ Brio that's afraid of a thirty-foot face?"

I smiled, converting the distance in my head. "One and the same. Clark, I've had some life-changing events. I've decided to abandon caution and just do the things I want to do. Not outright stupid stuff like being a medical doctor such as yourself, but activities like rock climbing. I'm all in. The guy I brought with me is sometimes a little rough around the edges. But I think you'll find him entertaining. If he's half as good a climber as he says he is, he'll push you. That can't be all bad."

Clark studied me. "Well, as long as he doesn't do anything dangerous. It's your call. We'll get you guys up. I think we should do a warm-up down in Bishop first. It'll be a good test. If it doesn't work out, we won't do the Hulk. If your friend is a fuckup, you're the one who's going to pay the price."

THE OPERATING ROOM TAKES A BITE

SIERRA LAKES, CALIFORNIA

AFTER MY BREAKFAST CHAT with Clark, I ran into a nurse colleague and neighbor, Ryka. She looked at me, shaking her head. "Bad news, VJ—your tendon repair is getting bumped. Dr. Fruman has an emergency add-on."

I spied Bart Fruman as he wandered into the post-anesthesia care unit. "Hey, Bart, how are you?"

He deadpanned, "Another day above dirt, so it's a good day." Bart was a tell-it-like-it-is kind of guy. I admired him immensely.

I continued, "The grapevine says that you've got a case and you need to delay me. What's the verdict?"

Bart said, "VJ, you just can't make this shit up. I've got this twenty-two-year-old here who's got a minor problem. His friends shoved a tube up his backside so they could pour vodka in it. Apparently, it's a thing. They call it boofing—a way to get drunk faster. Now he's got blood coming out his anus. I'm not sure yet what I'm going to find. I'm going to scope him first and we'll see. Sorry, I can't give you a better idea how long I'll be."

I couldn't help chuckling. "He really put a tube up his rectum?"

Bart cracked, "Rectum? Might kill 'em."

I shook my head, stifling a belly laugh. "Bart, you have fun in there. Don't fall in."

Ryka added her own two cents. "You know, there were women in college that would soak tampons in vodka and put them in their vaginas to avoid the calories but get the same buzz." Bart and I both looked at her with equal amazement.

With no alcohol-absorbing tricks to add, I decided to use the extra time to dive into the rock-climbing book I'd brought with me. What I lacked in skill, I hoped to partially make up in knowledge. I knew I was fooling myself. Like surgery, there was no actual substitute for hands-on experience. Enter YouTube. A true godsend.

Ultimately, I started and finished prisoner tendon/nerve man. I performed the repair with sutures twice as thick as normal. Though I was hoping the fix would withstand everything jail would throw at him, I wasn't confident.

The next big challenge was choosing the correct wrist ligament reconstruction for Bear, one of the other local rock-climbing maniacs. Despite having full license from him to do anything I deemed necessary, the decision was a puzzler: Do I go for stiffer but more secure, or better motion with the greater possibility of later failure? I settled on stiffer. So, in addition to the wrist tendon I borrowed part of to substitute for the damaged ligament, I used a narrow but ultra-strong synthetic tape as a supplement. On top of all that, I tightened the tissue surrounding all the bones. I got it bombproof. Bear was a stud; he'd make anything work. Black and white in medicine is a fabrication of television and novels; life in our world is grayscale.

I wasn't done. A car, a wall, an errant deer, a fractured femur, and my availability on the surgical floor created our own collision. The young man was a good person who got penalized for trying to not kill an animal. Getting ready for a case of this type is like getting ready for a battle. We strap on our lead armor to shield us from the mandatory live X-ray, tray after tray of custom instruments are unwrapped, the fracture table and its multiple appendages are constructed, rolls of tape and padding are unfurled, the patient is positioned, and only then can we start. I'm always tense at this point. I think of all the parts of the case that can go wrong.

Having done hundreds, I've learned to never be complacent. The smallest problem can rapidly become a very large problem. This was not one of those times. Once the rod was secure within the marrow of the femur, I inserted the interlocking screws at the top and bottom of the titanium implant to prevent the bone from shortening or rotating. This task accomplished, I relaxed and asked those in the room who were still paying any attention to me the obvious question: "What do you do if you're a hydrophobic fish?"

My contentment was short-lived. The lords of trauma were not done. Bart Fruman walked in from next door. "Hi, VJ, sorry to be the bearer of bad news. You've still got more work to do. Here's the short version of today's excitement. The woman you're going to have to fix took two .45 rounds to her arm and one to her belly. I just finished exploring her. Lucky lady, nothing too awful. She'll have an ostomy. Better that than dead. Her humerus is pretty blotto, though. The other woman wasn't so fortunate. Her name is Alexandra Kandinsky, our now-former neighbor. She had a terrible, no good, very bad day. She's probably making new friends right now. I didn't know her, so I can't tell you if she's in the good place or the bad place.

"These fine ladies got into it over something, some sort of love triangle deal. Likely there was a little alcohol involved. The original shooter, Alexandra, isn't huge, and the one you're going to work on isn't small. Once our gal got hit, she apparently became extremely angry, took the gun with her good hand, and turned the tables on Alexandra. That's how she ended up in the morgue. The best part—they live four houses up from you. First, the guy who owned your house before you dies in a lightning strike; then, your next-door neighbor dies under questionable circumstances; after that, the porno king's house blows up; and now this. Makes you wonder, doesn't it? You inhabit the unlucky side of the street."

I interrupted, "For the record, Bart, the porno king was on your side of the street."

Bart thought for a moment. "Correct you are—maybe we should both move. Our mutual friend, police chief Johan, called me right after this woman rolled in. He asked if she said anything to us. He was wondering if an active-shooter situation still existed and wanted to hold off going into the house until he knew. Our street is going to be blocked off for the investigation. Hopefully, we'll be able to go home when we finish."

Two hours later, after most of the hard fracture work was done, a call came in on speaker. The voice was distinctive. "VJ, I try come home. Many police, sheriff car, highway patrol. Not appear they know what they doing. Many standing around talking. Not let me in house. They not tell me what wrong. You know man in charge?"

Just what I needed—Slobodan getting into Johan's grille. That would be a volatile mix of personalities. "Listen, Slobodan. Walk over to the Village. Grab a drink. I think they'll let you get by soon. I'm relatively certain of it. I'll fill you in on the details. Give me an hour. I have to finish this case and deal with the EMR garbage."

It was already too late. A new, familiar voice came on. It was Johan. "Hey, VJ, tell your friend he has to settle down or I'm going to throw him in a jail cell. Obviously, you know what happened. We're trying to get this crime scene nailed down, and we don't need him interfering."

"Please don't arrest him," I pleaded. "Put him back on the

phone. I'll get this worked out." I heard rustling as the phone changed hands again.

"Slobodan, for fuck's sake, I have to finish this case. Stay out of their way. Go to the bar like I told you, and it will be fine. I'll catch up with you." I heard an assenting grunt. As I had gotten to know Slobodan better, I increasingly got the sense that there was a deeper, darker side. The skiing event had seemed like a one-off, but I didn't like the sense of discomfort starting to develop.

Once I placed the final sutures and put on the bulky dressing, I walked down the hallway to speak to the patient's family. I was exhausted. Slim Stall, one of the sports medicine gurus, spied me.

"Hey, VJ, how ya doing? Word on the street is that you're going on a rock-climbing tour with Clark and Lachlin. And you give *me* shit for letting Burch take me heli-skiing? Man, you are insane. You might as well plunge a scalpel in your throat and save us the trouble of fixing up all the bones you break. That is, of course, if you don't die. We both know you don't belong on a wall with those two. There aren't too many people in this town who do. You're being misled into a sense of security because you work with so many of them in the PACU. The climbs they do are not routine."

Before I had a chance to respond, Renaldo Bilmer, the other supreme jock doc, sauntered up. He, Slim, Burch, and Sam helped keep the U.S. ski team patched up.

"You're right, Slim," he said. "I'm glad I did that extra three months of hand during residency. We might as well start advertising for someone else to take over for our associate here. VJ, when are you going out? I would have thought that getting shot would have been enough for you. Neither of us will be around when you need to get your new fractures fixed. We're all headed to that course in Taos. You'll be okay, though, we have a ringer coming in from San Diego tonight. He loves staying up doing trauma. You'll make him happier than a bass fisherman here on opening day."

Both of them smirked at me with the knowledge that I was

probably about to do something really stupid and neither of them would have to pay the price for it.

I played dumb. "I don't have the slightest idea what you're talking about. Everyone here knows how afraid of heights I am. I would never do something like that."

Bilmer shook his head. "That's not what we just heard in the cafeteria."

There was no out now. "Glad to know Clark kept this climb under his hat. I was going to tell you about it *after* I finished," I said. "I appreciate the great confidence you have in me. It warms my heart to know I have such supportive friends. I'm thinking of some wonderful Christmas gifts right now—perhaps all-expense-paid trips to Siberia for both of you, winter clothes not included. Seriously, Lach and Clark are going to watch out for me. What could go wrong?"

"You mean other than everything?" Bilmer laughed. "VJ, just stay focused. It's a tough climb. Those guys are in amazing shape. If you have problems, don't worry about stopping. Believe it or not, we still like having you here to do these hand weenie cases."

Slim added, "Yeah, VJ, you're much more useful to us with a functioning brain and two functioning hands."

I studied my friends. They were genuinely concerned with my well-being. I listened but decided not to hear. Given the late hour and the day's adventures, all I wanted to do was nothing. I definitely wasn't in the mood for any more mental challenges. However, there wasn't a choice. I called Slobodan back. Fortunately, he'd settled down. The vodka helped. We arranged to meet at the Rib Rattler in thirty minutes.

The ringer, David Harkey, called me the second he arrived. When I told him about the case I'd just finished, I heard the disappointment in his voice that he'd missed doing it. The exuberance of youth—what a thing. But now I was officially off call for the rest of the trip. Freedom! I loved that feeling.

Once I reached my place, I threw on some street clothes and made my way to the bar. My charge was whooping it up with a big crowd. He yelled in his distinctive Serbian accent, "Another round on house." Then he spied me coming in. "There you are. I thought you waste entire night working. What wrong with you? Join us. Have fun!"

The writing was on the wall: If I stayed, I would regret every minute the next day. If I left, all bets were off the board, and I might never see Slobodan again. Of course, there might be something to be said for that.

A MAN WITH A POCKMARKED FACE wearing a fresh-off-the-shelf SKI SIERRA LAKES hat occupied a back table in the Rib Rattler. Gwinevere's uniquely gifted contact from Las Vegas had arrived. The pulled-down bill was a clear and intentional signal that he was not to be bothered. Miro had never been a good person, nor had that ever been a problem for him. He had all the standard excuses—abusive father, negligent mother, run-ins at an early age with the criminal justice system, poor educational opportunities. The reality was he didn't give a damn about other people, and killing them gave him no pause. He practiced his craft for the self-satisfaction of doing it well. He also liked the generous paychecks and the indulgences they afforded. This particular job would require finesse and the utmost attention to detail.

Here at the behest of his boss, Miro had been watching Slobodan and now eyed Brio as he sidled up to the bar. He'd casually kept tabs on both of them. The server placed a new Dewar's in front of him and started to chat. The ice-cold stare stopped the unfocused babble. She slunk away. The man radiated danger.

WITH A WARM SMILE, Lexi, the uber fabulous barkeep, greeted me: "So how's the king of Boston faring these days, now that you're a married man?"

I declared proudly, "I'm happy beyond belief. God threw away the mold when she made Leila. To think I had to come all the way here to find her."

She responded with authority, "You do know that *the best* people have always been in Sierra Lakes. Of *course* you met her here."

Slobodan piped up loudly, "I single, Lexi. How you feel about trading Swede for Serbian? VJ not half man I am. Give me chance. I take care of all need you have. Make you happy inside and out."

From the end of the bar a swarthy patron, looking moderately drunk, got up and started walking toward us. I didn't recognize him. I know he had no idea how big Slobodan was. Menacingly he said, "Hey, you Eurotrash douchebag. My friend doesn't want to listen to that bullshit. Why don't you shut the fuck up!"

Those words were a mistake. In seconds Slobodan had the man in a headlock, appearing quite ready to smash his skull like a tomato. I yelled, "Don't do it! DON'T!"

Slobodan looked at me, smiled wickedly, and released the man he'd subdued, but not before viciously kneeing him in the groin. The loudmouth collapsed on the ground. Except for the sound of his groaning, the bar was absolutely silent. The people there had no doubt seen brawls. Yet this one-sided fight had a different flavor. Would Slobodan have really killed him? I wasn't sure. Maybe he himself didn't know. I gently took his arm and guided him toward the door. The conversation about what had happened would get back to me soon enough.

The walk up the hill to my house passed without words. Both of us were mad. Once inside, I said, "Slobodan. I work here. You have to respect that."

His answer was straightforward. "I understand. That why man need lesson. He not bother any friend of yours again."

In his world, the rules were different from mine. How to negotiate these differences was my problem.

I admitted, "That was impressive. Where did you learn to fight like that?"

He grinned maliciously. "I learn in service. Many things you not know about me, VJ."

I nodded. "Indeed, I don't. You surprise me every day." The feeling I had earlier had instantly amplified. It was the same sense I got when a rattlesnake suddenly appeared on a trail I'm hiking.

ONCE THE DUST SETTLED at the restaurant, Miro covered himself with a nondescript black coat and took his own leave. The man who'd created the disturbance was currently slumped on a nearby bench outside. Though altogether unhappy and still in moderate distress, he saw the hardened man in the SKI SIERRA LAKES hat glance at him. As a consequence of skipping school on the day brains were distributed, he said, "What're you looking at?"

Miro turned back, considered his options, then ferociously smashed his elbow into the obtuse man's face. Blood rushed out of the freshly broken nose. Racked with new pain, the Neanderthal didn't see the fist that delivered the knockout blow. He hit the ground and stayed there, not moving at all. In fact, he would never move again.

Miro went to his room to get some aspirin and sleep. An altitude-induced headache was killing him. The man he had just bludgeoned was a mere speed bump. He wanted to be sharp for the real work ahead.

THE BOARDROOM

BOSTON, MASSACHUSETTS

AN IMPECCABLY DRESSED MAN sat quietly on one of the richly embroidered chairs in the executive's office—the same man who'd been wearing the scintillating black suit at Hackford-Regan's bar. The twenty hours of travel seemed to have had no effect on him. His other boss had sent him to complete the business deal, a task he was thrilled to assume.

Sitting behind the elegant oak desk, the stern-looking Mikalyn de Grom creased her brow, wondering if she could trust this man with the beautiful smile. She had sensed a difference in his attitude over the past twelve months. It was always clear that he was all about himself; now it was just more obvious. She decided to keep tabs on what he was up to. If there was a power play to be made, she would be the one to do it. Her association with the Marjanovics and their allies in the Russian mafia, the Bratva, had started years earlier, and she'd morphed into a near clone—direct and absolutely ruthless.

"Now that this Ebola drug has tanked," de Grom said, "the takeover proposal you pitched for Red Mountain needs to go through, quickly. Our Russian associates are quite insistent. We want to keep them happy. Some of our mutual acquaintances have had issues when they're not. According to what you've told me, all the pieces are in place, correct?"

The junior emissary responded assertively, "Yes, we've got that under control now. The other issues as well. It took doing, but soon they will be permanently resolved."

De Grom pensively stroked her hair, so tightly pulled back it made her visitor's scalp hurt. "I suppose it's better if I don't ask you how those tasks were accomplished. Just make sure that whatever you did doesn't come back to bite us. Petra Lewis and I used to work out at the same club. We got to be pretty good friends. She was killing it. That is, up to the minute when that SOB Brio got involved. I think you know how matters ended. We were lucky not to get pulled into that mess. Our stake was a small one. I don't think even her partner, Rick, knew we were involved. That is the way it must be on this deal—a light touch. Brio didn't do anything with that data he *accidently* took, did he?"

"Not to worry, Ms. de Grom," the man responded. "He will not be a problem. The financials are solid on the deal, and all the other particulars are covered. Your monetary situation will soon be extremely bright."

The man brimmed with the confidence of someone accustomed to things going his way. Although he was adopted, for him, they always did. It had been so since he was a child. He grew up with everything he wanted. The fire still burned inside. His connections in South Africa were invaluable. That's why de Grom had recruited him as a liaison. Though she'd helped to push him forward, he did not care for her. Serving two masters on opposite ends of the globe was an extreme challenge; so far, he'd navigated the crocodile-infested waters successfully. But he also knew that if circumstances dictated, either one of his chiefs would not hesitate to literally cut his heart out. That was a sobering fact.

He had grown weary of the commute between Cape Town and Boston. With the merger in play, the trips had become even more frequent. He'd do it until the job was completed, then continue his climb up the ladder. He was already highly skilled in the art of meeting new people, gaining their confidence, then taking what he needed. Who he had to step on was of no concern.

SECRETS OF THE MEADOW

SIERRA LAKES, CALIFORNIA

WAKING UP AT SIX, I looked outside at the brilliant sunrise. The sky quickly turned deep blue. What a nice show.

My obligation to the Sierra Lakes Orthopaedic Institute was morning office only. That was about all I was up for. Thankfully, there wasn't any fallout from the events the previous evening at the Rib Rattler. Today I was going to leave Slobodan to his own devices. I was hoping he'd keep his nose clean.

Plenty of daylight remained when I said goodbye to my last patient. I bribed one of the techs to finish my EMR data entry so I could make a stat exit. In the middle of the night I'd had a sudden pang of anxiety about events from the previous year. The same worry had occurred too often. I couldn't put it aside any longer. Strapping on my trail shoes, I launched my reconnaissance mission.

First I ran to the site where I took down the two Luciano brothers who had been sent to kill me. That had happened during a vicious snowstorm. Meters of snow on the ground were no longer an impediment. A search of the remote area where I'd shot the assassin who had been driving the snowmobile was initially fruitless. I didn't even know if what I was looking for existed. I shook my head at my own paranoia.

Out of the corner of my eye I spotted the outline of something familiar nestled by a tree. It was unmistakable. Guns are like that. I experienced simultaneous relief and anger at myself. In my rush to load the bodies and incinerate them, I'd neglected to verify that the snowmobile driver wasn't carrying a rifle like his partner had been. I hadn't seen one when I originally identified him through my binoculars. This was a twin of the Remington 700 SPS that I'd grabbed from his brother. Now the question was what to do with it. The problem was solved a lot more quickly than I anticipated.

The voice from behind me caught my attention. "Yo, VJ, how are you? Interesting piece you've got there. Do you always do trail runs carrying a rifle?" It was Johan, my friend the police chief. His presence was too unlikely to be a coincidence.

I gently laid down the death instrument and walked over to greet my buddy. "Good to see you. I have to speak to your lovely wife about all these cases I've been doing. Lorraine's about to get very busy. Thank God she's the best hand therapist there is. My guess is you're curious about what I just found. So am I. It's a hell of a bear swatter. I wonder who left it here. Has anyone reported one missing?"

"Yeah, it's sort of a funny thing to leave lying around."

Still surprised to see the police chief in this specific place, I asked, "Johan, I know what I'm doing out here. What brings you to this lovely place?"

He sat down on a nearby log. "Odd situation. Some stray camper was walking through here with her son a couple of hours ago. The boy found some live rounds. The lady saw exactly what you just did. I don't think guns are her thing. She called the office and reported it, so I thought I'd come take a look.

"By the way, thanks for mucking the thing up with your prints. That should make dusting it so much easier. Do you run this way a lot? It's not where most of the trail folks like to go."

I stuttered for a second. "Yeah, I know. I wanted to check out something new. I like to cross-country here in the winter, so I thought it'd be nice. Johan, if it's okay I'm going to keep going. I've got some distance to cover yet. Are you guys still coming over for barbecue?"

The chief nodded yes. "See ya soon, VJ. Try to keep that friend of yours out of my hair until then. He's a real gem. And give me a heads-up if you find any more cannons."

"Will do."

I left the reference to Slobodan alone, nodded to Johan, then made my exit. I suspected he was on to me. I had thought as much when he called me in the hospital after I got shot the year before. The two of us were involved in a dance with a partner we didn't want. Thankfully, he was crafty enough to avoid asking me any direct questions that would force his hand. The timing today was unlucky, but my midnight ruminations for once were justified.

I decided to wait until we next connected to see if there was any other fallout from this chance discovery. I did make one personal resolution: If I ever had to cover up something again, I'd certainly be more compulsive about doing it right.

THE HULK BECKONS

MONO COUNTY, CALIFORNIA

NEXT ON THE THREAT LIST was the rock-climbing warm-up in the Owens River Gorge. I knew Lach and Clark wanted to verify that I wouldn't be a major liability on the Hulk, a decision I tremendously appreciated. As we made the drive down the hill toward Bishop, I prayed my Boston guest wouldn't screw up. Under the category of "Wonders never cease," Slobodan was an angel. Everything went letter-perfect. I practiced each hold and maneuver for the umpteenth time. Best of all, I didn't freak out from the heights. Slobodan demonstrated skill and oratory constraint I hadn't witnessed. I wondered if he had a twin that had secretly switched places with him in the middle of the night.

The trial passed, we launched our attack on the Hulk at zero dark thirty the following morning. Except Clark wasn't in the car. Lach explained that his mountaineering partner's young son had spiked a high fever during the night. For obvious reasons, that responsibility took priority. In his stead was Sara "the Spider" Snowden, one of the operating room nurses I often worked with. I was genuinely sorry about Clark's family emergency, but seeing Sara there was a big smile. The Peruvian wonder was yet another legend in the Sierra Lakes climbing community. There was nothing she wouldn't tackle—all 1.6 meters, 48 kilograms of her.

Our diminutive new team member was dwarfed by Lach and Slobodan in stature only. The woman was solid muscle. She was also a fountain of information. During the car ride Sara provided an abridged description of the hike to get to the Hulk. She described it as beautiful and fun. Of course she would. She wasn't capable of a negative thought. Just wasn't part of her DNA. Clearly, we had no genetic relationship.

The trail in was about eight kilometers and 860 meters of elevation gain. In other words, it was going to be a bitch just to get there. Like approaching a replantation, I steeled myself for all that was about to come.

After parking at Twin Lakes, we hiked along Robinson Creek. Two kilometers into the climb, we passed an aspen grove. Had it been light outside, the trees would have been resplendent. I could still hear the distinctive sound of their leaves as the wind rustled through. I love that sound. It conjures a sense of serenity. As it was, nature's music was just a small distraction. My adrenaline was pumping too hard.

The waterfalls roaring from above did garner my attention. The water was high and fast from the abundant snow melt. There was a big log crossing we had to negotiate in short order. Falling into ice-cold water this early in the climb would have been a problem. Per usual, I hadn't slept well the night before, so I was trying to be as attentive as possible to the trail.

Thank God Sara was leading. The path was in no way obvious, particularly in the dark. My headlight was a little like my brain—not as bright as it should've been. We were looking for the critical two-meter-by-one-meter rock that indicated the turn to get to Little Slide Canyon. After identifying the key marker, we started up a series of steep switchbacks and then finally reached the opening of the canyon. The trees were sparse. I was able to make out the scooped-out sheer rock walls on each side and the large boulders in the path ahead. On the right, I took note of Kettle Peak. Sure enough, I caught my boot and stumbled, but I did a roll, and fortunately, only my pride was damaged.

Lach said, “Hey, VJ, you okay there? Those rocks will just jump right out there at you, won’t they?”

Slobodan couldn’t resist a jab too. “VJ, maybe you leave climbing to big boys. Fall like that on climb bad for all of us.”

I frowned. Before the conversation took a more negative turn, Lach restored the peace. “Boys, this is going to be fantastic! We’re going to kill it up there.” Lach defined excellence in every way, as an athlete and as a person.

We resumed the hike, and I could see the outlines of the magnificent canyons with their spires. We had to cross a large snowfield skirting to the right, closer to the rock. There was still quite a bit of snow left from the late winter and spring storms. The problem with the snowfield was that if you lost your footing, you slid down to the base, picking up speed on the way. The stopping point could be a boulder or tree, resulting in very sudden deceleration. A tibia might then look more like broken china. I had taken care of my share of those unlucky climbers. Fortunately, nothing like that happened today. Doing what we could to avoid the snow, we cut back left to pick up the trail again through the rocks and boulders. As we passed by the cave I’d been briefed on, I knew we were close. There were four souls inside readying themselves. They waved and politely nodded. No words were exchanged. Everyone was focused on the task at hand.

We reached the base of the Incredible Hulk at around six fifteen. Sara gave me a visual tour. "To the south you'll see Matterhorn Peak." Pointing farther, she said, "There's the Duck, Reggie Pole, the Turret, and next to it is the Outguard Spire. We'll save those for your next trip. Welcome to the Sawtooth Range."

She calmly gave me the full description of the area, knowing how nervous I was. Unfortunately, I became way too distracted the second I looked up at the 450-meter granite wall. Momentary terror invaded. It was the same feeling I had the day I started my internship in the surgical intensive care unit. I asked myself, "Am I up for this?" The flight/fight response was screaming "flight." But the answer had to be yes. Why I'd agreed to this risky challenge could not be answered. But I didn't run. I was hell-bent on conquering my own demons as well as the wall. There was no choice.

The sun had begun to rise, and there were no visible signs of thunderstorms. That was good. I'd been ambushed on the top of Mount Whitney by thunder, lightning, and a vicious hailstorm. Running down the ninety-nine switchbacks in a torrent of water with lightning bolts striking was harrowing enough. I had no interest in repeating the experience. The west-facing beast we were poised to scale was known for ferocious wind. I was mentally prepared.

Lach said, "VJ, this is the best 5.10 route in the Sierras. Just like a sweet black-diamond bump run on the mountain. You're going to love it. We will mainly be following a continuous crack system to the top. There will be a little face climbing, but there will be bolts there to link to the next cracks." Translation—this was going to be a helluva tough climb, but intensely rewarding.

"Now, how far up are we going?" I asked.

Sara filled in the details. "The true summit is eleven thousand, three hundred feet. We're going to top out there." Per usual, I had to mentally convert feet to meters—3,444 meters, to be exact.

She continued, supplying some beta, rock-climbing lingo for

critical information: "The climb is a walk in the park. It's going to require some thumbs-up and thumbs-down jams that Lach told me he showed you. Also, keep your feet outside of your rope. If you fall and the rope is outside your leg, you'll flip backward. That's no bueno. The entire route protects naturally, except one old button-head quarter-inch anchor on the way up. It's more like mental gear. Watch that; it can crack. Clip it, but don't count on it. All the belay anchors will be secure. I'll make sure there'll be plenty of redundancy in the system. You'll be very safe. There are twelve pitches on the Red Dihedral route we're taking, but we're going to link a few of them."

Lach chimed in, "This whole climb will be about creating friction with your hands and your feet. You're going to use your feet, body, and hands to work as a unit. Remember to just focus on what's in front of you. That will get you to the top. I've done it a lot." The last comment was stated without a hint of cockiness. It was just fact. He was trying to help me settle.

I tried to seem confident. "Okay, guys, show me the line. I've been working on my visualization technique." I channeled Alex Honnold in his TED Talk about his monumental free solo of El Capitan in Yosemite. His words were "I accepted what I had to do and did it. The best part? I didn't slip, so I didn't die."

Slobodan piped up, "VJ, so what if this your last day on Earth? If you go out, it will be glorious death." I glared at him, wondering again about the sagacity of inviting him in the first place.

The equipment was checked, double-checked, and triple-checked. We all racked up with our gear on the side of the harnesses, chalk bags on the waist, smaller spring-loaded cams in front to reach more easily and bigger ones in the back. The cams were inserted in the cracks to support the rope as we progressed up the wall. Sara checked the rope to make sure there were no knots. Then she scanned to see that my figure-eight knot was dressed properly, going through the leg loops and waist loops, and that my harness was double-backed for extra safety. These steps were just two of many important check mechanisms.

The last step was to put on my climbing shoes. They fit like a glove, and therefore would be perfect to wear all day. Before moving ahead, Lach threw me a pair of crack gloves, affectionately known as hand jammies. "VJ, don't forget these. They'll prevent you from chewing up those delicate surgeon fingers of yours. Don't worry, I won't tell everyone you're a cheese dick for wearing them." In this case I was willing to accept the anticipated razzing for the extra help. I was never going to be a professional rock climber but did intend to continue to do operative procedures.

Given that we would take a lot longer to do the ascent because of me, all of us thought it would be best to stagger ourselves as two different parties and let Slobodan and Lach go first. I watched them tackle the wall with fearless abandon. If they continued at that pace, they'd be able to do it twice before we got through once. I ceded this battle to Slobodan.

When it was our turn, we reached the 5.8 bulge on the first pitch—sort of like a blue/black ski run. This one was definitely challenging, but not full-on like what was awaiting. As Sara had just informed me, with the new seventy-meter dynamic ropes, we'd be linking several of the normal pitches. I'd learned that the ropes were shorter "back in the day." Since the number of pitches—the sections of the climb between stops—were determined by the rope length, the stronger, longer, more reliable ropes permitted longer belays, and therefore fewer unique pitches. None of this meant the ropes couldn't still get caught on sharp rocks and fray. It was a fact I decided to ignore.

I breathed a sigh of relief when the site for our second belay was reached. The big yellow ball in the sky started to grow more fully. I was pretty chilly and looked forward to some warmth. I was only slightly less anxious.

Sara pointed out the best holds as we progressed up the wall. We worked through each problem with her continuing to coach me. She expertly controlled the rope drag and every aspect of the climb. She was wonderful. By the third pitch the wind really kicked up. Thankfully, the rays of sun warmed us while we were buffeted. Sara took the line of least resistance, following the natural cracks. When there were no cracks, I searched for hand- and footholds, which my hands and feet found in the natural features. I reminded myself about remaining a slave to good technique and maintaining absolute focus. The finger and hand jamming I'd practiced worked better than I'd anticipated. Climbing a wall of this magnitude is like doing a lengthy surgical case. It has to be conquered in small pieces. Adherence to sound principles yields good outcomes. Impatience compounds difficulties.

Grasping for the next hold, I pondered the pull-out strength of the spring-loaded cams Sara embedded in the cracks every three to four meters. The three-point anchors she'd built dramatically increased our safety. In the words of the greats, they were absolutely "bomber." As I gathered the anchors on the way up, known as "cleaning," I studied the rope snaking through the carabiners above. There was no choice—either trust the protection or spend the next few hours fearing immediate death.

I made a move and thought my foot had a good hold. It didn't. Neither did my hands. Sooner than expected, I tested what I'd been contemplating seconds earlier. The fall was sudden.

SARA LOOKED DOWN, but the ledge was blocking her view. She said to herself, *Uh-oh, where is he?*

Far above, Slobodan and Lach were moving through the pitches with expert efficiency. A quiet competition had germinated. Lach acknowledged a particularly difficult move that Slobodan successfully executed. "Nice! You having some fun?"

The Serbian gracefully accepted the compliment and with uncharacteristic humility acknowledged the truth. "You still better. I like that you push me."

Lach surveyed the majesty of the scenery all around him. "We're just lucky to be able to enjoy this. It doesn't get any more special. Let's give Sara and VJ a chance to catch up."

IT WAS OVER QUICKLY. I dangled but didn't panic. I came to rest back against the wall. Sara was intentionally keeping the rope tight. If she'd been making a traverse, I would've swung like a pendulum, which would've been a lot more dangerous. It was a sobering moment. In a way, though, the slip was helpful. I'd made a mistake, and the safety features did their job.

I thought again of what the illustrious Honnold said: "I didn't want to be a lucky climber, I wanted to be a great climber." Unlike that international phenomenon, I was completely willing to settle for lucky. I started back up and regained my bearings. Lach and Sara's voices were in my head, instructing me about what features to look for and how to conquer them using all body parts. I looked up and realized that Lach and Slobodan had stopped and apparently decided to wait for us. They must have seen that we were doing better than expected. All at once, they were off again.

I was halfway through the pitch I'd just fallen on. Then it happened.

I heard a noise, then a loud, emphatic call from above: "ROCK, ROCK, ROCK!" I knew to keep my head down, but my brain reacted in the opposite direction. I committed the cardinal sin and looked up just as rocks the size of small asteroids sped by my face. Fortunately, they smashed into a nearby ledge instead of me. I was lucky to still have a face.

When the pitch was finished, Sara was there waiting, shaking her head. "That was an unexpected treat, wasn't it? With all the thawing and freezing, there must be some loose rocks. I'm pretty certain Slobodan accidently set off that little slide. They barely missed both of us. We're pretty lucky. I'm still surprised that they got dislodged. I should ask Slobodan about it when we summit. I didn't hear you scream and didn't feel a tug on the rope, so I decided you must be okay. How close did those rocks get to you?"

I had no intention of telling the truth. "They bounced. They didn't come anywhere near me. Thanks for the heads-up. I'm ready. Let's keep going."

Silently I was beginning to wonder. Now two separate events on this trip, both caused by Slobodan, each of which could have left me severely hurt or dead. I had to put those thoughts aside and refocus. It was the only way I was going to scale the wall before me. Going down was not an option. The discussion with Slobodan would have to be tabled for later, assuming I got the opportunity.

I saw another party of climbers laboring through the ascent on the Positive Vibrations route. It gave me some reassurance that I wasn't the only one having to exert myself.

We reached a natural ledge below the splitter crack, then progressed up to the base of the Shattered Pillar. We pressed on. I searched for face holds—the features and irregularities on the wall—with my hand as I watched Sara scurry up. I was convinced that my mentors were gifted with rock-climbing telepathy. They were poetry in motion.

I reached a section where completing the next move demanded that I lift my leg high, very high. I thought my adductor muscles were going to rip. After several strained attempts, I did it. That move marked the hardest part of the climb. I was elated. It even beat the nirvana of a ski run on a fresh-powder day. Well, actually not, but damn close. Nothing beats a fluffy powder day.

We came to the next pitch, where the rock formation created a ninety-degree right angle, or dihedral. This was a left-facing, inside corner red dihedral—hence the route name. It looked like a very long open book. Now I was both warm and warmed up. I shed my layers down to a breathable climbing shirt. I was holding my fear in check and ready to finish the ascent. The falling rock had unnerved me more than I wanted to admit, and the concern about Slobodan gnawed at me despite my best efforts to keep it at bay.

I had to clear my head, so I took time to look around at the vast space. Trees dotted the neighboring light-gray peaks, none as elegant as the one we were on. The sparse lichen on the granite rock reminded me how foreign we humans were on this terrain. It was not a place man was meant to be.

Sara yelled down, "You're on belay. Climb on." That was her signal that the ropes and anchors were set for me to progress safely. When I didn't respond right away, I got a rope tug to make certain I was ready.

In my loudest voice I responded, "I'm climbing." I gave my own rope a tug to make sure the message was transferred. She yelled again, "Climb on!" That is precisely what I continued to do and do and do. I didn't fall again, which in and of itself was both a miracle and a triumph. I was setting no land speed records, but as the minutes and hours passed I saw the top grow nearer.

We tackled the last pitch, which required stemming through the chimney—a technique of pushing oneself up the space with both hands and feet spread out in opposition to create force on both sides. Eventually, I saw the body-sized hole in the rock and made my way through. Then, all at once, I'd done it. I'd topped out. The view was phenomenal. My absolute joy at reaching the summit was so overwhelming that I could have been in the middle of doing a ten-digit replant and still been out of my mind with happiness. Nothing could touch me. We paid homage to the mountain, took pictures primarily for my benefit, and hung out for a short time in the small space.

Lach and Slobodan had passed the time waiting for us discussing the finer points of free-climbing. They seemed to be genuinely enjoying each other's company. I thanked God that my friend Lach would remain a friend. For that moment, I shelved any anger directed toward my houseguest. It was evident that Lach had no idea what had happened with the rockslide. So, neither Sara nor I made mention of the trifling event that almost decapitated us. Details, details.

Eventually the descent had to be tackled. The road back was not a cakewalk. "Scary" and "sketchy" were two words bandied about to describe it. Sara and Lach reemphasized the critical importance of staying focused. It was not uncommon for good climbers to get hurt or killed when the descent wasn't taken as seriously as the climb up. In the climbing world, as elsewhere, complacency and fatigue are two major factors contributing to accidents. We had the necessary discussion about our teams. Sara had willed me up the Hulk and was ready to hand the reins to Lach. Slobodan had proved every bit as capable as he claimed, and I knew my Sierra Lakes friends were impressed. Lach even asked, "Slobodan, you interested in free-climbing in Yosemite next week?"

The response was classic. "No, I save myself to kick VJ ass back in Boston. I take him to mountain in New Hampshire. I show him real workout. In fact, we start work together now. Sara, Lach, you go down. We follow. I take good care VJ. You watch." He glanced over and caught the look of doubt in my eyes. "What, VJ, you not trust me?" Gesturing to my friends, he continued, "I take better care of you than these guys."

None of us wanted to dispute that Slobodan was capable of helping me get down. He obviously was. If I argued, it would make for a very uncomfortable remainder of the trip. Trust and intimacy are paramount with a climbing partner. I had neither. I was tired, but still mentally sharp. The climb to the top of the Hulk didn't seem to have affected Slobodan at all. He appeared primed and ready for the next adventure. I answered the lingering question simply, "Let's do it." And so we did.

We watched Lach and Sara descend with grace. Our own path started that way. There was enough snow and ice that our return would be slick and much trickier than it would have been even a month later. We down-climbed along the ridgeline. Slobodan took control when we reached the section that called for the rappel.

"Now VJ, you check harness carefully. I rigged rappel for you. Do not let go rope with brake hand. Very important remember that."

I checked my brake-assisted rappel device. It was attached through the harness belay loop with a solid locking carabiner. I made *certain* it was locked. Now I was committed. This equipment would be the deciding factor if I fell on the rappel. There was, of course, another variable I still wasn't considering.

I put my feet on the ledge, worked my butt down, then took a short leap of faith. I was gratified that everything held and I was not plunging into the abyss. The anchor Slobodan placed was strong and reliable. Now mentally fortified, I worked my way down slowly and steadily. There was a snag in the rope about three meters below me. I flipped it free and was feeling good.

Slobodan called down to me, "VJ, how you doing down there? See, everything just fine." I resumed the descent, growing more comfortable by the second. I was still staring at a sheer sixty-five-meter drop.

SLOBODAN PEERED DOWN to monitor VJ's progress. As he saw the top of the white climbing helmet disappear, his eyes became slits.

At almost the same moment far below, Sara stopped. She felt unusually queasy. She really didn't know why. Yet, the feeling was there, knowing at her. This wasn't altitude playing games with her stomach. It was a deeper unease. The thought crept in and played on her mind. Had she done the right thing, leaving VJ under the Serbian's guidance?

Lach glanced at his partner, noticing the obvious concern on her face. He said, "I know what you're thinking. I'm a little worried too. But you know what? They're big boys. Slobodan will take good care of him. His climbing was almost flawless. So, let's try to get down from here without killing ourselves." Sara turned her head again toward the descent path they had just completed, which VJ and Slobodan were now negotiating. Holding her doubts in check, she followed Lach down. But the gnawing sensation inside didn't go away.

FREE FALL

MONO COUNTY, CALIFORNIA

DISASTER STRUCK WITHIN SECONDS. Unknown to me, when Slobodan guided the rope through the rappel rings, he hadn't used the middle mark that signifies the halfway point in the cord. One end of the seventy-meter rope was only about twenty meters through the anchor. It was fatally uneven. I believed there was a much longer distance I could safely rappel down than I actually had.

Relying exclusively on the safety provided by the rope, I descended the steep drop oblivious to the peril awaiting. Without warning, the short end slipped through my hand, a huge problem. There was no stopper knot—a critical addition that would have also prevented what happened next. I literally rappelled right off the end of the rope, launching into a sudden, heart-stopping drop into the abyss.

A plummet into the gulley filled with loose rock was a death sentence. There wasn't even time to scream. It's amazing what goes through your brain in those few seconds. I once saw a movie that unfolded just as a soldier was about to be hung. His entire life played out before the trapdoor opened and his days on Earth ceased. I thought of Leila and Tess and all the joy we'd had in the short time we were together.

Violently, my unplanned descent came to a sudden stop, and I snapped back to reality. Serendipity had intervened. My harness caught on a just-large-enough outcropping. There I dangled for a few minutes trying to decide if I was broken. I had a large number of cuts and scrapes. Nothing obviously bad.

I marveled at my narrow escape from certain death, and was reminded of an incident that occurred during my residency. A steel worker had fallen seven stories onto rebar. He was stopped when it impaled him. The irony of that wasn't lost on me. He had some nonthreatening spinal issues afterward; however, he was otherwise spared.

I found myself engulfed in a wave of emotions—immensely grateful to be alive and still intact, and simultaneously enraged. *What the hell is going on with Slobodan?* I asked myself. There's no way that fall should've happened. I knew it in my core. I didn't allow myself to ask the obvious: *Was it intentional?*

I focused on repositioning myself into a more stable hold.

Using some of the permanent bolt anchors that Lach had told him were in place, my so-called partner started his own rappel toward me. When he reached my perch, Slobodan was contrite, but not quite to the extent that I would've expected from someone who was responsible for my almost getting smashed into a million pieces.

After asking me if I was okay, he said, "VJ, maybe your leg not as good as you say."

I struggled to maintain my composure, channeling my inner operating room professor self. "Slobodan, that fall had nothing to do with my femur and you know it. Let's just get down and get the fuck out of here."

We established a new anchor system and reset the rappel. This time, I let Slobodan go down first. When we finished that section, we were hardly done; we had to advance through endless loose scree to get to the bottom. That was an adventure in and of itself. Several times I misstepped and almost catapulted downward. But we safely reached the base and connected with Lach and Sara. One look at me, and our faces, and they knew something had happened. I told them briefly that the rappel had gone sideways, but didn't dwell on details. I decided to save that for a later conversation. This was the last rock-climbing experience I would share with Slobodan. I would make sure that would also be the case for anyone I cared about.

The ride back was not the exhausted but boisterous, self-congratulatory event I'd expected. We were all quiet. I could tell that Sara and Lach were mad at themselves for entrusting my safety to Slobodan. I heard Sara muttering to Lach about Slobodan not putting in a backup Prusik—an extra measure of knotting that should have been done. I stewed about my wholly unnecessary brush with death—again. As for Slobodan, who knows what he was thinking? He seemed to have retreated into his own mental Siberia.

We did have one discussion, though. Before we reached my house, I said, "All of us need to agree that what happened today is not to be shared with anyone, and I do mean *anyone.* If I even breathe a word of the truth, Leila will have my head on a platter. Worse, I'll never hear the end of the I-told-you-so from Stall and Bilmer. If anyone says anything to you, just back up what I've decided to say. Is that a deal?"

Lach and Sara promised they would comply with my request. Neither had anything to gain by doing otherwise. Slobodan didn't comment.

Few pursuits put instant death up close and personal. Astronauts, Marines, test pilots, and free-climbers all share that unique perspective. I hardly put myself in the same league as those people. But, somehow, circumstances continued to arise that made me appreciate the tenuous nature of life. I was suspicious that, yet again, bad luck and nature were not the sole forces in play, and vowed to be more circumspect about the people I invited to hang out with me. Asking Slobodan to come to Sierra Lakes had been impulsive, a theme of my life. His devil-may-care attitude had appealed to me. So often I chastised myself for being too anxious and too cautious, admiring those who seemed to be less burdened. Therein lay the explanation for my being so ready to adopt Slobodan as a pal. For the remainder of this trip, however, I had no intention of pursuing anything more potentially dangerous than driving.

SIERRA LAKES TRAGEDY

SIERRA LAKES, CALIFORNIA

THE NEXT MORNING, Slobodan sat at the table downing cups of coffee. I asked, "So, what are you doing today while I'm working?"

"I think I go back north 395 to Bodie," he responded quickly. "I notice sign for it yesterday while we driving to Hulk. Seem like interesting place. See ghost town. Drink beer. I must use car I rent here. Get value for money I spend." The decision to visit the historic site was a good one. Everyone came back raving. It would also take him far from me.

"Believe it or not, I've never been there. There are some hikes nearby that are exceptional. They're close to where you almost killed me. You've got my trail book. I have to go protect Sierra Lakes from the scourge of hand afflictions. See you at dinner."

Slobodan looked at me with piercing eyes. "VJ, you fine. That what make life interesting. What not kill you, make you stronger." I had grown to understand Slobodan much better. He was vastly entertaining on his terms, but essentially immune to the feelings or needs of others. In essence, a classic sociopath. He was also fiercely independent and very resourceful. Leaving him on his own without me as tour guide was a non-issue.

About three o'clock I got a disconcerting call from Johan. "VJ, we have a problem. In fact, we have two problems. You know the guy your asshole friend got into it with at the bar the other night? Guess what—maintenance found him dead in the Village the next morning. His face was smashed. From what I was told, he was blackout drunk. I think he choked on his own blood. The Village cam showed some guy in a hat bludgeoning him. The footage didn't show me what he looked like. The bartender told me you two left together, so I know Slobodan didn't do it, but I still wish I could have talked to him.

"That leads me to the second problem. A car went over the guardrail going north on the 395 near Conway Summit. The vehicle crossed the two southbound lanes just before that lookout point. Maybe the driver was trying to avoid hitting a deer. The car fell a couple of hundred feet, smashed into boulders, and then burned to a crisp. So did the driver. Whoever it was wasn't wearing a seat belt. Not that it matters in the end, but there's another detail. The victim also got decapitated in the process. Haven't found the head yet. It must have rolled under some rocks. We'll keep looking."

Feeling a chill, I suddenly had an odd sense of where the conversation was going. "Johan, are you about to tell me that it was Slobodan's car?"

"I'm sorry to break it to you this way, but in a word—yes. We did ID the vehicle and traced it to him. Have you spoken to Slobodan today?"

The information was bizarre. With what had happened while skiing and rock climbing, my first thought was that some greater force was looking out for me. I couldn't quite put my finger on the emotions I was experiencing. Slobodan was too cavalier, and his overconfidence had almost gotten me killed as recently as a day ago. I wasn't happy or sad; I felt disoriented, so I just sat down.

"Johan, give me a minute. Let me see if I can reach him." As I anticipated, the call went straight to voicemail. My brain was stuck on the randomness of the course of events. I called Johan back. "I can't raise him. Is there anything that you found on the body? Slobodan had a very distinctive ring."

On the other end of the phone, the response was simple. "The coroner has what she found. Can you come over and take a look?" I jumped in the truck and sped over.

The moment I saw the scorpion ring, the reality and gravity of the situation struck me. I also realized how little information I had about the man. Slobodan had rarely mentioned a family, when he did, it was vague. I never even knew what city he was from. Somehow, we always spoke about current world affairs, medicine, economics, or other topical subjects.

His interactions with women suggested he had no wife, at least in the States. Like it or not, I was tasked with the job of figuring out what to do with his body. I made a call to his boss, Dr. Tribolsi. In all probability a similar call was made to my department chairman when I "died."

Tribolsi wasn't my favorite. I think his bow tie reduced the blood supply to his brain. We had gotten into heated exchanges more than once. Still, I had to face the music. I wanted to leave a message, but unfortunately, he picked up the phone. "Dr. Tribolsi, this is VJ Brio. I need to talk to you about Slobodan."

Before I could get more words out, I was interrupted. "Has he done something bad to one of your patients, Dr. Brio?"

I was taken aback. Slobodan was many things, but he struck

me as a very astute physician. Maybe Tribolsi was threatened. It was easy to understand—he was a weasel. Slobodan had probably abused him mercilessly in the lab. I summoned the will to speak further. "Well, Dr. Tribolsi, that is actually not why I'm calling. Slobodan died today in a car accident. He was visiting with me here in Sierra Lakes, California. I wanted to inform you. I was also hoping you could access his file and help me locate his next of kin."

There was silence on the other end of the phone. I said, "Dr. Tribolsi, did you hear what I said?"

"Well, Dr. Brio, I can't assist you with that. You'll have to call administration in the morning. Good evening." With that, he hung up.

Out loud I said, "What the fuck?!" I didn't expect an outpouring of compassion. I just needed help. Everything about the conversation was so strange, I almost forgot the purpose of the exchange.

DR. TRIBOLSI had other troubles on his mind. The man with the beautiful smile and enchanting South African accent sat in the comfortable armchair directly across from him. He eyed the doctor as he sipped his tea.

Tribolsi might be brilliant, but he was weak. In the wild, he wouldn't last long. Nor was he going to fare any better here in the epicenter of higher learning. He'd helped this representative of the Cape Town–based Ebola Foundation immensely, but now his services were no longer needed.

This specific conversation would be a short one. The facts of the case were simple, and the decision easy. Too bad for Tribolsi.

The brilliantly dressed man proceeded with the task at hand.

When the job was complete, this most unwelcome visitor glanced back at the property. Tribolsi's Back Bay house was lovely, a perfect place to retire. The Charles River was just steps away. He made a mental note to try to pick it up before the listing officially hit the market.

NUISANCE WORK

SIERRA LAKES, CALIFORNIA

HAVING ACHIEVED NOTHING, I figured I'd have to wait until morning to try to unravel the mystery swirling around Slobodan's intentions toward me, and his untimely death. It was odd to contemplate the demise of a person I'd been spending so much time with. I was processing my thoughts when Johan stopped by the house.

"Hey, VJ. Rough day. You want to grab some dinner? Lorraine is teaching a church class tonight."

I didn't hesitate, seizing the opportunity to learn more about the day's events. "Let me snag a sweatshirt." Even in the middle of summer, evenings in Sierra Lakes were often chilly.

We walked across the street to the Rib Rattler and settled in for dinner. We talked for a few minutes about superficial things like sports before turning to the more obvious topic. "VJ, your buddy Slobodan—he sure didn't go out of his way to make friends here during his short visit. What was his story?"

I semi-shrugged. "Like I told you. I didn't really know him that well. I'm aware he was into some business deals; the guy had energy. He was just a cowboy. Think about how many doctors run their planes into mountains. There's a reason for that. Misguided arrogance. I'm not immune. Wish I was."

Johan narrowed his eyes just slightly. "Yeah, VJ, I can see that. Funny, once I found out all about your friend Petra and what happened between you two, I completely wrote off those assholes she had contacted me about. There was no reason to do anything different. Still, they're sort of like a missing puzzle piece—bothers me on some unconscious level. I'm wondering if that rifle we found belonged to one of them. I can't prove it, but I don't think they ever left Sierra Lakes. Course I'm not going to ask you about it, because then you might feel obligated to lie to me. I don't want that."

I kept my gaze steady, and tried not to betray any emotion, shrugging but saying nothing. Johan was a brilliant detective.

He sat back. "Okay then, book closed—for now." His smile gave me heartburn. "About this new case. Is there any reason to believe your friend's misfortune wasn't an accident?"

Deep in thought, I gazed across the table. "I presume you're not asking if I was involved. I wasn't. Ironically, I felt like I wanted to kill him on several occasions this past week, like when he was causing trouble with you the other day. But I mean that, of course, only as a manner of speech.

"Leila and I both accidently read some data that Slobodan was taking to London for a meeting. It clearly had business significance. I think there were big dollars riding on the information. In fact, the company he was working for tanked. I could think of a scenario where some heavily invested parties would be upset. It's an interesting question, and definitely possible that someone was after him. Did you find anything at the scene that seemed odd—I mean other than the fact that there was no head on the body?"

Johan played with his fork, twirling it this way and that. "That's hard to say. Cars don't usually blow up, but it's certainly not unheard of. Remember, though, I'm just the police chief in Sierra Lakes. This wasn't my crime scene. It's the sheriff's, Bobby Wilson. I don't think you know him. He's a smart cookie. Don't be alarmed if he gives you a call. I'm surprised he hasn't already. I told him the reported victim was here visiting with you."

I normally would have downed another piece of the loaded corn bread. I could exist the rest of my life on that alone. But the circumstances had dampened my appetite.

"Sure, I'll tell the sheriff what I know. Slobodan's laptop should be at the house. I'll turn it over and the sheriff can see what he finds out. Let's talk about something else—how are the kids?"

Johan filled me in. The words penetrated my skull but didn't register. I was now focused on the information that Leila and I had seen and the question of whether it had cost Slobodan his life.

When I got home I went to Slobodan's room and gathered his things. He traveled light. The computer was not there, though. I figured that given what had happened with the bag switch, he didn't trust leaving it anywhere near me. He had apparently taken that and a day pack with him on his ill-fated excursion. There were a few clothes, some toiletries, a Serbian novel that looked like a murder mystery, and not much else. I decided to contact the sheriff in the morning and tell him to look for the computer.

The next day I placed the dreaded call to MRMC administration. My absolute favorite people on the planet. I spoke to several mid-level individuals who were useless. Finally, I got bumped up to Hymie Tucker (whom I preferred to think of as "Hymen Tuchus"), the secretary to the COO. He was a cold fish, and a bit of an SOB, but at least he would talk to me. "Yes, Dr. Brio. I understand you have a situation. I suppose these problems have become normal for you. Not so much for us. Please tell me what happened to this Dr. Marjanovic."

The personal attack was not unanticipated. I disregarded the comment of the whining dweeb and focused on the information I needed. "Mr. Tucker, I need to have you examine Dr. Marjanovic's file and direct me to his next of kin."

There was a long pause. "Dr. Brio, about that, we have been searching our database. We have nothing at all in our records about a Dr. Marjanovic. Who is this man?"

I was starting to get angry. "For fuck's sake, Tuchus, I mean Tucker, I know no one there likes me, but can you just forward the information so I can do something with this body!"

"Dr. Brio, another comment like that and I will have to refer you to the physicians' well-being committee. I cannot provide you information I do not have. You say the man worked in Infectious Disease. Perhaps you should try to contact Dr. Tribolsi. He may know something we don't. I have nothing further for you."

I hung up the phone with no resolution of my problem and now a number of new questions. I decided to take the plunge and call Tribolsi's office again. I actually had a good relationship with his assistant, Manny. He had worked with one of my orthopaedic colleagues before getting wooed to the ID Department.

"Hey, buddy, are they treating you okay? I need to speak to Tribolsi. Is he around?"

He was not his usual jovial self. "VJ, I guess you didn't hear. Dr. Tribolsi had a stroke. He's in the neuro ICU. They don't think he's going to make it."

I put the phone down without saying anything but a stammered goodbye. Clearly, something was very wrong.

With no personal information about Slobodan and no way to obtain any, and no one to pass the buck to, I called the sheriff and told him what I had observed and been told. He listened carefully, asked me a few questions, and finally said, "I agree that things don't add up. I'm gonna get the boys to look for that head and that computer. We'll see what we find. This is not gonna be an easy one. Either that or the obvious explanation is staring us right in the face—the man got distracted by a deer, ran off the road, and got his ass torched. You let me know if you find out something else. I'll keep working on it for now."

He did not seem too enthusiastic. He'd had some heart problems, I knew, and was set to retire in a few months. I can't say I was hell-bent to find out anything more myself. If someone had killed Slobodan, then that was someone I didn't want to cross. Fool me once . . .

I called Johan and told him about Tribolsi's stroke and my conversation with the sheriff. I had another day of office scheduled, and there seemed to be no reason not to do it. The whole thing was crazy. I could think of little else as I zipped from patient to patient.

As expected, within a day, Tribolsi was dead. I might be the only person who would try to connect the two unfortunate incidents. The thought occurred to me that, yet again, I might be at some personal risk. That was unsettling.

THE DANGER OF SPEEDING

GARDNERVILLE, NEVADA

WHILE DRIVING DOWN the empty highway, Miro contemplated his latest accomplishment. Beautiful in its simplicity and execution. The technical achievement of a proper assassination was not to be underestimated. Any moron could shoot somebody. The key was to perform the act without suggesting that a real murder was being committed. Miro was a virtuoso in his field. They hired him for that reason. A messy hit would ruin the billion-dollar deal. Completely unacceptable.

A clunking noise in the trunk interrupted his train of thought. He quickly realized the severed head had gone rogue and was not staying where he'd put it. He'd planned to dispose of it in Reno, but the damn thing was irritating him. A roadside burial now seemed necessary.

As he searched for a convenient turnoff on a remote stretch of 395, Miro peered at the sky. There was no moon, but the stars shone brightly. The Big Dipper was particularly luminescent despite the season. He passed a sign indicating that Gardnerville was five miles ahead. When blue lights appeared in the rearview mirror, Miro checked the holographic projection on the windshield. Sixty-four miles per hour. The speed limit was fifty-five. He thought, *You're kidding me with this bullshit—right?* Apparently not; the official vehicle continued to follow him.

Miro pulled over onto the dirt shoulder but kept driving along the side of the road. The voice on the loudspeaker impatiently directed him to stop his vehicle. Not wishing to frustrate the interloper, Miro complied as he fingered the lethal steel instrument.

The unsuspecting highway patrol officer barely had peach fuzz. He gestured for the blond man to roll down the window and suggested he hand over the customary "license and registration." Those were his last words. The knife rendered his trachea nonfunctional and his carotids useless. Sounds from his mouth and oxygen to his brain were a thing of the past.

Miro shook his head while he wiped the blade clean, thinking, *Stupid kid. Popped me for nine miles per hour over the limit. Not his day.*

Swiftly, Miro jumped out of his car, dragged the body into the Nevada Highway Patrol cruiser, stripped, quickly changed into new clothes, and deposited his old ones and gloves into the vehicle. He put a rag in the gas tank and lit it, allowing enough time to clear the area before the ensuing immolation. When the car burst into flames, Miro was already well on his way to the nearby sleepy town. He knew he could easily exchange vehicles and plates. By the time anyone noticed the new missing car he'd be in Reno. Miro was not a man who ever looked back.

PART II

DEPARTURE

LOS ANGELES, CALIFORNIA

YET AGAIN I'd had an unforgettable experience in Sierra Lakes marked by anxiety and death. This was the place I was supposed to come to relax. I still loved it, but I was beginning to wonder. What should've been a glowing feeling of triumph from conquering the Incredible Hulk was instead a sense of foreboding.

The morning news described the gruesome murder of a highway patrolman, torched near Gardnerville. The bodies were starting to pile up. I didn't call Johan to see if he knew any of the details. I couldn't bear it. I just wanted to escape.

During the truck ride back to LA I spent the five hours flipping channels on satellite radio. I couldn't focus. Finally, I settled on comedy, which gave me a chance to put aside the anxiety gnawing inside my gut. Laughing is definitely good therapy for just about anything. Once I docked, the ride share came quickly, and I was back wandering the vast expanses of LAX.

Walking down a random concourse, bleary-eyed from the constant sleep deprivation, I looked up. A hundred feet ahead, a familiar face was strolling toward me. Despite my brain fog I recognized Asiya Banerjee, the fascinating physician from a wedding we'd all attended just two months earlier. She'd dressed Leila and Tess in traditional saris for the culturally rich event. After meeting, we became fast friends.

Asiya had been at a medical meeting in San Francisco and was now headed to see relatives in Washington, D.C., before returning home to Kashmir. Her husband, Nithan Banerjee, was the new chief minister of that Indian state. Her flight out of SFO had been cancelled, and the one through Chicago was also cancelled, so she had finally been rerouted through LAX. The casual decisions of an agent sitting at a computer in Kansas City and now, here we both were. A shared coffee seemed right, so coffee it was.

We talked first about her children and the wedding, then restarted a political discussion that had been interrupted at the wedding. To our mutual dismay, we still weren't able to solve all the planet's ills. As our conversation continued, Asiya began to look very anxious.

"Asiya, my apologies—we certainly don't have to talk about politics."

She responded with a soft smile. "VJ, this is not on you. There is an issue that I can't get out of my mind. Nithan is fighting a battle at home with one of the major crime bosses. This man, Bhaduri, is very powerful and extremely dangerous. I don't think Nithan is taking the risk seriously enough. He thinks he can save the world and nothing will touch him."

I felt for her. "Asiya, I know about those types of people. I would love to tell you that you're wrong to be concerned. You're not. They're vicious. Money and domination rule every decision they make. Other people's lives mean nothing."

I didn't have time to share my own story. The overhead speaker indicated that both our flights were boarding. I gave Asiya a hug, and we were off. I hoped our worlds would intersect again.

THE FORCE

JAMMU, INDIAN TERRITORY OF KASHMIR

THE CAPITAL CITY was teeming with activity. Tourists streamed along the banks of the Tawi River, providing much-needed cash to the small businesses that lined it. Cooler winds prevailed at a time when it was normally brutally hot. There was at least a sense of temporary political stability. People were generally happy—save one.

The lackey turned to his boss. "Mr. Bhaduri, sir, I regret to tell you that our enterprise in the Sialkot District was just raided. They confiscated the heroin and arrested our employees. This new man in charge, Banerjee, seems to be quite serious about making our lives difficult. The police we bought were not able to stop him. I do not think that he understands the proper role he should play as chief minister."

The small, thin man did not respond as he looked out the window at the sun setting over the Siwalik Hills, but the informant noted a small shake in his hand. It was clear that Bhaduri was furious. What he lacked in size, he compensated for in unrelenting force of will, mercilessly dominating rivals. His base of operations was perfect, nestled between China, Afghanistan, and Pakistan. He was literally in the center of the action, his scope of activity rapidly expanding. The impending deal represented a major step forward for him in the international market.

Bhaduri was a transplant from Tamil Nadu. As a Tamil Brahmin, superior achievement was expected from him by his parents. Bhaduri's family was dominated by physicians and engineers. Even as a boy, though, he had known he was on a different trajectory. He had every belief that he would do great things, but his religious teachings meant nothing to him, and math and science were a struggle. Manipulating people was not. Morality was not. He didn't believe in it. By the time he was sixteen he'd already become established in the drug trade. When it came to be time to replace his mentor, the man's liquidation was an easy step. Bhaduri had built his business carefully, never overstepping. Gradually his power base and influence expanded. He also possessed a strong appetite for pleasures of the flesh. The international prostitution ring he headed rewarded him financially and otherwise. Now he'd reached a crossroad.

Chief Minister Banerjee had come to Jammu intent on exerting his own moral authority—the crime boss be damned. Even the lowlife who bore the bad news understood that the two men were headed for a direct confrontation. Banerjee had fired the first salvo. Bhaduri plotted his response. It would not be subtle.

NEW RICHES

BOSTON, MASSACHUSETTS

THE CERTIFIED LETTERS came in the mail to each of us. It was a fact I couldn't quite wrap my brain around. Leila, Tess, Axel, and I were in line for huge whistleblower payout checks. The insurance carriers and government were extremely thankful for our collective work. Axel had led them directly to Petra's accounts and to those of most of the co-conspirators. Rick's accounts and the dollars he made were gone with the wind. That cybermagic was not Axel's work. Rick had his own computer warriors.

A big chunk of my cash was targeted for Doctors Without Borders and the Hand Society's Touching Hands Project, but I had an idea for another way to spend some of the money. The whole mess with Slobodan in Sierra Lakes had affected me, and the day-to-day grind in the office was burning me out. Nothing about it felt right. I wanted an escape and needed to do something different.

The financial windfall created the chance for a soft landing. When I'd seen my South African friend Solomon Mizrahi the previous year at the annual Hand Society meeting, he'd offered to let me take a sabbatical, of sorts. I first met him when he joined my hand study group for one of our conferences. Copious amounts of splendid red wine led to a series of entertaining conversations. He was an extraordinarily intelligent, talented surgeon in charge of a busy hand surgery department. The idea was to work with him at the public Onderskeid Hospitaal in Cape Town. The time to do that had arrived.

One afternoon while Leila and I were relaxing on the Adirondack chairs, I brought it up, laying out my plan and reasoning.

Leila took a sip of her beer then spoke: "My first take is that you're trying to escape something that's hard to escape. But it does sound intriguing. It would certainly give me the opportunity to connect with the South African branch of my family. My dad has been pushing me to do that for years. His parents brought him to the U.S. when he was young. They settled in Atlanta, but almost everyone else he's related to is still there. What are the logistics? We can't take Vika or Cat. Do you think someone would temporarily adopt them?"

"I've got that covered. If that's your biggest issue, we don't have an issue. Living in Cape Town would feel like complete decadence. The place is supposedly just like La Jolla. Although residency was a grind, I have only great memories of the six years I lived in Southern California. How can you argue with beautiful beaches and perfect weather? There is a huge need for medical volunteers with your skills. You can literally do anything you want. It's a no-brainer. I don't know why it's taken all this trauma to make such an intelligent decision."

"Hold on there, VJ," Leila objected. "Don't you think you're getting a little ahead of yourself? I haven't even said yes yet. My guess is that you've already planned this move and that you're not really asking my consent but just telling me what we're going to do. Would that be accurate?"

I answered honestly. "Leila, darling, life is about perspective. From my perspective, I just wanted to make sure that all the bases were covered before I presented you with your choice. If you give the okay, I'm going to run it by Tess. It would be a great opportunity for her to do some amazing subinternships in a very unique place."

Fortunately, Tess was very excited by the prospect of this experience, and promised to look into her own options. She was halfway through her required clinical rotations. She'd finished internal medicine and was almost done with surgery.

After she presented a detailed academic plan, her dean granted her a special waiver to permit her to do several electives at the same South African hospital where I was going to volunteer. Infectious disease, nephrology, and neurology offered unique views of an entirely different medical world than Boston. The hands-on decision-making opportunities would be amazing. She acknowledged the special nature of what was ahead and intended to take full advantage.

Leila made big plans for Tess to meet the Akekawanzie extended family. In fact, she had one particular cousin in mind. According to Leila, he was a man with an irresistible smile. Tess would sniff out the setup immediately, but since I wasn't responsible, it would be okay. Tess and Axel had stayed close, but on a strictly platonic level. The short-term romance that had followed the takedown of the Cooperative didn't suit either of them. But we worked out a nice agreement with Axel. He would live in our town house rent-free; in turn, he'd supervise the care of Vika and Cat. I liked the idea of having him in our place.

Among the myriad details I addressed prior to leaving was the phone call to my younger sister, Kari, in Israel. I thought she and her husband, Mark, might want to take a vacation and join us for a week or two in Cape Town. He was an executive in a pharma company just outside of Tel Aviv. I was pleased to learn he was already doing work in Cape Town and had several upcoming trips planned there. Unfortunately, Kari had her own obligations and didn't see a good opportunity to take time off while we'd be there. I looked forward to seeing Mark in South Africa, whom I admired greatly, albeit without my sister, and perhaps taking a trip to Tel Aviv at some point to see Kari too.

POWER PLAY

BOSTON, MASSACHUSETTS

CLOSE TO OUR DEPARTURE DATE, while driving home from a show, Leila offered an idea. "VJ, how would you feel about going on a small detour before we start in Cape Town? My father mentioned this game park resort, Wengonyama. I checked it out. It's incredible. All the reviews say it's *the* place to go for a photo safari."

I was happy with Leila's plan. It's not as if there was a chance I'd change her mind even if I wasn't. "Like I planned this sabbatical, my assumption is that you've already booked this photo safari for the three of us, yes? And you've told Solomon?"

She looked at me demurely. "However did you guess, love? Turnabout is fair play." The conversation stopped abruptly as an ambulance screamed by, no doubt headed to MRMC. Our street was awash with blue flashing lights. Although I hadn't taken call in months, my first impulse was to contact the trauma unit to see what I might get sucked into. Old habits are hard to break.

The road wasn't blocked, and there was no one there to direct us, so I slowed to a crawl and carefully negotiated a path around the multitude of parked patrol cars. The next second a flashlight was banging on my window and someone was screaming at me: "You're driving on the wrong side of the road. Give me your license and registration now." I quickly handed him the documents, but before I could get out a word he was gone. Five minutes later he returned with the ticket. I was seething. Leila wisely reached across and completed the one-way transaction.

We looked at each other, wondering what had just happened.

"Honey," she said, "this is just a taste of what it feels like to be a person of color. That cop was a complete dick to you because he could be. For once you weren't *knowingly* breaking traffic laws. He gave you that ticket to punish you for past sins."

I suspected there would be no way to contest it, since we would be in Cape Town by the time the court date rolled around. Although I'd try to postpone it, the idea of having to capitulate made me even more angry. This time I couldn't even get Axel to help me.

We were close enough to home that we could walk. I threw the car in reverse and found a place to stash it about five hundred meters away. While we walked back, Leila checked her cell and picked up the local news station feed. A gunfight had followed a chase with the car thief who had landed in our neighborhood. Unconsciously I rubbed the area on my thigh where I'd been shot. I was reminded again how lucky I was even to be around to get bothered by this adrenaline-driven officer.

I realize certain things about myself. Outrage and reactivity burn quietly inside me like the pilot light in a stove. They can ignite instantly. Situations that would simply irritate most rational people spark absolute fire inside me. I look at it as justified righteous indignation. Sometimes it's good, and sometimes destructive. I can't help how I feel, but I continue to struggle to maintain balance. But this time, an unnecessary car chase and shooting in the middle of a residential area—really? Absolute stupidity. I decided I couldn't entirely let this one go. Letters to the mayor and police chief would have to be written. The entire event also reminded me how desperately I needed a change of scenery. Our foray into South Africa couldn't come soon enough.

As we approached our townhouse, we noticed the front door was cracked open. I didn't think we'd left earlier that evening without closing it. Rather than do the obvious and ask one of the police officers in the area to check, both of us charged in, warning the potential intruder we were home. The perpetrator of the break-in stood defiantly at the top of the stairs, holding a baseball bat. Once Tess realized we were no threat, she walked down and collapsed on the couch.

Sitting opposite, I asked, "So Tess, were you here preparing for your tryout with the Sox, or is there a different reason you're holding that bat?"

"VJ, don't be a jerk," Tess snapped. "You know I'm tough. I didn't particularly like it when bullets started flying. The bat was the only protection I could find. By the way, having the combination to the safe where you keep the pistols would be helpful in the future."

Following our dustup with the Cooperative the previous year, with so many people threatening our lives, the three of us had decided that concentrated self-defense training would be useful. One of my patients was a recently retired Navy SEAL. He was very happy to help. He insisted that the family Brio spend time at the gun range. No one argued. We purchased several 9mm Sig Sauer P938s that we'd all practiced with, and I stored them in our bedroom.

I had experience using a variety of weapons during my time

in my Swedish military unit. Leila's father had exposed her to guns from an early age. After the episode during her teens when intruders assaulted her mother, only to be thwarted by her father and a .44 Magnum, Leila redoubled her efforts to familiarize herself with handguns. Tess's situation was different. The Cooperative was the first direct threat she'd ever faced. The initial concept of learning to use a gun was totally foreign. Suddenly, the need became imperative to her. Tess spent concentrated, quality time with our instructor and reached the point where her skills eclipsed those of Leila and me. She loved having bragging rights over the two of us.

The bat remained in her hand as she explained. "I was worried. I came over to pick up the clothes Leila got me for the trip. Before I was even through the door, I heard all these sirens and then gunshots right behind me. I ran upstairs, grabbed the Louisville Slugger that you keep by the door, and jumped in your tub. I figured that was the safest place. I didn't want to get hit by a stray shot or flying glass. I just came out of the bathroom. Do you have any idea what's going on? I left my phone somewhere in the excitement."

I just shook my head. "Tess, I thought you would've glued that thing to your body by now."

She glared daggers at me. "As if you should talk, VJ."

Instantly I apologized. I was still amped up from my dealings with the ticket wanker and was taking my frustration out on her. "Sorry, sweetheart. Apparently, the police took care of your shooter. He stole a car, and they managed to chase him here from Storrow Drive. I can't explain the logic of pursuing him onto this street. He's either dead or getting operated on now. My blue friends just gave me a ticket. That made me happy. But now that I know you were in the firing line, I'm just relieved you're okay. Apology accepted?"

Tess sniffed. "I'll think about it. This neighborhood does seem like the smart place to have a gun battle. Maybe next time they can do it in the middle of the hospital. At least it will be easy to get the wounded to the OR. Whatever—I'm glad the drama's over."

ANOTHER AIRPORT POLTERGEIST

ZURICH, SWITZERLAND

BEFORE WE COULD leave behind the everyday Boston chaos and wing our way to the bush adjacent to Kruger National Park, where the true fun would begin, I had to create my own personal drama. It started with my carry-on luggage, the kind I've used for years. I had clothes in it that I didn't want the airline to lose at our stopover in Zurich.

"Sir," the counter person said, "this bag weighs eight pounds too much. You'll have to check it. There's no charge."

I protested, "I've taken this bag filled with the same clothes weighing the same amount the last four international flights."

She didn't budge. "It's a safety issue. If it falls on someone's head it will hurt them. Either you check this or it doesn't go."

I had no chance of winning, so I entertained myself by insulting her in Swedish. I gathered certain critical belongings and stuffed them into the personal item they would allow me to take. Before we took off, I said to myself, *Put your computer in the bag.* My brain countered, *No, don't put it in the bag. You'll want it during the flight—everything will fall out again.* So there I put it, easy to get, under my bag in the overhead. As soon as we sat, I was reviewing articles for my board recertification. So, I read intensely and never even looked at my computer.

After a night of fitful sleep on the plane, it landed, and I merrily grabbed my bag, sans the underlying computer. We had a six-hour layover, and it was only forty minutes later that I discovered my mistake. I was simultaneously furious with myself, General Patton at the first airline counter, and the Orthopaedic Board. Relatively calmly, I ran up to the airline counter hoping for a miracle. No miracle. "Sir, there is no one at the gate. You will have to wait to see if the cleaning crew finds it."

"But you don't understand. I know exactly where it is. Can you have someone radio them and tell them so they can grab it?"

With her fake smile and brusque Swiss-German accent, she politely quashed me.

"No, that isn't possible. You can try Lost and Found. They're downstairs. Next customer, please."

I ran downstairs, feeling like the clock was ticking ever faster. Finally, it was my turn. "Ma'am, I left my computer on the plane. Is there any way you can contact the cleaning crew to see if they can get it?"

Blank stare. She handed me a card with a website.

"Sir, you must go online and make a claim."

"Ma'am, you don't understand, the computer isn't lost. I just left it behind."

"Sir, make the claim online."

"Can I do that here?"

"No."

My phone data wasn't working. Again a small tirade of Swedish curse words passed through my lips. I left in search of an airport computer to make the claim. I am nothing if not persistent.

I checked the Lost and Found office every half hour for the next three hours. The granite-faced clerk was not endeared to my presence.

Just before we had to leave to catch our next flight, the clerks changed. The new clerk made a call. I stood expectantly at the desk. The back door opened, and my computer case serendipitously appeared. I was saved. A man who looked slightly familiar delivered my coveted laptop and quickly exited. He reminded me of someone I had seen somewhere in Boston, but I couldn't place him.

Quickly I took a peek at the lost treasure. There were grease smudges on the keyboard that I didn't remember, but lord knows how many people had handled the computer on its not-so-short-walk back to me. I had to rush to the gate, so I emptied the clothes in my bag, treating the viewing public to my pink llama boxers, and stuffed the computer inside.

Leila and Tess had been knocking down drinks in the lounge. For them, the need to indulge in another glass of wine was no problem at all. And thus began our journey to a new world buried in the old.

WENGONYAMA

JOHANNESBURG, SOUTH AFRICA

THE FINAL LEG routed us to Johannesburg, where we were scheduled to pick up our connection to Kruger the next day. It proved completely uneventful. Business class was still a treat for the ten-and-a-half-hour flight. I devoured Swiss chocolates and watched movies. Tess and Leila knocked down more wine—pre-game training for the game park. The three of us were glassy-eyed when we departed the craft.

We breezed off the plane. Then the efficiency stopped. We were mired in a forever line. People from all parts of the globe stood with us on the decades-old yellow linoleum floor. I had ample time to study the vast array of clothing styles and listen to the different languages. Like Finnish, most of it sounded nonsensical. I amused myself by making up conversations and telling Tess what person X was saying to person Y. She wasn't as entertained. Weariness from the twenty-four hours of travel was beginning to take its toll—particularly as time passed. It turns out that thousands of people from all over the world don't smell great.

Each of us entering the country was being screened for all manner of infectious diseases. It was a perfect entrée for what Tess would be doing. We did get to know the people behind us. They were newlyweds taking two months to experience Africa. Their plan didn't involve guides or hotels. Javier and Amanda were going to rent a vehicle and hit the parks. He was a native Peruvian, she was from Canada. They met on a failed climbing expedition up K2. Day after day in tents in wicked storm conditions spawned the romance. This was their third continent. Naturally, rock climbing was a huge passion, Torres del Paine in Patagonia the latest conquest. I was only surprised that they weren't Sierra Lakes natives. The Incredible Hulk came up. They were intrigued, taking great interest in each of us, asking many questions. They seemed particularly focused on what Tess and I planned to do at our new hospital. We exchanged contact information and promised to host them if they made their way to Cape Town. They assured us we would meet again.

Finally, we reached the front of the line. We had our eyes checked, our temperatures taken, and got officially passed. By this time we were thoroughly exhausted. Plans to go to the Mandela museum were scuttled. I thanked God that we'd had the foresight to ship most of our belongings ahead of time. Dragging around multiple heavy bags at that point would have been too painful. We were going to stay at a hotel on-site and fly out the next day on a bush plane.

The next thing I knew Leila was sitting on top of me grabbing my shoulders. "Are you going to sleep forever? Tess and I both did a workout and we're ready to get going. We need to at least go out and get some food here." The exercise thing was beyond my comprehension. I still felt like I was in a fog. The two wonderful women I was with were clearly insane.

Once my eyes focused, I realized that I'd been dead to the world for over eight hours. I rallied enough to take a shower and put on my clothes. The hotel directed us to a place that turned out to be a faux Caesars Palace. It was completely bizarre to be halfway around the world and yet not away from the influence of the States at all. But then we saw the menu at the restaurant we chose. There were exotic dishes of all types. We settled on platters of grilled meats, fish, and vegetables—a tremendous feast. Dessert was even better.

Tess jostled my arm when I got the bill. "We've been gluttons—are you going to have any money left for the rest of the trip?"

I did the calculation and smiled. "In Sweden we could get three Big Macs for what we paid here. This is definitely the place for us!" Just as we were leaving, who did we see? Amanda and Javier from the airport.

"VJ, Leila, Tess, fancy meeting you here. Did you indulge? We went to town." All of us laughed and traded food war stories. Indeed, they were an extremely intriguing couple.

The well-worn bush plane waited for us the next morning. Tess cracked, "Is it safe?" I looked over the aircraft. Its wings seemed as if they might fall off at any moment. "Safe as an egg in the nest of an eagle." Silently I was praying that we would just successfully take off and land. The time in the air was slightly choppy, but all things being equal, not bad. Then we were there, squarely in the middle of the Wengonyama private game reserve that abutted Kruger National Park. The strangeness of the environment was both bewildering and enchanting. I thought of the group entering Jurassic Park for the first time. Full of wonder and curiosity. Knowing there was danger, but not letting it penetrate the aura of excitement.

Leila was all over it. "Wow! It's beautiful! What a place!" I looked around and there was nothing but nature. It was a perfect introduction to the wild. The best part—it wasn't even that hot, and there was virtually no humidity. I hate hot and humid. I have no idea how I ever survived the long summers in Durham.

The people greeting us introduced us to the rules of the road. At night there would be absolutely NO walking to our luxurious individual dwellings without being escorted by an armed ranger. There would be absolutely NO standing up in the observation jeeps. Both absolutely verboten. Separation from the dangerous animals we'd be viewing was not negotiable.

Our plan that first evening in Wengonyama was to connect with Leila's cousin's wife, Ayanda Akekawanzie, and their son, Noah. I'd been informed that her husband, Samson, was on a science expedition in the Arctic with a group that was heavily involved in a climate change study. It was unlikely he'd be back while we were in South Africa. Ayanda was a political science professor at the University of Cape Town, where her husband was also based. Her focus was revolution. I was keen on getting her impression of the evolution of politics in Europe and the United States. Noah had avoided the academic yoke shared by his parents. His calling was government—a profession the Akekawanzie clan had staked out. According to Leila, he was a bright young star, a man on the express elevator up. I was hoping he'd just be a nice guy and not too full of himself.

We entered the expansive lobby area filled with rustically elegant furniture, where Leila spied the pair, already standing up to give hugs. The young man was beautiful. He also looked strangely familiar. He smiled directly at Tess, and for that moment nobody else in the world existed. Slowly he made his way to the place we were standing. Tess was transfixed. Leila made the introduction.

"Tess, VJ, this is my second cousin, Noah. He works in the government, doing what, I don't know. I'll leave that for him to explain." In less time than it takes to do a carpal tunnel release, it was apparent that he and Tess had chemistry. They found a pair of overstuffed chairs in the corner of the huge lobby and set up camp as if they had known each other for years. Leila and I sat down to get acquainted with Ayanda.

After an afternoon adventure in the park and a delicious dinner, the five of us gathered in front of the fire. Noah had a certain charisma, sporting that brilliant smile and exuding confidence, intelligence, and wit. This package was tied up neatly with a bow of sincere humility. Obviously, the support and contacts his parents provided were a huge bonus, but it was clear this was a man who would indeed quickly climb the ladder of influence. Perhaps even become president one day.

Noah was an official in the Cape Town office of the Department of Health and possessed an interesting perspective on the system. He was intimately aware of the long-standing history of graft, nepotism, and deceit, practices not so easily eradicated.

"Yes, VJ, we have an imperfect set of circumstances that we deal with every day. Sometimes it is quite a struggle. You will find this out firsthand. My sources suggest to me that matters are not so different in the United States—yes?"

I smiled widely. "Well stated. Greed and humanity will be forever joined. We make rules to try to change what happens, but we all know how clever people can be when they want power, sex, or money. It is our curse. We've come here to escape all that."

Noah settled back in his chair with a glass of fine Merlot. "And so you shall. Our extended family will see to it that you learn all about how wonderful South Africa can be. I have specific ideas how cousin Leila can help our department. There is so much need." Then, abruptly, Noah shifted gears. "Tess tells me that you are her biological father, but you have only known each other for a relatively short time. She says her mother is not in the picture." I glanced to Tess to see how much she'd told him. Seeing that Noah was momentarily distracted, she mouthed the words "He doesn't know who she is." I raised my eyebrows nonetheless, surprised at the turn in conversation.

Noah continued, "I am pleased you found each other. I too am adopted. Unfortunately, I have no knowledge of either biological parent."

Before I could comment, Ayanda spoke up. "We never wanted to hide anything from Noah. We did everything we could to get information from the adoption agency, which we had learned about from a university friend." She shifted, seeming uncomfortable as she told us the story.

Leila asked, "Did they put you through the wringer like they do in the States?"

Ayanda crinkled her face and shook her head. "Strangely, they were most interested in our economic status and apparently impressed that we were professors. Those details seemed to be more important than what kind of parents we would be."

I interjected, "I understand what you're saying, but it would take about two seconds to figure out that you are wonderful."

Ayanda smiled broadly. "Thank you for the compliment. We were fortunate. They told us a baby would be ours in weeks. Both of us were thrilled. We didn't really care who or where he came from. We asked them about the parents of the baby, and they assured us that drug addiction was not a problem in the birth mother, but told us nothing else of her. It seems that the birth father died in a diamond-mining accident soon after the conception. The birth mother was leaving Cape Town immediately after the delivery. We were not permitted to be present for the event."

Leila asked, "If you don't mind me asking, have any of you ever tried to follow up with the agency to find the birth mother?"

Ayanda again looked somewhat ill at ease. "We later tried to contact the agency representative who helped us get Noah. He was still a baby. We thought when he got older he would want to know.

Obviously, that was before all these DNA tracking tests. Our effort was in vain. She and the group she worked with literally vanished about a year after we brought him home. Very odd. We have made several inquiries, but all to no avail. The hospital records had neither a birthdate nor an address for the mother. Her name was recorded as Jane Smith. Look at Noah. The boy is black as night. Does he look like his birth mother would be someone named Jane Smith? We didn't think so either. Ultimately, it didn't seem that the matter would be worth pursuing further. So we haven't."

Noah offered, "I did end up doing the DNA tests. Oddly, I seem to be related to almost no one. Still, I feel extraordinarily lucky. Whoever my birth parents actually were, they must have felt I would live a better life with my adoptive parents. They sacrificed for me. Yet, I do wonder about them."

Tess piped up, "Cheers to adoptive parents!"

I held up my glass. "Skoal."

Leila added, *"L'chaim."* The pronunciation was perfect. I gave her a loving squeeze of approval. She'd been working on her "ch"s. She was ready for the side vacation we'd planned to visit Kari and Mark in Tel Aviv.

Noah placed his glass on the table. "Alas, I must turn in. I have only recently returned from your country. The department has required too many trips for a project I am working on. The technology group is in New Hampshire. I have been back and forth so many times through your Logan Airport. On its best day, it is a difficult place."

I commiserated. "We had no idea you were so close. When we go back, you must stay with us! Logan is a phenomenal pain in the butt. I understand wanting to get out of there as quickly as you possibly can."

We all lifted ourselves out of our chairs with great effort. They were so comfortable, and each of us was somewhat unsteady from the wine.

Then it hit me—Hackford-Regan's, the Boston bar. That's where I'd seen Noah. The sense of déjà vu had been tugging at me all evening.

I blurted out, "Noah, I just realized. I saw you at that bar on Charles Street. You were with that South African lady—de Grom."

Noah shook his head slowly. "Sorry, VJ. I have never been to any bar on Charles Street, and I do not know a soul with that last name. You have probably mistaken me for someone else."

There was a sudden commotion. A known female adolescent leopard had decided to make her way into the camp. We learned quickly that these animals necessitate immediate attention. How she passed through the electrical fencing was a small mystery, but here she was nonetheless. Her business seemed to be focused exclusively on getting water from the swimming pool, demonstrating no interest in us. How long that would last was anyone's guess. The guides and trackers sprang into action, coaxing the elegant but deadly feline to return to her normal habitat. She had to be convinced first that this was not the best location for hydration. No one, least of all the guides, wanted to take her down. Eventually, with patience and the proper incentive from the kitchen, they escorted her out. It was quite the show. When the excitement died down, we retreated to our individual, secluded palaces. No one needed to be reminded how important it was to have the armed escort safely tuck us in to our sleeping quarters.

I was fascinated with Leila's cousins. "So, it seems like your family has the market cornered on smarts. Very impressive people. I'm really looking forward to spending time with them."

Leila smiled demurely. "Fortunately, they liked you too. So maybe they're not that wise after all. What was all that about you seeing Noah in Boston? Then again, maybe all of us black people look alike to you white-bread Vikings."

I pushed her gently toward the doorway. "So funny you are,

wife of mine. Seriously, I could swear it was him. That said, I did have a few drinks that night."

She commented, "Judging from the way Tess and Noah hit it off, I think we'll probably be seeing him a lot now. You'll get your chance to really get to know him. I think they look very sweet together."

I nodded in agreement. "Tess sure locked it in. It would be a nice thing if he's her Prince Charming. Logistically it would be a challenge, though. Maybe we'd have to relocate here permanently. Ironic that they're both adopted, isn't it? What're the odds?"

Leila laughed out loud. "In our crazy world, high. Let's not plan the wedding just yet. Give them at least until the end of the week. Plus, I'm not sure someone so genetically compromised is the right person for my cousin's son. That could be a major deal breaker." I looked at my wife like *Are you serious?* She snickered. "Oh, you thought I was referring to Petra's contribution. No chance. I meant yours, big boy. Two of you married into one family may be overwhelming for the Akekawanzies. By the way, no playtime tonight. I'm just putting it out there in case you were having any ideas. I had way too much to drink."

In about two minutes she was passed out. Snoring quietly on top of the sheets, with her flowing black hair adorning the pillow, she was beautiful. I was reminded how fortunate I was to find her.

Sadly, the rest of the night did not reinforce my general feeling of well-being. I woke up sweating profusely, struggling to catch my breath. Leila stirred next to me but remained asleep under the canopy of our triple-king-size bed. Silently I thanked God that it really was just a dream. Still in a fog, though, I looked around the room just to be absolutely certain.

Yes, I was still in the Wengonyama resort, next to Kruger National Park. Yes, I was still in South Africa. It was the second night in a row that my brain had conjured up this nightmare about being in a mental hospital on the verge of being disemboweled by my nemesis. I found the bottle of Malarone pills on the night table and thought about heaving it across the room, but didn't want to wake Leila. The explosion against the wall would have given me at least a small measure of satisfaction. Moving forward, it would have to be environmentally unfriendly DEET. The mosquitoes weren't that thick, but I had nonetheless decided to take the drug to stave off the risk of getting malaria. Unfortunately, the medicine was notorious for inducing bad dreams in some people. This one had been a doozy.

Here I'd come halfway around the world to de-stress, and the ghost of Petra was still haunting me. Tess had stood up to her on that Boston rooftop in what seemed like an eternity ago. The end result was a dramatic fall punctuated by a spike of rebar through Petra's chest. The she-devil was dead. Still, here I was, lying next to my wife in a splendid resort, having night terrors about the evil banshee. It was a psychiatrist's dream case. Literally and figuratively. Finally I went back to sleep. I had to be ready for the next morning's adventure, rested or not.

Fortified with coffee and pastries, we were off at six thirty. Once we gathered in the modified Land Rovers with their broad rear rows of seats, we wanted to focus exclusively on the amazing world that surrounded us. The vast South African savanna was most beautiful in the early morning and evening. There was a special quality to the light that accented the vegetation and wild animals inhabiting the space. The sunrises were as classically stunning as the sunsets—a color extravaganza emanating through the branches of the acacia trees.

We were assigned a ranger and a tracker to maximize our experience. While the ranger drove and answered questions, the tracker scanned for signs of wildlife from a specially designed seat attached at the Rover's front end. Both rangers and trackers were highly trained. Sometimes the process of obtaining the highest certification took years. A tracking position at any of the game parks was a prized job.

Phuti, the man assigned to our contingent, was Tsongan. During lunch I'd learned a little about his background. Economic troubles drove a number of men from his village to jobs in the mines or urban areas. Cash from agriculture and cattle often wasn't enough to support a family. Without adequate food many suffered, some turning to crime. Phuti's pathway had steered him away from darker elements. He was gregarious, and his love for the country infectious.

The Rover carried our five-person contingent and a family of four. The Fishers turned out to be a nice match. Now living in Indianapolis, they were originally from Mexico City, but shared my Jewish heritage. Everyone in their family had keen intelligence and huge personality. We were collectively awed by the wildlife: rhinos, leopards, rare painted dogs, and the array of exotic birds.

About an hour into the excursion, I realized that the morning beverage hadn't been such a great idea. After another forty-five minutes, I was near the breaking point. If you are parked next to a herd of elephants or a pride of lions, getting out of the Land Rover to answer nature's call is not an option.

Diego Fisher eventually saved me by querying the ranger: "Umm, Jakob, is there a place we can pull off to take care of a bit of personal business?"

He laughed. "Of course, that was part of the plan. I was just waiting to see who would break down first."

I tracked Diego down during our pit stop. "Thank God you said something! Man, I thought I was going to burst. Can you believe these animals?"

He looked into the distance. "They are phenomenal! It's funny that you are in our jeep. We routed through Johannesburg on the way here and met the most intriguing young newlyweds, Javier and Amanda. When we told them we were coming to this fine place, they mentioned that they had met you several times. They said to say hello if we connected. Nice people."

Suddenly I felt like one of the animals being tracked. All I said was "Yeah, very nice people."

Collectively we were moved by the quiet splendor in the broad expanse of the African plain. When our Rover came upon a troop of baboons hanging out in the trees, the volume turned up dramatically. It was such a kick seeing them do their baboon thing in their native environment. For that matter, it was completely gratifying to just sit back and watch all the animals behave naturally, not in some contrived zoo setting.

And so went the next few days—touring in the morning, gorging afterward, touring in the afternoon, taking a siesta, gorging again, and drinking, sometimes heavily. One evening we took an excursion into the park, gazing at the brilliant, diamond-like stars. Without light pollution to contend with, the views were unparalleled. Leila took my hand and grasped it gently. In that moment, I recognized all that I'd missed for decades. It was the sense of fulfillment. I was sad and ecstatic all at once. Life with Leila would never be dull. No question. There wasn't a minute of it I wanted to miss.

Existing in a game park wasn't a sustainable lifestyle, but it was definitely both unique and energizing. The group bonded famously. The fact that Noah and Tess had become inseparable didn't escape anyone's attention. Nascent love is a wonderful thing to witness.

THE HUNT

LIMPOPO PROVINCE, SOUTH AFRICA

ON A SECLUDED SIDE of the same game reserve the tall, blond, blue-eyed Afrikaner chewed springbok biltong, a dried-meat delicacy.

From the moment Adriaan Vanderweiss could raise a gun, his elders had taught him to use firearms properly and skillfully. In the expansive veld, he learned to track and hunt. Any time he strayed from the vast open space, he felt ill at ease. This was his kingdom. Often at night, he lay in bed awake, pondering how he had allowed himself to drift into his present role as an enforcer. He no longer liked himself or what he was doing. The same dream visited him night after night. He was in quicksand with no saving tree branch to grasp. A tall, wiry, indistinct figure would toss him a rope. As he struggled to reach it, the man would pull it suddenly away, fiendishly laughing. Such was the peril of involvement with the Foundation.

Today was particularly hot and dry. There was little breeze, making the flies all the more irritating. The whole landscape looked parched. Drought was never good. Tension amongst the people and other animals throughout the country was palpable. To Adriaan, it felt like he was in the middle of a simmering pot. He thought the random vagaries of the elements were probably in some way responsible for what was about to occur. He watched his prey run. It didn't matter. He was going to win, and the rather slow, dull-witted creature wasn't.

Off to the left, a pride of lions slept. A particularly skillful lioness had provided the group with a fresh wildebeest kill. Having just fed, the male, a veteran of many wars, watched with indifference. He was a beast Adriaan knew well. One of his teeth jutted out at a ninety-degree angle, compliments of a giraffe kick. To add insult to injury, the poor bastard had also been gored by a water buffalo. A difficult life for the king of beasts. Still, the lion had to maintain his usefulness. That was Adriaan's job too. His Cape Town boss demanded it. He turned to watch his own target. Animals responded to danger with three primary senses—smell, sight, and sound. None of these were going to save this one.

Perched in the specially designed seat attached to the front of the vehicle was Joseph, Adriaan's tracker. He also had his eyes trained on the fleeing game. Then he spied a ten-foot-long greenish black fiend with a white underbelly, and then another. Through his binoculars he followed the vicious attack. "Mr. Adriaan, black mambas. A shame for our friend that he found that nest." These venomous snakes struck so fast that few prey could escape them. Death was certain and rapid. Only two drops of venom can kill an animal. Babies carried two to three per fang; the adults stored up to twenty. They also tended to bite repeatedly.

Joseph shook his head as he contemplated the prey's demise. "The hyenas will take care of the body, bones and all."

Acidly, Vanderweiss remarked, "Yes, I know. Fortunately even human ones." Here in the park, nature was unforgiving, and ultra-efficient. The fallen target, Queenie, had stolen a computer containing critical information about a new Ebola drug that was being tested. Big cash had been offered for the industrial espionage by a representative of a competing pharmaceutical group. The theft was a desperate play by the man. He knew the risks were considerable. But, his wife and brother were disabled, the former from a car accident, the latter a victim of a mine silicosis. Queenie had to take care of two families. Compounding the hardship, his parents were both ill. His was a classic tale of economic distress. Despite having what most considered to be a good job, every day was a struggle to feed his extended family. Whatever he tried was just not enough. The money offered was more than he could make in a lifetime. The temptation was too great.

Once Queenie became aware that his treachery had been discovered, he knew his death was inevitable. Like the scripted conclusion of a Greek tragedy, it was over. Only the exact *how* had been uncertain. Now that question was resolved too.

AN UNEXPECTED DISCOVERY

LIMPOPO PROVINCE, SOUTH AFRICA

THE NEXT-TO-LAST MORNING I opened the door to our bungalow. The combination of the previous night's alcohol and interrupted sleep had me disoriented. Two monkeys greeted me with loud screeches. After I almost had a heart attack, I headed for the pre-safari nourishment. Yet another spectacular, full breakfast buffet would await us on our return.

Not seeing my daughter, I took the short walk to Tess's digs and knocked on her door. After a delay, I heard movement, and the door slowly opened. Wearing Bowdoin College sweatpants, a Cadbury chocolate T-shirt and looking somewhat ragged with glasses askew, she motioned me to enter. The wine from the previous night had gotten her too.

"VJ, this place is great, but it's going to kill me. How much time do I have before we start?"

I felt her pain. "We have about twenty minutes. See you then." Tess acknowledged the directive and padded deliberately toward the shower. I went back to our rooms to make sure Leila was ready. In contrast to Tess and me, she was filled with energy. Where she got it, I couldn't fathom.

On this particular morning, we weren't the only mammals considering breakfast. Our tracker's radio crackled. Word was that a leopard had made a fresh baboon kill during the night. The big cat had invaded the troop near the river line bush and come away victorious.

We raced to the scene, knocking down brush, small trees, and anything else in our path to view the carnage. Before we got there, however, Leila spied something unusual, even for Africa, and she yelled, "Stop! There's an arm lying over there!"

Tess spun around and gasped. Our tracker, Phuti, had a horrified look on his face. I saw him whisper and cross himself. He grabbed his rifle and launched out of the jeep. A quick sweep of the area turned up no other body parts. Holding the arm, he radioed the camp to report the find. We never did get to see the leopard's kill. Later, other people in the camp said it was jaw-dropping.

I reflected that the savagery of nature takes place daily. Sport is not part of the equation; survival dictates behavior. Human savagery is so different. I was convinced the unfortunate dismembered person was a victim of the latter.

More radio calls were made, rangers converged, and the investigation began. The scene turned quickly into a conflagration of activity. We were surrounded by official vehicles filled with heavily armed men and women from the State Security Agency. It seemed obvious there was more to this story than a random death, but the SSA did not reveal why they were so interested.

I felt decidedly uncomfortable. I was also unsure about the purpose for the hardware they carried. What did they plan to do—machine-gun the big cats? These same officials wanted to speak to everyone in our jeep. I guess it was a formality. This wasn't our normal playground. Since Leila spotted the arm first, she was the prime witness. No, she didn't see anyone outside the jeep; no, she didn't see an animal running from the scene; no, she didn't need to talk to a PTSD counselor.

Their independent search apparently revealed no further information. The arm was bagged and sent for analysis. There were no reports of anyone missing from any of the nearby resorts. Speculation ran rampant about the original source of the extremity. No one could offer a shred of insight into why there was a dismembered, mostly eaten man in the wild. The event obviously altered the tenor of the excursion. In the short term, we moved on. But I still wanted to follow up with Phuti later.

Since the morning ride got cut short and the afternoon completely blown out, the trackers and guides generously gifted us another special night session. The splendor of the birds and animals in their native habitat cannot be properly described; it's only properly experienced. When the sun went down, the game park was utterly flawless. The guides gave us a tour of the southern constellations. I felt very privileged to share their beautiful outdoor office, if only for a few days.

At the late dinner that night, I cornered Phuti and asked him about his dramatic response to the day's strange turn. With the focus on the arm, I didn't think anyone but me had noticed. I was stunned to learn that he'd immediately recognized the arm, confessing it belonged to his cousin Queenie. The distinctive leopard tattoo was the giveaway. He confided in me that a week earlier Queenie had come to the resort begging to be hidden. The man who had offered to pay him handsomely to steal the computer from work had completely disappeared. He didn't know where to go. Traveling to Wengonyama was a desperate act.

I asked about his cousin's workplace, and the answer deepened the mystery: Onderskeid Hospitaal in Cape Town, where Tess and I were both slated to volunteer once we finished our game park experience.

Phuti didn't want to get officially involved at all. Nothing positive would follow for him or his family if he did. I agreed to keep under wraps what he had told me about his cousin smuggling the computer out of the hospital. Getting immersed in an investigation was also the last thing I wanted or needed. My curiosity about the story was already turning into worry. Since I worry about everything all the time, my new concerns were not a giant leap.

Before going to bed, Leila and I had a frank discussion. My deal with Phuti did not extend to withholding potentially critical information from my family. After I told her about Phuti's cousin fleeing the hospital with stolen information, I said, "Something is going on that clearly isn't kosher. Is it still a good idea for us to be heading to Onderskeid?"

Leila matched the concern in my eyes with her own. "VJ, I hear you loud and clear. But your friend Solomon has been at Onderskeid a long time, and I think he would tell you if there was anything really problematic. You and Tess are doing straight clinical work. Even if there is something going on, realistically, I don't see how it would affect us."

I agreed and hoped that I wasn't getting torqued for no reason. "I'm still going to let Tess know about all of this. If either of us gets the idea that there's a problem, we'll pull out."

"VJ, I want this to work more than you can imagine. I want us all to have the best possible experience. But I agree totally: We're gone if there are any issues."

The last morning at the resort was drama-free, the unbelievable splendor restored. Everyone was still talking about what had happened. Phuti's secret remained just that. We took a larger plane to Cape Town, my catastrophic thinking held at bay for at least a short time. Just as we were about to touch down, we caught a view of Table Mountain and its nonidentical twin, Lion's Head Mountain—the two iconic peaks that lord above the city. Leila and Tess both gasped at the beauty. Solomon was right. We were going to love this place.

Our passage through the airport this go-round was infinitely easier. There were no fewer people, nor lack of strange tongues. However, we had flown in domestically, so there was no awful queue to hold us back. We were outside in minutes. Although technically winter, the weather was perfect. Warm sunshine and a cool ocean breeze simultaneously met us. I smiled inside. It was the same feeling I always get when I walk through the airport exits in Hawaii.

A prearranged driver whisked us to our new digs. I couldn't help but notice a large, impoverished living area just as we left. The township was one of the most obvious markers of years of apartheid. Those who weren't white and privileged suffered enormous hardships. Society, as I understood it, continued to be in flux. Perspective would definitely be important to maintain. In case I forgot to do that, Leila would be there to remind me. I was now in a place with *her* family and *her* people. I celebrated that fact.

PART III

ONDERSKEID

CAPE TOWN, SOUTH AFRICA

IN THE FACILITY where Tess and I now walked, unique medical events were part of everyday reality. Groundbreaking procedures were pioneered within these walls. This knowledge penetrated deeply, filling me with excitement.

Each of the dated hallways was teeming with activity. The signs for the Porphyria Clinic brought a smile to my face. This rare blood disorder can result in an infinite number of bizarre consequences, causing some poor souls to look like vampires and others like werewolves, for instance. As a student, my very first internal medicine patient was a West Virginia man with seizures who reacted badly to everything we gave him. Turns out he had porphyria. He was referred to us because no one there knew what was wrong with him. We nearly killed him trying to make him better. Thankfully one of the hotshot newbies on staff had just read an article on the topic and made the diagnosis on rounds. A Dutch orphan had gifted the disorder to South Africa in the late 1600s. As a student, I knew a lot more about porphyria than I did about high blood pressure. Nothing has changed. I still knew almost nothing about hypertension or most other medical diseases. Before my sabbatical was over, I planned to spend time pumping the knowledge of the specialists seeing these patients.

I nudged Tess. "You're going to learn so much here, and you know what—so am I." She peeled off and went to the Infectious Disease Clinic.

Solomon was detained with a case more difficult than anticipated. I hung out in the OR lounge waiting for him to finish. We had a number of issues to discuss before I started my first day.

As I tried to get acquainted in Onderskeid, I had the sense that everything at the hospital was foreign and familiar at once. I sat down in a worn but comfortable lounge chair and closed my eyes. It had been a long couple of days. Then I caught the sounds of a day gone by. It was none other than Patsy Cline, singing "Walkin After Midnight" in that rich, distinctive voice. I pinched myself to make sure I wasn't back in Durham. She was a goddess there. One of my primary mentors, attending physician, Jessica Derosa, played her music during every surgical case. The words were etched in my brain forever.

My daydream ended when my friend and colleague walked in. Solomon was a head taller than me and probably twenty kilos heavier, all of which was muscle. He had a commanding presence. That he was a rugby star in his past life was no surprise. Unlike many Jews who had fled Lithuania and landed in South Africa to escape the Nazis, Solomon's family originated in Northern Africa. Business opportunities drew them to the tip of the continent. His darker complexion and almost jet-black hair made him look years younger than me. I can't say I wasn't jealous. The only flaw was a large scar on his face courtesy of a rugby brawl. In reality, it only made him look tougher. There was no doubt who was in command of this army.

Solomon greeted me with a bear hug and wide smile. "VJ, so you are finally here! Wow—Patsy Cline! She's great! I heard her first in Hendersonville, Tennessee. I was moonlighting there during a rotation I did at Vanderbilt. Bet you didn't know I was in the South too. Both of us—strangers in a strange land."

I chuckled, knowing exactly what *that* felt like.

"By the way," he continued, "I caught wind of a bit of a scrape up there by Kruger Game Park. Did you hear? Strange, huh?"

"News travels fast," I said with surprise. "How did you know about it?"

"How could I not? The poor fellow worked here in the Infectious Disease Department."

I was curious. "Yeah, but it's not like his arm was stamped with his name and address."

Solomon answered me with information I already knew but was keeping to myself: "No, but the arm did have a very distinctive tattoo, which helped them identify him quickly when they cross-checked his DNA. He was on one of those commercial databases. Boom, done." He perceived my look of consternation and asked, "Is there something I don't know about?"

I certainly wasn't prepared on our first meeting to have a conversation about my own paranoid thinking. "Solomon, Tess is about to do an ID rotation, that's all. It's just a strange coincidence."

He sat me down. "It's one of our premier departments. The attendings and fellows are all top-drawer. Africa is blessed in many ways. From an infectious disease physician's standpoint, it's absolute nirvana. Dr. Sherako's clinic has some of the most fascinating cases on the planet. Whether it's malaria, rabies, congenital cytomegalovirus, or any of the hundred other bad actors, they arrive from everywhere in southern Africa. Sherako is in the middle of some serious Ebola research—game-changing stuff. Patients from the DRC are streaming down. Huge grant money from some pharmaceutical company. Tess can decide if she wants to get involved on that front. It's not classic medical student territory. Although they have some stellar new medications, Ebola is still pretty scary."

Solomon took me on an official tour of the hospital and the facilities. I saw all the places I was accustomed to seeing. An instant favorite was the tea room. Inside, there was an assortment of cookies accompanied by steaming hot vanilla rooibos tea. The entire surgical team was hanging out there between cases. It was such a nice refuge to recharge one's clinical batteries.

Then we came to the clinic. The setup was absolutely fascinating. There was a long table. On one side sat the physicians; on the other, the patients. Getting a second opinion required only that you tap on the shoulder of your neighboring colleague. No one had to consider the patient privacy rules practiced in the States. We were able to freely exchange ideas and information to help the person being treated. What a novel concept. The care was excellent, and the physicians deeply engaged. The free part for the patients didn't hurt, either. I loved the intellectual challenge.

Immediately I became a part of it. One of the hand fellows was asked to give up his seat to me. I can't say I wasn't intimidated at first. Now in the thick of the battle, I was surrounded by people speaking multiple, completely foreign tongues. The range of problems would be entirely different from what I was used to seeing. I asked myself the same question I asked myself before climbing the Hulk and at the beginning of first grade, high school, college, medical school, residency, and fellowship: "Are you going to measure up? This isn't the same as what you're used to doing."

The first patient was a small child with a previously undiagnosed birth nerve palsy. The self-doubt subsided, and I regained my footing. This was an issue I understood. As the morning continued, I grew more comfortable. I was amazed that so many of the patients had endured physical hardships the Boston crowd couldn't possibly imagine. Best of all, there was no attitude. One man had had his hand cut off by a machete. Another young lady experienced a bone infection as a youth that went untreated. Her forearm now took a virtual U-turn. Yet another had long lost tendon use in four fingers. All three were just looking for a way to improve their function. No one stood to gain financially from their affliction. It was completely refreshing.

Virtually everyone needed something done. I was going to be a busy boy, and the prospect was thrilling. Every hand surgeon wants to use her or his skills to fix something gone wrong. The reconstructive possibilities in this setting were going to blow anything I had done previously out of the water.

Just before I walked out the door of the clinic, I realized I had left my phone sitting on one of the desks. I turned back suddenly and saw a physically impressive man in scrubs who seemed to be following me. He immediately averted his eyes and walked down a separate hallway. The event happened far too quickly for me to see the name on his hospital badge. I figured my delusional thinking was at work again, and elected to just write it off.

That evening Leila and I were sharing a meal on an outdoor restaurant patio with Solomon and his lovely wife, Karina. It was to be the first of many culinary indulgences to come in Cape Town. The shish kebab was to die for. Conversation flowed freely. While we reveled in an extremely decadent chocolate mousse, I asked a vexing question. "Solomon, Karina—your families have moved abroad; you have teenage children. Are you two going to stay here in Cape Town?"

Solomon looked at me with a glint of the devil in his eyes. "VJ, that answer is simple. If you decide to make this your permanent home, of course we'll have no choice but to leave." Then with a sigh of resignation he added, more seriously, "My friend, that is not an easy question to respond to. Both of our families have been here for generations. South Africa is ingrained in our identity. I'll give you an analogy. It's like being at a party. When you arrive, it's completely festive; everyone is having a marvelous time. As the hours pass, people start to filter out. But you're still having fun, and there's no reason not to stay longer. Gradually, more and more people leave. If you stay too long, there's a sense you've worn out your welcome. The key is to try to leave at the best time before the end of the party. Some of my friends have said, 'Better ten years too early than one minute too late.' That is where we are in our lives now. What shall we do with our children? We're not sure, and no one can tell us. This country, this continent, seeps into your soul. You have been here a short time and already I know you feel it. VJ, you willingly left Sweden. It's a very special place if you like freezing your butt off and eating foul herring. Nowhere is perfect. We don't want to be pushed out of here if we can help it."

I said to myself, *VJ, coming to South Africa was an excellent decision.* Having friends and family there made it all the better.

The next day Leila and I headed home after a long, lovely, invigorating walk by the ocean. It was nice to get acquainted with Cape Town. The city was a jewel. We happened upon an outdoor dance festival. Competing groups from throughout the country were performing. The talented participants wore brightly colored, free-flowing outfits. It was like watching a raging fire—we were mesmerized. South African culture was starting to work its way into my subconscious. I understood what Karina and Solomon had meant. It was such a nice, warm feeling. I remained acutely aware of the overwhelming inequities in the Cape Town world—the hospital was a daily reminder. Still, I couldn't resist the positive vibe. This place versus Boston? Not even a conversation.

When we finally got back to our temporary home, both of us collapsed on the couch. I started to pick up a book, then thought of a better plan. The boudoir seemed to be a far superior place to cap off the day. I gave Leila the eye and took her hand. It didn't take much convincing.

We were rudely interrupted when my phone went off. I'd committed the unforgivable crime of failing to silence it. It should be the first lesson taught in residency. If you're not on call, turn off the damn phone or leave it overnight in your locker. A normal person would have learned this concept after the first fifty times being interrupted. So many of us still believe we are indispensable and therefore must be available all the time. If I hadn't answered Nick's call that night and subsequently reattached his four cut-off fingers, my life would have been far different. I wouldn't have found out about the Cooperative. They wouldn't have identified me for termination. Virtually everything about the world that I thought was true had changed, the simple consequence of answering a phone call. I thought I'd learned my lesson.

Undeterred by the annoying ring, we pressed on. When the thing went off again, we were forced to temporarily cease and desist. Leila whispered, "Sweetheart, it's okay, get it. We have the rest of the night." Not.

Solomon was on the other end of the call. "Hi, VJ, are you around? I've got an arm sitting in a bag here at the hospital. The unfortunate soul it's detached from got it clipped off on a sign while driving down the road. He had his arm hanging out the window. Bad decision. The funny thing is that the arm showed up first. A Good Samaritan found it on the road and brought it here about fifteen minutes before our guy came. We figured he'd show up sooner than later. A missing arm usually gets someone's attention pretty quickly. I didn't even ask him what he was doing in the meantime. He's hopped up on something. My guess is heroin. We've been seeing a lot more of that recently. His vessels will probably be shit from what he's using, but I want to at least give him a chance. I'm wondering if you could lend a hand."

Unlike the prank call from Chi several months earlier, this was the real deal. Though I was frustrated sexually and otherwise, the prospects of helping on this case were far less threatening than a multiple-digit replant or mid-palm amputation. We just had to suture large vessels, tendons, and nerves, and fix a large bone. Most important, I wasn't the one who was primarily responsible.

When I hit the OR, Solomon was already getting started. One of the fellows was locating and tagging the structures we needed to repair. The humerus was shortened, and rapidly we applied the requisite steel plate and screws while the brachial artery had been temporarily shunted to feed blood to the arm. Lack of oxygen does disastrous things to the muscles in an amputated limb. The clock is even more critical in major amputations like this, versus fingers where there are only tendons—the structures that connect muscle to bone. Our clock had been running.

We set to work on repairing everything. Once the arm was on and the anatomy restored to its pre-collision status, we took the important step of doing the compartment fasciotomies. Arms and legs are like grapefruit sections. If a portion swells too much and the pressure isn't released, the muscle will die. Not only is that a functional problem, but the breakdown products can cause the kidneys to fail and the patient to die. Other than making someone look better in a casket, a successfully replanted arm is of no benefit to a dead person.

It was a treat to help someone so skilled. Cases like this forge lasting bonds. Solomon was indebted to me for providing able assistance, and I to him for the opportunity to be there at all.

Even though it was late, or early, depending on one's perspective, when we finished we took a walk to the lounge to decompress with some hot tea. After tonight's operation, I couldn't help thinking about the other fellow whose detached arm was found in the Wengonyama reserve.

"I wasn't going to say anything, but may I tell you something in complete confidence? Apparently, the man whose arm turned up in the reserve was carrying a stolen computer. His cousin, who was our tracker, told me when we were at the game park. You haven't heard anything else, have you?"

Solomon regarded me seriously. "Is this information in the hands of the SAP?" I looked at him, questioning. He said, "SAP—the South African Police."

I gave him an answer he probably didn't want to hear. "I'm not certain what they were told. After everything that happened in Boston, I decided to stay out of situations that didn't involve me. If you don't mind, I'd prefer you keep that information under your hat. I think it's better if our family stays away from anything controversial. Tess and I are so happy to be here at Onderskeid. I want it to stay positive."

"VJ, I understand why you feel the way you do, and I share your desire to maintain some distance from whatever he was up to," Solomon said. "I don't know anything more, but I promise to keep my ears open." He thought for a minute. "My friend, tonight we did good. It was a pleasure to work with you. I think it is ideal for both of us to focus on medicine. It's what we do best."

I was satisfied with the surgery and the answer Solomon gave me. At least for the night, I would sleep. That said, I still hadn't given up entirely on the idea of consummating the unfinished business with Leila. Testosterone can be such a demanding master.

SUPPER'S READY

CAPE TOWN, SOUTH AFRICA

DAYS LATER, we gathered for the evening culinary adventure. Leila asked Tess if she was enjoying herself on the infectious disease service. She nodded an enthusiastic yes between bites of stew and chakalaka, a South African vegetarian relish.

"You would not believe what I've already seen," Tess said after swallowing. "We've been looking at a number of cases of intestinal parasites. *Cryptosporodium* and Blastocystis hominis are wicked. But there's a ton more gnarly critters. You were right. This place is ground zero for everything cool."

My stomach did a little somersault. Both Leila and I had the same disgusted response to the idea of intestinal parasites, and I suggested, "Tess, let's table this discussion until we finish. Let's get back to something more normal, like writing a book about embalmed humans returning to Earth as medical students. I hope it will be fun for you to do. If it's not, then there's no point."

For a moment Tess had that far-away, deep-in-thought look,

then responded, "Another classic case of type two fun. I dread writing a book, because I'm not sure if I can. I'm worried that even if I can finish it, people won't think it's any good. That will kill me. But I really want to. I feel like I have a story to tell."

Leila weighed in. "Tess, then you don't have a choice. Who gives a damn if other people don't like it? I *know* you have money in the bank, so it's not as if you need book sales to pay your bills. Just go with it. If it doesn't happen, it doesn't happen. No one you care about is going to judge you. I didn't think you'd want to do anything VJ wanted you to do. By the way, I started working on something myself." Tess chimed in, "That's fantastic! What's it about?"

Leila paused for a moment then said with authority, "The clash of cultures. Reuniting with my family here has made me think so much about the African half of me. The Korean part is equally strong. I believe I have something important to say, living in Boston, now more than ever. I considered a biographical approach, but honestly how many people would I reach? I settled on a fictional character. That's who I'm fleshing out right now. "

I thought about how wonderful it was to be able to spend time with these two strong women. "Well, if there's anyone who has the credibility to tell that kind story it's you. Needless to say, there will be brilliant Swedish doctor in the plot."

Leila couldn't resist a dig. "You wish! Okay, enough about my indulgence. Tess, what are you going to call your masterpiece?"

Tess responded, "I've been kicking it around. What do you think of *Anatomy Lab Meets Night*?"

Leila pondered the name. "Intriguing. Simple, clean. I like it."

"Tess," I said, "you and Leila are going to be a best-selling authors, and I'm going to be relegated to the dishes. That noise you probably heard a minute ago is one of those chocolate chip cookies Leila tried to hide from me in the freezer. It's calling my name. I do have another question, though. Have you met a guy named Harrison Sherako? He's supposedly an expert on the Ebola virus."

"Yes, I have," Tess said. "He's a great person, incredibly smart but not full of himself, really down to earth. You can't miss him—he has this diamond ring that puts anything I've ever seen to shame. Apparently, his son works in the diamond industry and just took a new job up in Kimberley at the Whitefire mine. VJ, you're rubbing off on me—I'm digressing. Dr. Sherako has been putting me to work with his Ebola patients. They get flown down from the DRC. In fact, he just took a trip up there yesterday. He has a special grant from a drug company."

I held off on the cookie and focused on what Tess had just revealed. "Tell me. Exactly what kind of contact are you having?"

Tess smiled. "What do you think? The full Monty—special gowns, special gloves, full coverage. I'm telling you, though, the team here is doing exceptional work. People are getting better.

"I found out they'd been collaborating with the group at MRMC," she continued after another bite of food. "I had no idea. They mentioned they'd met Dr. Tribolsi, but not Slobodan—now both are dead. A really spooky coincidence. It's usually the patients with Ebola that die, not the doctors doing the research on the disease. Don't you think that's kind of weird? When I told Dr. Sherako that Slobodan bought it when he was visiting you in Sierra Lakes, he said he wanted to meet you."

Nothing about what Tess said warmed my heart.

SITUATION CRITICAL

NORTH KIVU PROVINCE, DRC

FAR TO THE NORTH, in the Medecins Sans Frontieres/Doctors Without Borders tent, Harrison Sherako sat wearily. The team he was consulting with was nestled in an area of the North Kivu Province in the Democratic Republic of the Congo. They'd done their best to limit this latest Ebola outbreak, identifying the cases early, then isolating and treating infected patients. Infection control practices meant stopping the unsafe washing and ritual manipulation of the ones who'd already died. These burial practices were killing Ebola containment efforts, but were ingrained in the culture. The conversations with those affected were necessarily very delicate.

Every day, contact-tracing teams were going out to locate those people most at risk. But there remained tremendous resistance from the population. Political groups were stirring the pot to promote their own agendas. They were not helping. Sherako's work with victims of the COVID-19 virus in Brazil had taught him many lessons. He hoped to avoid massive quarantines and the resulting hysteria.

The goal was to vaccinate and treat as many people as possible. This new recombinant VSV-Ebola vaccine was the ticket. Still, the emotionally taxing nature of the work was overwhelming and was wearing down the staff. Yonaker-Wood, the company that had worked with them to provide drugs, was on the outs. The newest iteration of their study drug had killed too many of Sherako's patients. An angel grant from Red Mountain Pharmaceuticals had allowed him to funnel many more infected patients to South Africa. They supplied a specially outfitted plane to do the transport. But Cape Town was a long way from the DRC and from the strain of *Bundibugyo ebolavirus* he was desperately trying to stop.

Still wearing a mask, Sherako gathered the energy to walk outside, where he surveyed the blighted terrain with weary eyes. Garbage and broken cars pocked the site. The DRC was a beautiful country, but this was not one of the highlights. The Ministry of Public Health had finally okayed the new site, after he'd been told twice before that a different location for the central Ebola Treatment Unit was approved. After all, no one really wanted one of the scariest infectious diseases on the planet in their backyard. Playing the game had required great savvy and patience. The massive sets of supplies and tents were finally being put in their proper places. Sherako was optimistic, though. He didn't have a choice. If he didn't make this work, hundreds of thousands if not millions of people would be at risk. Hemorrhagic fever on that scale was unfathomable.

One of the local government bureaucrats approached. "Dr. Sherako, sir, we have located the perfect place for your work, have we not?"

"Yes," he responded, with the slightest hint of sarcasm while glaring down at the man. "Yes, it is perfect. Now, what can you do to discourage the rebels? They have been actively opposing our mission to suit their needs. The physicians and the other health workers are exasperated! We've had to abandon our scrubs and dress formally, like lawyers. We can't travel in our cars but only on motorcycles to blend in. Otherwise we're at risk for attack.

"That doctor the rebels killed several weeks ago—he was my friend, a truly dedicated man. All of us are here to do one thing: save people from this terrible virus. Do you really understand what we are talking about? Bleeding from every part of your body and dying a horrible death is something I know you don't want to experience yourself. Am I correct? Do you want to be the one responsible for the next global pandemic—not one that kills just millions, but tens or hundreds of millions? Can you even imagine the scope of that?"

The man appeared visibly shaken and coughed before saying, "Yes, Dr. Sherako. You will have the full support of the government. I will see to it myself."

The doctor regarded the official with disdain born of constant frustration. "Thank you. Please make certain there are army personnel with guns here to protect us, starting tomorrow. By the way, I think you might want to come in now yourself. Your eyes look red."

SIPHO MOBUTO, one of the workers setting up the equipment, watched the conversation from afar. This was his last night in the DRC. His cousin had arranged a job for him at the Whitefire Diamond Mine near Kimberley, South Africa. Possible dangerous exposure to toxic dust and asbestos from the new job would be no picnic, but anything would better than what he was dealing with here at home. The arrangement with the human smugglers was in place. His passage would be arduous, but he felt confident he would reach his destination.

The population was on the move. Rival rebel groups fighting for turf and control forced the issue. Originally from Tchomia on the shore of Lake Albert, Sipho was one of the many affected by the trouble. Government corruption and the endless armed conflict in his adopted city had driven him to leave. The regular job he'd had was gone, a casualty of the ongoing violence. With no real family attachments, he was willing to do whatever it took to make his life better. He was glad to be making an exit while he still felt healthy. The cough he was just starting to develop was a mere trifle. Getting away from this Ebola virus made the dangerous trip all the more worthwhile.

The Russian crime syndicate that was handling his transit had spent the requisite money on bribes for the right officials and police. People like Sipho were just a small part of the pie. Most of their human trafficking business involved moving in young woman from Africa, Asia, and Europe as sex workers. This particular Russian crew had another strong business ally in Cape Town—Red Mountain Pharmaceuticals.

HOME SWEET HOME

CAPE TOWN, SOUTH AFRICA

ONE SATURDAY, Solomon and Karina hosted the Brio clan at their Bishopscourt estate in the southern suburbs of Cape Town. It made any place I had ever lived in seem like a hovel. The sprawling home was set back from the tennis court and swimming pool. Majestic trees filled the landscape along with a well-manicured flower garden. I thought to myself, *I sure chose the wrong country to emigrate to.* How could anyone not be overwhelmed?

Solomon saw the look in my eyes as I scanned the beautiful property. "VJ, I am quite fortunate that my family has done well in the business world here. I can't take credit for what they have provided for us. That's one of the reasons I prefer working at a public hospital. It gives me a chance to give back to the people who have allowed us to enjoy this life."

I raised my glass to Solomon. "Sir, you are a mensch." Tess glanced my way as if I had just insulted our host. "Sweetheart, that's a Yiddish term. It means a person of integrity and honor, also someone who is generally thoughtful and intelligent." I laughed and explained to Solomon, "She's got my blood, but didn't grow up with the culture. But like Leila, she's got the toast down."

Karina and Leila simultaneously gestured with their own goblets, saying *"L'chaim."* We settled in for a relaxing evening. Tess brought up our plan to go to several rural areas to do primary care. One of her professors at Harvard had paved the way for her to do this, and she had coopted me to help. I didn't object to her plan. I looked at it as good bonding experience. Leila wasn't excluded; she was already committed to her own volunteer activities in one of the townships.

While Tess was speaking, I saw Karina glance sideways at Solomon. The conversation quickly turned to Leila's highly political family. Our hosts were fascinated with what they were learning about their own government.

After dessert, Solomon beckoned me to go with him to the garage, where he opened a small case and handed me a sleek handgun wrapped in cloth.

"VJ, I know this is not what you want to hear, but if you insist on going out to some of those clinics in the bush, you should have this." It was a Vektor CP1 9mm semi-automatic pistol with a double-stack ten-round magazine, and it was made to be concealed.

I looked at him questioningly but took the piece. "Solomon," I asked, "should I be worried?"

He smiled. "No more so than you would be in parts of Los Angeles or Chicago. I believe in preventive measures. By the way, don't drop that gun. They stopped making them because they'll sometimes accidently discharge. I picked it up from a friend a few decades ago. You know how to shoot, don't you?"

I nodded my head yes. "Funny you should say that. If I learned nothing else from the Cooperative, it was that certain skills are important to master. I think you'd be very impressed to see how the women in my life can also handle a weapon."

Solomon replaced the prize in its carrier. "From what I gather, there is nothing those two can't do if they put their mind to it." So right he was.

When we departed later in the evening, Leila asked about the contents of the case I was holding. I was tired and didn't feel like going into details, although I knew I would have to at some point.

"My darling," I said, "Solomon is very happy to have me as free labor. This is a bit of insurance that I won't make a sudden exit." Surprisingly, she let me off the hook without another comment. I looked into the passenger seat and got my answer. She was sound asleep. Saved by the fruit of the vine.

For a moment I had forgotten Tess was in the back. She wouldn't take no for an answer, so I handed over the case preemptively. "Solomon suggested we carry this for the outreach clinic work we're going to do."

She opened it up and inspected the package. "Nice piece. Extra ammo too. Very generous. Where are you going to keep it?"

I thought for a moment. "We'll put it in the glove box. With all of Leila's family traipsing through the house, I think it will be safest there." In the rearview mirror I saw Tess nod in agreement. "When we get back to the house I'll put it in there. Leila will get upset if she knows we're carrying a concealed weapon."

DIAMONDS ARE FOREVER

NORTHERN CAPE PROVINCE, SOUTH AFRICA

AT THE WHITEFIRE DIAMOND MINE, sitting on the edge of the Northern Cape and Free State provinces in South Africa, life was proceeding much as it had since the late 1860s, when the first of the Kimberley mines opened. De Beers, brought to prominence by Cecil Rhodes, had boosted consumer desire with its brilliant "A Diamond Is Forever" advertising campaign in 1947. Before then, these gems were not the *chosen* sign of engagement and matrimony. Diamond mining blossomed into a multibillion-dollar industry employing tens of thousands. De Beers routed many of its rough stones to the Israel Diamond Exchange in Ramat Gan. Diamond cutting and trading was centered in a group of four huge interconnected buildings in the city. South Africa and Israel maintained a strained relationship, but business was business.

Unlike the gold, platinum, and coal mines, few from other countries were given diamond mining jobs. Though working conditions could be undeniably dangerous, the gold mines posed greater risk because they were deeper. That industry was also beset by struggling families doing their own illegal private mining in abandoned shafts. Economic opportunity was a powerful draw for those in-country. Since the latest COVID-19 outbreak, work options were limited for many. With the Millennials' attention turning to synthetic engineered diamonds, jobs in the industry were now growing more scarce, with competition for them greater. In turn, those who were running the day-to-day operations were keen on getting the best people they could to max out production while there was still demand.

Whitefire was no exception. Foreman Zach Simpson and his associate, Ethan Smitheman, watched the new man, Sipho Mobuto, carefully. Neither was convinced he was in any shape to work in the mine below. His eyes were red and he was coughing. He looked like a hundred-year-old man. Zach was the first to speak, "You there, you cannot go inside coughing like that. Report to the infirmary. Ethan will assist you." Zach was decidedly unhappy. He had gone out of his way to get Sipho, a foreigner, credentials to labor in the camp, and now this.

Ethan glared at Zach. He too was both concerned and frustrated. To him, sick people represented danger. His father, Harrison Sherako, was the internationally renowned infectious disease specialist at Onderskeid Hospitaal in Cape Town. Ethan's natural father had died in a freak boating accident when he was only a year old. His mother married Sherako not long afterward. Although her son was officially adopted, Ethan's mother wanted to keep the Smitheman name for the sake of his paternal grandparents, so Smitheman it stayed.

Growing up, Ethan was inundated with disgusting pictures from medical magazines. His father reveled in talking about the patients he saw and the horrible manifestations of their ailments. From Ethan's perspective, the worst thing that ever happened was the picture-taking capacity of the cell phone. Sherako would innocently draw him close with the promise of the view of some beautiful scenery, then hit him a repulsive shot of the effects of some parasite. He knew only some of what his adopted father was up to with his Ebola studies but didn't want any part of it. He was even reluctant at times to touch him.

Ethan's world was completely different. He had recently obtained his master's in mining engineering and was determined to establish himself in the business. As much as he loved Sherako, he wanted to be completely separate from his world.

Ethan kept his distance from the red-eyed, coughing man as he led him to the medical area. The doctor wasn't there at the moment, so Ethan gave what little information he had to the new clerk and, before leaving, practically took a bath in the nearby hand sanitizer. He had done his job, now he was out of there. Sipho was someone else's problem.

Mvezelwa Crotta, the malevolent product of a former IRA bomb maker and a Xhosa mother, was sitting on the edge of a bed by the door in the infirmary. A slip on a wet floor had resulted in a fall and fractured wrist. The medic had manipulated his deformed forearm with no anesthesia. Mvezelwa wanted to hurt the man, but at least now with the bone in better position, he felt only minimal discomfort. He was just getting ready to leave. Work would be impossible, though, and that was a huge issue.

He studied the man being escorted in. He did not look well at all. Without warning, the new patient began coughing uncontrollably. A spatter of blood struck Mvezelwa in the face, hitting his mouth, nose, and eyes. Panic overwhelmed him as he struggled to find anything to clean himself with. He grabbed the bedsheet, wiping away the disgusting discharge while he ran from the building. He was horrified. What had this man assaulted him with? Whatever it was, he didn't want it. With no way to work and now an exposure to some unknown disease, he decided he'd return to his family home in Cape Town. He had a friend who worked at Onderskeid. Maybe he would help him.

The drama in the medical infirmary started a small firestorm. The physician on duty had returned and was appropriately concerned. Calls were made. Sipho was thrown in the back of a truck and transported to the same place the man he had spewed blood on was headed.

DIAMOND MINE CRISIS

CAPE TOWN, SOUTH AFRICA

WEARING A SPACE SUIT EQUIVALENT, Sherako examined Sipho in his isolation chamber. At times like this he wanted to do everything possible to not make a patient feel like an animal in the zoo, but he felt relatively powerless. The mandatory protocols were what they were. Next to him was the new American medical student, Tess Ryssdal. She had already proven to be sharp, highly capable, and calm beyond her years. The lab work confirmed what the mine doctor had suspected—Ebola.

His desperate eyes begging for help, Sipho looked at the man, who said, "I am Dr. Sherako. I am here for you. I know how terrible you feel. The good news is that there is a medication we are trying on people who are already infected like you. It is not a guarantee, but we think it may help." When he informed Sipho that the chances of living were around thirty percent, the response was muted and stoic. Sherako continued, "Please tell me where you have come from." Sipho detailed his path from the DRC to South Africa.

Sherako mentally catalogued all the contacts he would have to track down. The human smugglers were a disaster. They represented possible game-changing vectors. He was going to have to rope in Mikele Erikson, the epidemiologist in the department, to see if she could lend a hand. If the people who brought in Sipho were transmitting the virus, it might become unstoppable.

The infected man's story concluded with his brief sojourn at Whitefire Diamond Mine, the event at the infirmary, and the trip to Cape Town. Sherako's eyes betrayed concern. "Excuse me, I have to leave you for just a moment. Tess, why don't you get a little more medical history from Sipho? Also, we need a detailed contact list."

Sherako went through the decontamination protocol as rapidly as possible. When the laborious equipment removal and body cleansing was finished, he ran to get his phone and called his son, Ethan. He got only the message machine. He furiously searched for another contact number at the mine. Finally, he located the number of the chief mine manager, Chrisjan Jaars. The phone rang and rang. At last there was an answer.

"This is Dr. Harrison Sherako at Onderskeid Hospitaal. I need to speak to Mr. Jaars urgently."

"I'm sorry, Doctor. He is in a meeting. Can I take a message?"

Sherako was not in the mood for the classic "He's not interested in whatever you're selling" response he'd received. "Yes, please tell him that I am seeing a patient who just came from your facility. He has Ebola virus. It is possible that everyone there, including you, has been exposed. Dying from Ebola is very unpleasant—blood coming out of every orifice of your body." There was a gasp on the other end of the line. "Now will you please get him for me?"

"Yes, right away." In an instant, a harried voice came on. "Dr. Chicago, what's this about Ebola virus at the mine? That cannot be. We only employ screened workers here. Is this some sort of game? And by the way, what kind of name is Chicago? It doesn't sound South African."

Sherako could sense the ineptitude over the phone. He'd heard enough about it from Ethan. "Listen, man. What I'm telling you is reality. I just interviewed a person who came to your facility from the DRC. I'm sending a team from Onderskeid to you immediately. You need to lock down the infirmary. I will send you the complete isolation and cleaning protocol. Jaars, you need to follow these instructions to the letter. Remember, this is not just for the safety of the workers, but yours as well. Take what I'm saying very seriously.

"For the record, my name is Harrison Sherako—SHERAKO! I am in charge of the Ebola research clinic here. If you ignore what I'm saying, there is a good chance that many people there will become infected and die. You must immediately locate Ethan Smitheman. I believe he has critical information about this patient's contacts while he was there. I need to speak with him. As of this moment, your mine is under strict quarantine. No one goes out, no one comes in until our team arrives. Got it, Jaars?" The manager consented to the directive, almost whimpering.

In less than fifteen minutes Sherako's phone rang. "Dad, the manager grabbed me and told me I had to speak with you immediately. What the hell is going on?"

Sherako was relieved to speak to his son. "Listen to me, Ethan, I need you to tell me everything you know about this man you sent us. Who he had contact with, where he went."

There was a long pause. "Dad, I had contact with him."

Sherako remained cool. "Okay then, this is what we will do." He explained a detailed plan to his boy. During the few minutes that the conversations took place, another man from the mine showed up at the hospital with early symptoms of the virus. Sherako quickly isolated him and dispatched a contact-tracing team. Ebola loose in Cape Town would be an unmitigated disaster.

Next, Sherako immediately went to the office of the director, who, for a change, was actually there. "Mr. Mashaba, there was a significant Ebola exposure at the Whitefire Diamond Mine, and now it's coming here. We need to move quickly to try to contain it. I'm mobilizing a team right now. The Foundation will have to foot the bill for the helicopters."

Kgalema Mashaba looked distracted and didn't respond.

"Mashaba, did you hear what I said? This could be a total horror show! We're going, and you have to release the funds."

Finally, sound emanated from the director's mouth. "Sherako, we do not have the money to do what you are asking. We now have to pay twice as much for the drug."

Sherako could not restrain himself. He grabbed Mashaba by the collar and slammed him against the wall. "Now listen to me, you fat lowlife piece of human garbage. I know you've been taking most of those donations for yourself and your cronies. I've been forced to do nothing. Not this time. If you don't release the money, I will be on the phone with every news outlet in this city in five seconds. Don't believe for a moment I won't do it!"

The director was cowed but hissed, "That would be unwise, Dr. Sherako. There are forces at work that you do not understand. However, I will see what I can do. Please excuse me."

Sherako stepped out of the office. Behind the closed door he could hear a decidedly one-sided conversation. When it was over, Mashaba stepped out. "Dr. Sherako, you can have your team and your drugs. But *never* threaten me again like that. It might not play out well for you."

Evidently the person the director answered to thought the diamond miners at Whitefire were worth trying to save. Sherako stormed away. He now had to focus on logistics. They had an emergency plan and supplies in place for this eventuality. He knew he'd pay a price for the outburst in Mashaba's office, but he'd been left with no choice. His son's life and those of many others were at stake.

PROBLEMS

NORTHERN CAPE PROVINCE, SOUTH AFRICA

THE CONVERSATION at the mine was not going well.

"How do you let a man with Ebola into our mine?!" Jaars yelled at his underlings. "This will kill our production. At least a forty-two-day quarantine period. Someone will pay mightily for this fuckup. I have a mind to drown all of you in a bath of Ebola virus."

One courageous employee spoke up. "Sir, what do you want me to tell the families of the staff? They will be asking a lot of questions."

This inquiry made the manager even more furious. "What do I care what you tell them? None of these people matter. What is important is getting the mine running again. This man Sherako is coming here. He is a flaming asshole. We have to convince him to make this happen more quickly. As soon as he arrives, make sure you find me. We have a business to run! Now get out."

When the office was empty, Jaars dialed the number he was

afraid to dial. The man he had to speak with maintained absolute power over the empire. In a business world filled with great white sharks, this man was a killer whale. No one had crossed him and successfully navigated to the other side. There was no shortage of people who'd tried. When Jaars had been approached about laundering a share of the heroin money for diamonds, he was not strong enough to decline. Heroin itself had also gotten into the camp for transit elsewhere. Even worse, not all of it left. Production was compromised. He felt trapped.

The call connected, and Marjanovic's serpent voice filled the room. "Jaars, I understand we have small issue at mine. Ebola virus. Not smart you have Ebola there. Kill you fast." The call was excruciating for the heavy, bald man, who was sweating profusely.

"Mining start again soon, important deal in works," Marjanovic continued. "We move merchandise you already got there for you. Small fee needed to do that. You understand. Doctor coming with drug. Cure most your worker. Our man part of team. He make sure everything go right. You not worry."

Jaars did worry. He was about to get raked over the coals—again—and there wasn't a damn thing he could do about it.

FAMILY TIES

CAPE TOWN, SOUTH AFRICA

WE WERE AT THE TABLE waiting to get served, surrounded by hordes of Akekawanzies. Many were ranking government officials. Leila had warned me before we came to the country that her family was part of the new political landscape. I took in the gathering, thinking about who was pulling what levers. These people were society's movers and shakers. I was fascinated. This was going to be a semi-traditional midday Zulu wedding. They did forgo the slaughter of two cows and a goat, but per protocol, the event was at the groom's family home. Leila explained that the bride arrived early wearing the customary blanket, circling the house to meet her betrothed's ancestors before entering through the kitchen. I spied the surrounding tables adorned with small rhinoceros figurines, artistically decorated pots filled with indigenous flowers, and wildly colorful place mats, table coverings, and glassware. This was not going to be a stiff Boston Brahmin event.

Once the ceremony started, I saw the bride and groom for the first time. I was blown away. She wore an embroidered, beaded red conical beret and flowing red dress with a wide rainbow beaded necklace and belt. The groom wore matching red clothing, the right side of which was marked with a distinctive gold-and-black diamond pattern. They were unbelievably elegant. As part of the wedding ritual, the groom sat on a grass mat while the bride pretended to make a bed that he would then lie in. Unexpectedly, the bridesmaids and several other young women began to hit him with small sticks, forcing him to run away. It was the most entertaining ceremony I'd ever witnessed.

Now it was time for the meal. The hors d'oeuvres had been wonderful, so it wasn't like we were super hungry. Nonetheless, with the soup service I was anticipating something delicious. It was a variation on something I wasn't sure of. After one spoonful, I looked over at Leila. "What is this? It's cold and tastes like a mix of Spam and haggis. It's disgusting."

Her face told me she felt the same way, but she was more diplomatic. "Sweetheart, I'll agree it's not particularly tasty. Pretend for a second that you're not a child and just don't eat it."

I was undeterred. "Jesus, I hope the rest of the meal is better than this. Maybe I should use my phone and order some takeout. Do you think that would bother anyone?"

Leila gave me a reproachful scowl. "VJ, stop it!"

I couldn't help laughing as I looked around the room. On the faces of the other guests, the reaction to the soup was similar. We didn't have time to explore the topic further. There was a commotion at the table next to us. A large, older gentleman was on the floor. Leila and I rushed over. Thank God there was a real doctor attending to the guy. Soon a small army of qualified physicians were involved. Leila helped them code the man while I supervised. The EMTs came and carted him out. It was pretty obvious that he wasn't going to do well. The bride and groom knew nothing of what happened. They'd been kidnapped by the photographer. I wasn't sure which was worse—getting coded at a wedding or having to suffer through an endless photo barrage.

Finally, we did get back to our meal. I nudged Leila and whispered, "I'll bet that guy ate *all* his soup." She punched me, but I could see her smiling. "Inappropriate" is my middle name. Fortunately, the rest of the food was really good, particularly the dessert. Now on my third glass of special beer, I decided to push the limit.

"Hey, Leila, can you ask the waiter for another piece of that chocolate-coconut king cake?" Eyeing the empty seat at the table next to us that the stricken man had occupied, I continued, "I know there's an extra one available."

Leila just shook her head, as she's often forced to do when she's with me in public. "You know you're going to burn in hell, don't you?"

"Darling, that's the benefit of being Jewish. We don't believe in that place. By the way, did you find out who he was?"

"It seems he's a government big shot at the health department," Leila said. "Noah works with him. I think he has something to do with research funding."

"Do you suppose he has anything to do with the Ebola Foundation, the group that's funding the research here?" Leila shrugged her shoulders, indicating her lack of information. I made a mental note to ask Noah about it.

We walked into the courtyard, where the dancing was already well underway. They were doing it in groups and individually. These new friends and relatives knew how to have fun. The spectacle was entirely un-Swedish. Our time in Cape Town had been dominated by events like this. I felt like royalty, even though Tess and I were riding exclusively on Leila's coattails. Tess and Noah remained joined at the hip. That didn't hurt her integration into the fold. I surveyed the landscape, trying to figure out what to do with myself before committing to dancing to music I didn't like.

I spotted a young woman with a crazy, beautiful mane of black hair. I stared at Leila, I stared at the teenager and then again at Leila. "Leila, sweetheart, is there something about your past that you're not telling me? Is she a Tess redux?"

Leila laughed at me. "Oh, you mean my daughter. Didn't I mention her?" My mouth was unable to form words. "Ha! Got ya. No, VJ, that's my niece, Eliza. I've told you about her before. I just didn't tell you she was a younger body double. My brother, Peyton, married the daughter of a close friend of my mother's family. They are Korean as well. And no, not a relative of my mother's. It's more of a crazy coincidence that we look so much alike."

Eliza came up and put her arm around Leila. "How are you, Auntie? It's been a long time. Who is this man you're with?" When she smiled, her face lit up in that very familiar way. Genetics.

"So pleased to meet you, Eliza. My name is Erik, but you can call me VJ. It's a nickname that attached itself a long time ago."

She reciprocated with a firm handshake beaming with self-confidence. Nonchalantly she said, "Hey, VJ, killed anyone recently?"

Feeling even more uncomfortable, and not knowing how to answer that question, my eyes shifted to my wife. She shook off the remark with a grin. "VJ, Eliza is somewhat precocious. She's just razzing you. I told her about Petra, that she had tragic flaws that necessitated her departure."

Indeed, this young woman was a Leila knockoff. "Eliza, you are no doubt a force to reckon with. I know just the right person to answer all your questions." I summoned my daughter to join us. "Tess, darling, there's someone we'd like you to meet. She's a cousin of sorts. Tess, say hi to Eliza."

Tess took one look. "You're a Leila mini-me. Cool. How's it going?"

I left them to grab another drink for myself. By the time I got back, they were deep in conversation, so I went to circulate with the other relatives. I quickly found Noah, who had been on another trip to the States and had only just returned. I decided to break the ice before asking about the departed guest. Clapping him on the shoulder, I joked, "So, you *are* being a gentleman with Tess, I trust."

He flashed that beautiful smile and responded, "What would make you think otherwise, VJ? So, tell me, how are things going at the hospital?"

"Curious that you ask. This story should interest someone in the government working in public health. A couple of nights ago the EMTs scooped up a man on the highway after a car wreck. They declared him dead on the scene and stuck him in the morgue refrigerator. The problem the pathologist encountered when she took him out was that he wasn't actually dead yet. In the medical world that's a problem. He did have an obvious forearm fracture that needed attention."

Noah looked at me with concern, although I genuinely thought it was a funny anecdote. "She told me there isn't great regulation of the ambulance services and these types of things happen not infrequently. It's certainly the first time I've been called to the morgue to do a consult on a live person. Is someone in the Department of Health looking into problems like this?"

He sighed. "Yes, VJ. There are so many difficult tasks we must address. The one you mentioned is but one of a multitude."

I could feel his embarrassment. Changing the subject, he said, "On a different note, I am curious. How do you feel about Tess working with those patients with Ebola virus? I am not sure it is such a good idea. It makes me very uncomfortable. Perhaps she should leave that unit."

Of course I agreed with him, but I tried not to betray my obvious displeasure that she was doing this and muted my comments. "Tess is an adult. She makes her own decisions. My influence is minuscule, if even that."

"They are doing excellent work," Noah continued. "That new drug they are testing is working wonders."

My interest was piqued. "Noah, you seem to know quite a bit about the unit. Do you happen to know anything about Dr. Sherako, the man in charge?"

He answered quickly, "Yes. He is quite the take-charge person. He takes no bullshit from anyone."

In the papers that I'd read from Slobodan's briefcase, "O.H." had been named as the research site. The results were outstanding. When I found out from Tess that Sherako knew of Slobodan, I had put together that Onderskeid Hospitaal was O.H. The world was very small.

"Noah, do you happen to work with that man who collapsed here and was taken to the hospital earlier? One of your cousins told me he works with the Ebola Foundation that supports the patients at the hospital where I work."

He looked at me with a blank stare and paused before answering. "VJ, I know his name, but I have no contact with him."

Something didn't feel right about the conversation. I decided to change subjects again to something safer. "Noah, you must take us to a rugby match. I hear the Springboks are splendid to watch."

Noah's face showed that he understood there was more on my mind than the national team, but he played along. "Yes, VJ, I will do that. If you will excuse me for a moment, there is a work matter I must address." I watched Noah retreat to a private place and initiate a phone call. I thought, *Curious behavior.*

I wandered back to find Leila. "So where is that brother of yours anyway? It shouldn't take more than two seconds to find him in a crowd."

Peyton had decided to use our stay as an excuse to visit South Africa. Leila pursed her lips. "He's on a conference call. It would probably take some type of world cataclysm for him not to be on the phone for at least half of any get-together. That boy drives me insane."

Peyton's wife had died of breast cancer a few years after Eliza was born. He had never remarried and remained one of Atlanta's most eligible bachelors. He'd confided in Leila that he was having trouble with his daughter. She was headstrong and forging an independent path quite immune to any influence he tried to exert. His world was divided between business and his daughter. He didn't make room for much else. This trip was a huge step.

As part of Peyton's social rehab, we were going to encourage him to participate in group activities like barbecues. I hoped to actually see him at some point. I'd met him briefly only once before, but had instantly liked him. One thing for sure, Eliza was about to become a more permanent fixture with our clan. Leila and Tess would have it no other way. Apparently, a massive shopping trip had already been planned by the trio. I anticipated a full-frontal assault on our credit cards.

Noah, now done with whatever important conversation had detained him, returned to our circle. He placed his arm delicately around Tess. She drew close to him and gave him a quick kiss. I felt slightly uneasy, but decided I couldn't say a word to Leila. I had no justification for my discomfort. It was just a gut feeling.

THE GAME

CAPE TOWN, SOUTH AFRICA

THE NEXT MORNING there was an envelope slipped under the door. Inside were two Springbok tickets for the evening match. The enclosed note was simple: "See you there." It was a wonderful surprise. I chastised myself for doubting Noah. The phone call he'd stepped out for was probably to arrange these tickets. Leila gave up her seat so I could take Solomon.

Newlands Stadium was curious. Rather than the angular or rounded arenas I was used to, this one was essentially a rectangle. We sat in the center, midway up the second tier of seats. Noah was sitting in the row directly in front of us with a friend. We had a terrific view of all the action, which was brutal. Textbook tackles were exchanged, padless bodies hammering each other with staggering blows. The ball flew about freely in the semi-controlled mayhem. Sweat, dirt, and blood marked the jerseys. Thousands of fans seething with subjugated anger lived out their fantasies of aggression through the men on the field. Highly entertaining.

At halftime, I turned to my friend and said, "Solomon, I'm always amazed to see how drawn people are to violent sports. I'm guessing it's the Neanderthal genes we share. Probably something about having to fight for food. Whadda ya think?

He pondered the question. "I agree, but there is more to the story. This is our tribe. If we were at a Duke basketball game, the roles would have been reversed. They are your tribe. We share the same tribe as hand surgeons, and we're both part of the twelve tribes of Israel as Jews. My fellow Springbok tribesmen would be thrilled to hug me to celebrate a drop goal. But the same person might not love me so much if he knew I was a Jew. That is one of the beauties of sport. Life station, profession, social status cease to matter when it is us versus them. There are only allies and opponents. We judge our own worth by the performance of these designated avatars. We scream for someone to get physically destroyed, but we don't really want them hurt. I agree we are Neanderthals, but slightly more sophisticated Neanderthals."

I launched into an analysis of my personal neurosis, not knowing if I was speaking to Solomon or myself. "If you scream at a television showing a random game in a random airport, then the people who are part of the greater sports tribe understand. The non-tribe, non-caring complete outsider can't comprehend it all. Leila fits into that category. Although she's fiercely competitive, she just laughs at my sports shenanigans."

I disappeared mentally while contemplating the human condition. People battling for their own definition of supremacy. Why should I care if a group of people who neither know nor care about me are successful at repetitively putting a ball into a cylinder or crossing a line with a differently shaped ball? I know it should not matter in the least, yet it does. Wholly absurd! Our memories process negative experiences far more precisely than positive ones. A significant loss, like a national championship, or even a game lost to the evil-empire-school-that-should-not-be-named-that-happens-to-wear-light-blue, tends to occupy a place in the brain for eternity. I am impressed that other sports people carry the same battle scars. We are a crazy group. Leila would never ruminate over a defeat by one of her favorite cooking channel chefs. Best to acknowledge professional sports for what they are—entertainment, a season-long reality television show with hopeful expectations of the outcome, but no truly defined script.

The sociologic data from the cessation of spectator sports during the COVID-19 experience were still being compiled. I remained curious what that would show. What will happen when all athletic events are computer generated? My guess is that nothing will change. People will remain rabid for whomever or whatever they choose to support.

Solomon stared at me. "Jesus, VJ, where did you go? Just enjoy the game."

I smiled. "Oh, my wise friend, I am. This is the best! I don't have to worry about who wins. I want them to win for you. Mental sports masturbation is one of my favorite pastimes. I am in constant pursuit of perspective. The fact that these musings are among my current biggest concerns is fabulous."

Solomon shook his head. "VJ, you're a very strange person. Thank God you can operate."

Ultimately, the Springboks carried the day. Solomon was visibly thrilled with his tribe's conquest. I continued to muse on the topic of my own disabling sports rapture as we made our way out. For some unknown reason, the entire crowd stopped, and we were caught in a crush of people inside the stadium. There was no way we could move in any direction.

Without warning, I felt pressure in the middle of my back and started to lose my footing. I was getting squeezed from all sides. My anxiety began to increase. A stampede was suddenly easy to understand. I started to look for escape routes.

All of a sudden I felt a strong shove. Now it wasn't the people that were the problem. I was perilously close to pitching over the rail onto the first level. If I survived, there would be little of me that wasn't broken.

At the last instant Solomon saw the problem, grabbed my arm, and I avoided disaster. It was terrifically unnerving. I looked around. Noah, who had been behind us, was now ahead. I asked Solomon, "Did you see someone push me?"

He shook his head no. "VJ, I just saw that you were about to fall. Someone was clearly in a hurry to get by you and out of here. They must not have realized that you were already getting pushed so hard." I was willing to accept that explanation but wasn't convinced it was entirely true.

The near "accident" colored my thoughts about the events of the day. I asked myself, *Is there someone in South Africa who wants me seriously hurt? Or worse?* I couldn't come up with anyone other than a relative of someone from Boston I had helped put in jail. That seemed highly implausible. I concluded Solomon had to be right. It's not like there's a shortage of mindless jerks at U.S. sporting events, either. I thought of Hanlon's razor: "Never attribute to malice that which is adequately explained by stupidity." I just didn't know if the guilty person was one of the crowd or myself.

When I got back to the house and walked inside, I spied Tess sitting on the couch, intent on an article. She barely looked up when I walked in. I asked what she was reading.

She hesitated at first, then came out with it: "Ring vaccinations for Ebola. It's for the work I'm doing with Dr. Sherako. He's brilliant and a great person. I can't *not* help him with these people. Plus, most of the team just left to try to deal with an outbreak at one of the diamond mines. I have to help hold down the fort."

I felt even more deflated. "We came here for a low-key, fun

experience. Today I almost got killed at the rugby match, and then you remind me you're doing substantial work with people who have one of the most horrible, deadly viruses on the planet." I proceeded to tell her what had happened at the end of the game.

Tess smiled as she walked to the fridge to get a beer. "VJ, calm down. You're just being dramatic. No one tried to push you over the edge. And I got vaccinated the first day I came. I've got it under control."

I was reminded of the scientist character's words in *Jurassic Park:* "You never had control. That's the illusion!"

I found Leila in the study, entranced by *The Splendid and the Vile,* an engrossing historical account of Churchill and Great Britain during the German Blitz. I gave her a hug and a smooch. She turned and smiled brightly. "Hey, how was the game? Did you have a fantastic time?"

"Yes, I had a lot of fun. But there's a story there. Tess seems to not care that I almost spent my last moments on Earth at the stadium. I'll tell you about it later. What do you think about her working this extensively with Ebola patients?"

She raised a single eyebrow.

I was looking for more than that and blurted out louder than I intended, "You know, Leila, Ebola isn't like a new boyfriend. Despite all that Tess has been through, I'm still not sure she has a mature enough idea of the true danger it poses to her. Do you have any idea how many health care workers have gotten sick and died from it?"

"VJ, *do not* lecture me about this," Leila snapped. "I don't think you're giving Tess enough credit. She got vaccinated, and this guy Sherako is an absolute stickler for adhering to protocol. There are so many infectious diseases here that could kill anyone at any given moment. Ebola just gets a lot of press."

Another voice entered the conversation. "Yeah, VJ, you shouldn't be in the business of censoring what we women do." It was Eliza.

She appeared out of nowhere, wearing what appeared to be elegant new clothes. The shopping trip had been an obvious success. Her presence was welcome, but now it was three against one. I had no hope. Any discussion of my concerns about Noah would definitely be a nonstarter.

VIRUS MINING

NORTHERN CAPE PROVINCE, SOUTH AFRICA

THE HELICOPTERS hit the ground, and Sherako's team swung into action. Immediate biocontainment was critical. Having practiced many times, they unloaded the gear quickly and efficiently. Here, unlike in the Congo, there were no rebels to contend with. That would make the task of performing medical care infinitely easier.

After locating the mine's management team, Sherako began the arduous process of setting up the laboratory and the isolation units, starting environmental decontamination, rounding up the workers and screening them, initiating treatment or vaccination. No one had any interest in experiencing the devastation of an Ebola virus infection, so cooperation was excellent. The GeneXpert machine they'd brought from Onderskeid Hospitaal was put into immediate action screening blood tests. A long line snaked around the camp. Anyone experiencing even the slightest evidence of red eyes, fever, sore throat, weakness, headache, or muscle pain was diverted to one of the treatment tents.

While the storm of activity was unleashed, Sherako finally was able to locate his son. His trained eyes searched for open cuts or sores—any pathway that Sipho's Ebola virus might have entered. Seeing none, he silently checked off that box. The questions came out like machine-gun fire.

"Did he cough on you? Wipe his nose and touch you? Vomit blood on you? Have you felt sick at all? Had a fever?" More boxes checked. Once all the questions were answered, Sherako breathed a small sigh of relief. In this new controlled chaos, he set about initiating treatment for the person at the camp he cared about most. "Ethan, go to the lab immediately. I will run the test myself."

Sherako had brought a staggering amount of the experimental drug from stockpiles at Onderskeid. He'd commandeered what he needed without dealing further with the useless Foundation director, Mr. Mashaba. This new antiviral from Red Mountain had shown significant promise in the clinic, and now was the time to use it on a large scale.

As the first day ended, Sherako sat in the makeshift command tent, poring over the screening data and the contact lists. Ethan interrupted his train of thought, sitting down next to him and saying, "Dad, there is something you need to know. The employees are acting strangely when they aren't working."

Sherako looked up. "What do you mean, 'strangely'?"

"Jaars told me to ignore it as long as they were doing their jobs, but I've been digging," Ethan continued. "There's heroin coming in. I think the boss is using it to get them hooked and stay working here essentially as slaves.

"That would be bad enough. But after I talked to you I read more about Ebola. I know needle sharing can spread the disease. I think some of the people who are bringing in the facility's supplies might have exposure. I just wanted you to be aware."

Sherako muttered, "Jesus Christ. This could be the perfect

storm. Do you have any idea how to find out who else, other than that man Crotta, might have come and gone since Sipho left?"

Ethan jumped up. "I'll get the logbooks. We know all the suppliers, distributors, and contractors that come through. That is at least a place to start. As you already found out, Jaars is something of an idiot. Hopefully there isn't some truck driver headed to God knows where, spreading Ebola around the country."

A few hours later Ethan came back to the tent. "Dad, there's something else. I found the books. I'm afraid that there seems to be a connection between the heroin and the people funding your research."

Sherako sat stunned. "I've had my suspicions that something wasn't right, but I didn't think they were involved in anything as serious as heroin. Are you sure? Where are you getting your information?"

Ethan held up his keys. "When I went to find the logs, I realized I'd left these in the office. When I went back to grab them, I overheard Jaars talking to someone on the phone. He sounded scared. He said there was a product shipment that should have arrived from Cape Town the day the quarantine started. I checked the logs. The only thing that came from there were medical supplies. The truck never left, but with all the confusion here it didn't get unloaded. I have no idea what happened to the driver. I just went to check."

He threw a package on the table. "This is what I found in the boxes."

The wrapping said RED MOUNTAIN PHARMACEUTICALS, INC. MEDICATION HIGHLY TOXIC TO SKIN. DO NOT TOUCH. Sherako did the honors of unveiling the package, which turned out to be a brick of heroin.

Ethan remarked sarcastically, "I suppose that's one way to take someone's mind off having Ebola. What was in the truck is a lot more than anyone here can consume. They must be moving it to other places using our distribution channels."

Sherako shook his head. "As if there aren't enough problems here. Come with me, Ethan. Let's have a small chat with Jaars."

When they reached the manager's outer office, they could see him pacing his room, talking to himself, sounding completely unglued. "He's going to kill me. I know it. He's going to torture me and kill me. I can't have that. I just can't."

Before the pair could enter the office, the man raised a sidearm to his temple and blew a hole in his skull. Sherako rushed in, but there was nothing to be done.

Ethan looked around in shock. "Oh shit! Oh shit! What an absolute mess. All of it." He reached for his phone to call the police.

Sherako gripped his son's forearm. "Hold on. Not yet. If the police storm in here, how many more people might be exposed? Who knows what will happen to these workers and our containment zone? No one is going in or out anyway. Jaars is dead, and nothing will change that. I think everyone is safer if we keep this quiet for the moment. There will be plenty of time to deal with everything.

"I have to get a shipment of methadone in here quickly. The last thing we need is a crush of people going through serious withdrawal symptoms. Ebola and heroin—it's an explosive mix."

DISCOVERED

CAPE TOWN, SOUTH AFRICA

"BOSS," SAID THE MAN with the beautiful smile, "my source tells me that Dr. Sherako knows about the heroin at Whitefire. I'm not sure how he found out. Jaars was sloppy. He failed to get the last shipment unloaded. I don't know what Sherako's going to do with the information. Our man at SAP tells me he hasn't talked with anyone there. There must be some reason he's staying quiet. Probably because he's buried in Ebola right now. But the good news is that the drug is working. We'll make a killing when the new data are released."

His mentor regarded the young man carefully. He was smart and chillingly cold-blooded, just like himself. "Put your contact there on him. Steal his phone. Make sure he *not* talk to anyone about heroin. Right now, he helping us. When he not, we take care of problem."

The protégé responded as he anticipated. "I've already done that. I thought you would want me to."

A faint smile crossed the boss's lips. "You do good job. Hope you get no ideas about taking mine."

UNWITTING SPY

CAPE TOWN, SOUTH AFRICA

NOT LONG AFTER the Ebola strike team departed Cape Town, Tess was holed up in one of the side rooms in the Infectious Disease office suite. The small adjoining spaces had no windows. A short hallway separated the administrative section from the medical portion. It was getting stuffy, so she opened the door to get some air circulating.

The Ebola outbreak in the Congo had worsened. There was talk that the effects could grow even more devastating than the incident several years earlier that had claimed over ten thousand lives in a very small area. Tess was determined to do anything she could to help. Dr. Sherako was an inspiration. The work he was doing was difficult on every level. Before he'd left on the emergency mission, she'd asked if she could go too, but he flat-out denied it. He didn't know exactly what he was facing and didn't want to place her at extraordinary risk.

Prior to departing, he had launched into a full-fledged tirade about the financial dealings of the director and the Ebola Foundation itself. The words resonated with Tess. She wasn't sure if he knew anything about her Boston experiences, but the fact that he said anything at all suggested he did. Sherako was a man who paid attention.

No one else was available, so Tess had stayed late to recheck the exposure timelines of the drug study patients and their medication responses. The man from Whitefire Diamond Mine, Sipho, had particularly interesting labs. All of his values had normalized. If this pattern held, the implications would be substantial. The other one from the mine, Crotta, was not so fortunate. It appeared he was headed directly to a conversation with his god.

Tess's head was buried in her computer when she heard a door open into the central office of the suite, then voices. One was clearly the Foundation director, Mashaba. The other one was muffled but sounded very familiar. They went into the director's office but left the door open. She heard Mashaba say, "My young friend, I am told we need to increase the dollars we pay your company for the new Ebola drug. It this truly necessary?"

The voice answering sounded a lot like Noah. Tess instinctively looked up and peered outside her room into the other office. She could only see the back of the man's head, but it certainly looked like Noah. Loudly enough and with distinct emphasis he said, "Director, yes, that is correct. We have made the decision. It is in all of our best interests." Immediately she ducked back into her own protected space, sensing they would not be having this conversation in her presence.

"Are you certain this change will not create problems?"

"Quite sure, Director. Please do as we ask. You know that we have evaluated our position carefully. This change maximizes profit. Your exposure will be somewhat greater, but you will not suffer. Be smart."

She heard the door close, then one set of footsteps that grew more faint, but not two. Tess didn't move. Finally, she heard the door open again and dared to sneak a look. She saw the bespectacled director stepping out and leaving with a large briefcase. He looked flustered and decidedly unhappy as he locked the door.

Tess impulsively decided to act. If this man was doing the things Sherako said he was doing, and if Noah was involved . . . she needed to know for sure. She took out the precision hook pick that she kept in her phone case. She'd purchased it after locking herself out of her Boston apartment for the fourth time. Deftly, she jimmied the lock and seconds later was inside.

Good fortune smiled on her. The laptop computer was still on the desk. Tess opened it and was initially frustrated by her inability to hack her way in. A call to Axel, friend, man-child, and computer wunderkind, removed that obstacle, the time difference notwithstanding. Fortunately, he was doing a radiology rotation and had the opportunity to take her through the steps. Her classmate was incredible; access was secured.

After a much-longer-than-desired search, an Excel spreadsheet with very curious data popped up. It didn't have the names she was trying to find, but there was a list of multimillion-dollar corporate donors to the Foundation. In turn, that revenue was being parsed out in cash to multiple individuals, but most was being routed to Red Mountain Pharmaceuticals. There were no entries for Money Launderers 'R' Us, but there might as well have been. The whole thing was scarily similar to the list of payments the Cooperative had been making to its cadre of providers. It smacked of impropriety. Tess slipped in her USB drive to copy the file. Then she noticed something else.

Three locations kept popping up—Grand Cayman, Panama, and the Bahamas. Import/export was the other common denominator. The big question in her mind was how a money-laundering scheme so obvious in its intent was continuing without government sanction. The equally obvious answer was someone or many someones on the take. She checked the payment list again for any clues. One big dollar amount was targeted to an N.A. Those initials caught her attention.

Engrossed in her mission, she failed to notice a member of the janitorial staff entering the outer office. When the woman opened the door to grab the waste can, Tess was startled into awareness. The rapid glance spoke volumes. The woman knew the student at the desk didn't belong there. Tess decided that telling a quick lie was better than saying nothing at all. She had never seen the woman before and hoped her presence wouldn't become an issue. "Um, hello! You surprised me. The director asked me to look up something for him. He had to take care of an urgent matter." As subtly as possible, she removed the USB drive. An immediate exit ensued.

CRISIS IN KASHMIR

JAMMU, KASMIR REGION OF INDIA

CHIEF MINISTER BANERJEE hung up the phone and sat quietly on his office couch. It wasn't enough that the centuries-long tensions between the Muslim majority and the Hindu minority were heating up, and that his state was yet again being used as a political football between Pakistan and India proper; he had a more immediate problem. There was an inside informant.

Every precaution had been taken, but the most recent raid had still gone down in flames. Bhaduri had escaped the trap. Banerjee swore he would not make the same mistake again and cursed himself for his naïveté. The agent from Mossad had suggested he allow them to handle the problem. They'd had a bead on Bhaduri recently. They just needed his blessing. Nithan had refused the help. Working with Israel posed political risk. He muttered to himself, "Stupid."

He rang for his assistant to bring him his favorite shir chai tea while pondering his next move. Absorbed in thought, he sipped.

The tea did not seem as hot as usual and tasted faintly bitter. To himself he said, "It's nothing a little honey can't help." He stirred the sweetener into the beverage, then drank it quickly, returning to the overflowing desk. The tea was not sitting well with him. Nithan elected to put the work aside and go to bed. Within ten hours he was doubled over in agonizing pain. Thoughts of work were immediately replaced with those of survival.

BHADURI REJOICED. The ricin had removed the annoying politician from the equation. Finally, he had free rein to act again. Since Nithan Banerjee had become chief minister, he'd had to alter every part of his operation. Despite several warnings, the man had not backed off. The first few attempts to get a mole placed had been unsuccessful, thwarted by the rigorous state screening process. Finally, the proper bribe worked, just in time to avoid the security service dragnet. The dashing economist turned public servant should have known better than to cross him. Foolish, very foolish.

This new business project in South Africa was very promising. He was being offered an enticing cache of diamonds to help move heroin from Afghanistan down to the new markets in South Africa. The fact that large amounts of dollars and weapons were also involved in the transaction posed difficulties. Bhaduri relished both the challenge and the payoff. Smiling inside, he made the call to assure that the man who had poisoned Banerjee would be himself liquidated. No loose ends.

ASIYA BRUSHED STRANDS of jet-black hair delicately from her face. She hadn't had the opportunity to have the conversation she'd intended to have. Work and the children had sidetracked her since her return.

Unfortunately, her worst fears were now being realized. Her visit to the intensive care unit earlier in the morning was difficult. The blood oxygen level monitors and recent lab work reconfirmed Nithan's life-threatening situation. The poison was insidiously defeating his lungs, liver, spleen, and kidneys. His gifted wife could seemingly do nothing to help him. He'd made a grave miscalculation, believing he was the indispensable man to clean up the corruption. Nithan had gone after the top dog in the Indian crime world and lost the gambit. Now they could only wait for the seemingly inevitable end.

As Asiya re-entered the ICU, alarms started to sound. There was a sudden rush of activity, doctors and nurses flocking to the patient who was coding. Asiya was terrified. She could only watch. The experience was excruciating. Slowly the team peeled away. She felt the acute agony of her husband's certain death. Then, unexpectedly, the attending critical care specialist turned to her and smiled. Nithan was back, at least for the moment.

When she was finally able, Asiya joined her husband at the side of his bed. Examining Nithan with probing, distraught eyes, she whispered, "Sweetheart, I'm with you. Don't leave me!" The endotracheal tube prevented him from answering. She thought she felt him weakly squeeze her hand.

BAD MAN DOING BAD THINGS

CAPE TOWN, AFRICA

THE KASHMIRI CRIME LORD was careful as he made his way through the foreign streets. Bhaduri's trip from Jammu was long and tiring, but he had finally arrived in Cape Town to close this crucial deal. His extensive organization in India was not here to protect him, but a standard contingent of bodyguards had made the journey. He was satisfied that safety would not be an issue. Just as he was thinking this, one of the myriad of unofficial minibuses almost ran him down. The city was rife with them. Though he did not need this type of transportation, apparently most individuals depended on them to get anywhere. Yet another vestige of Cape Town's segregation history. People of color were forced to live far from any form of work. The privately owned, schedule-free minibuses took them to the places they needed to go.

Bhaduri was not in the city to solve its civic planning woes. Heroin trade in Cape Town had exploded, the drug cheap enough that anyone could get it. Cocaine, amphetamines, and methaqualone also were abundantly available. South Africa's trade connections with countries around the world made it a particularly tantalizing place to move drugs. When apartheid ended and the new government took over, the market for drugs opened dramatically. No longer was South Africa a trading pariah with highly restricted land, sea, and air borders. Internationally based drug traffickers found a user-friendly environment with first-world infrastructure, relative affluence, rapidly changing social and economic factors, and generally porous borders. Organized crime saw huge opportunity and made its moves. South Africa became the largest market for illicit drugs in the sub-Saharan portion of the continent. The toxic infiltration was a very unfortunate, almost unavoidable consequence of the political regime change.

In this milieu Bhaduri sought to dominate a huge portion of the heroin business. The people they supplied were mixing it with oxycodone. "Bluetoothing" had also taken off: Users were taking hits, then sharing their blood with others. The resulting massive public health consequences were no concern to the small man wearing the nondescript brown sports coat.

Product was being routed from Afghanistan via Pakistan to South Africa. In the past, almost all of the drug had continued on to Europe, but now at least a third was staying in South Africa. Bhaduri had pivoted to this new group that offered a better, albeit more complex, deal than all their competitors. Diamonds were easier to move and harder for prying eyes to detect than monetary bank transfers. He didn't think anyone on the streets would have the slightest idea who he was, but he and his protection stayed vigilant.

Bhaduri was set to make the final negotiation in this hugely complex deal. Ali Wazeer, leader of an aggressive Hezbollah splinter group in Lebanon, had first contacted him months ago. The terrorist had arranged to acquire stolen United States military hardware from an Afghani group. Wazeer was desperate for the arms. A major incursion on the Israeli-Lebanese border was in the works. With the sophisticated weapons, they would be poised to inflict a massive blow, a statement that would make Wazeer a significant force in the convoluted Middle East calculus. He'd also established strong connections with heroin suppliers from Afghanistan. What he didn't have was an intermediary to off-load the heroin and get the cash he required to pay for the arms. That is where Bhaduri came into the equation.

Bhaduri had worked out the arms/heroin details with Wazeer and his bankers in Beirut. What remained was the cash/diamonds part of the exchange. Bhaduri had the capacity to readily convert the diamonds to cash. Several more days were necessary to make it all work, then the Indian crime lord would take the grand prize. His fee for making all this happen was enormous. The prestige return for the successful transaction—incalculable.

The South African organized crime contingent was led by the fierce Russian-backed Serbian, Matija Marjanovic. Bhaduri knew that this man was even more ruthless than himself—he'd even heard whispers that he'd had his own brother killed. There would be no skimming this time. The South Africans had their own means of converting drugs into laundered dollars. Bhaduri only had to get the product delivered to Cape Town. As the pieces fell into place, Bhaduri marveled at his own brilliance in making it work.

Despite gloating about the work he'd done, the Kashmiri visitor remained apprehensive about concluding the business with Marjanovic. His first several encounters had been brusque but smooth. To date he'd seen none of the savage tendencies Marjanovic was known for. He considered himself fortunate. Bhaduri had negotiated primarily with the man's associates. The woman, Gwinevere, was integrally involved, though he couldn't imagine sharing power with a woman, much less a former barmaid.

The other associate, the Black South African man with the broad smile, seemed altogether duplicitous. With all this in mind, Bhaduri punched in the lock pad numbers he'd been transmitted. Neither he nor his bodyguards noticed a short, tautly muscled man across the street watching.

MARK WILDSTEIN PEERED over the sports magazine he'd picked up. He immediately spotted the Kashmiri crime boss's cover team. This was an assignment he was enjoying. Bhaduri was the real reason Wildstein was gracing the streets of Cape Town. Masquerading as a pharma executive, Wildstein entered the country on a regular basis. Of course, the name on the British passport wasn't Mark Wildstein. Israeli passports tended to get flagged. To conduct its operations, Mossad used false or altered documents on a regular basis.

The dossier on Bhaduri was extensive. He was a cunning, deliberative man. He had acquired power with stealthy action and uncompromising cruelty. Up until this point his activities were reprehensible but did not affect the balance of power in the Middle East. This latest venture, however, was a miscalculation. Word had reached Israeli intelligence that he was brokering this arms deal for Wazeer, the Lebanese strongman. It was an uncustomary lapse in judgment that placed Bhaduri squarely in Mossad's crosshairs. There was critical information Mossad needed that only the crime boss could get. Once it was garnered, Bhaduri's personal expiration date would closely follow—a circumstance known in the intelligence world as "negative treatment." This type of sanctioned extrajudicial killing was born out of the need to respond to threats to the existence of Israel. Bhaduri easily checked that box.

Wildstein had tailed the Kashmiri to the nondescript building near the waterfront. There was no signage to suggest who worked inside. When Bhaduri departed Kashmir, he obviously thought he was entirely secure. He was mistaken. Wildstein's partner, Pinchas Saperstein, disguised as a flight attendant, had surreptitiously planted a bug. The ultrathin unit took up residence in the man's lower coat pocket, affixed to the liner. It represented a triumph of Israeli technology. The two Mossad agents had heard almost everything discussed with each of the players. They knew that the final negotiated portions of the deal were ready for execution. From the initial meeting, they learned about the connection with Onderskeid Hospitaal and the Ebola drug. They surmised this was one of the pathways through which the South African criminal's profits were being cleaned.

Wildstein and Saperstein sat together listening near the V&A Waterfront Marina. Situated at the foot of Table Mountain, they observed the constant flow of tugboats, fishing vessels, charter boats, and pleasure crafts. Luxurious yachts adorned the docks like five-carat diamonds. This pair's business had nothing to do with the maritime activity. The man in charge of the conversation being transmitted, the one with the thick Eastern European accent, was referred to only as Mr. White, which seemed likely to be an intentional homage to the movie *Reservoir Dogs*. The financial package being discussed was staggering in its magnitude.

Talking to their superiors in Tel Aviv, the two agents explained what they had learned about the Kashmiri crime boss's arrival. "Bhaduri is set to finish the deal. He's brokering all of this. The Afghanis route the heroin to the mafia here. It's already en route. Red Mountain will take delivery and use local distribution channels to sell it for consumption in South Africa and move just over half of it abroad. It looks like they're laundering a large portion of the cash from sales through the Ebola Research and Treatment Foundation. It also looks like the Russian Bratva is backing Red Mountain. We think 'Mr. White' is a dangerous guy named

Matija Marjanovic. From what we know, he cut his teeth in Bosnia indiscriminately killing people. He seems to be making the calls.

"Mr. White is arranging for Bhaduri to get the stones to pay for the heroin next week. Once those are in his hands, the Afghani militia will release the stolen American weapons to Wazeer. Bhaduri worked out a special deal with Wazeer's bankers in Beirut. He's fronting the money for the stolen American weapons. This way he can keep more of the profit, and Wazeer can get his weapons in time for their assault on our northern border. Our Kashmiri friend has a nice group of associates in Amsterdam and Zurich to off-load the diamonds and make another substantial profit. Wazeer is routing the armaments through the Afghani border into Pakistan. It's the same route they use to move the heroin.

"When we get more details, we'll tip the CIA. They'll confiscate the weapons and take down the Afghanis who stole them in the first place. Their assets are already in place. Then we have our conversation with Bhaduri. The diamonds should find their way back to the South African State Security Agency. The heroin and Mr. White will be their problem. The whole thing blows your mind. I thought Iran-Contra was complicated."

The upper-level Mossad major listened carefully to the words of his skilled operatives before advising, "The SSA can't know a thing about this until we confirm CIA has the weapons. Too many leaks where you are. You can't even trust your mother with this information. The diamonds will be a huge feather in the cap for them, and if we lead them to the heroin, all the better. They don't have to know you were ever there. Works for all parties concerned."

Pinchas said, "So simple. What could go wrong?" Mark shared a sardonic smile with his partner. Not every Mossad operation had gone letter perfect. This one had to.

Mark had another problem troubling him. His brother-in-law, Erik, and family were here in Cape Town as well. His wife, Kari, had told him about Erik's daughter, Tess, working in the Infectious Disease Department at the same hospital Red Mountain was using as part of their drug operation. She could be at risk. The question was how to warn Erik without compromising himself.

CHANCE ENCOUNTER

CAPE TOWN, SOUTH AFRICA

REGULAR LIFE IN CAPE TOWN was getting to be a pleasure. I was walking by the ocean on Sea Point Promenade, watching the waves pound the retaining wall. It reminded me so much of the time I spent during residency at the cove in La Jolla, sans the California sea lions. I'd always thought that La Jolla was one of the most splendid places on earth. Today was one of those completely lovely days. Beautiful azure sky, perfect temperature, cool ocean breeze, sparkling water, people embracing the coast.

I was lost in thought, considering the pediatric thumb reconstruction on the schedule for the next day. The child had a group of congenital issues, including absence of his thumbs. The pollicization would involve moving his index finger to the place where the thumb should have been. I looked forward to helping Solomon with the case. I hadn't done one since fellowship, having left these types of reconstructions to the skilled pediatric hand surgeons in Boston. The best part would be how well the little boy would do afterward. The family would be thrilled—total win for everyone.

All of a sudden, I stumbled on a crack in the sidewalk, tackling the concrete with a vengeance. I felt like an idiot, particularly when I looked at my palms and saw that they were both bleeding.

A Good Samaritan with a distinctive Israeli accent helped me to my feet. "You alright? That was quite a spill."

I recognized the familiar voice. It was my sister Kari's husband. "Mark?"

He acted as surprised as I was. "Erik, well, here you are. I planned to get in touch with you on my next business trip. This one has had far too many meetings. In fact, I only have a minute or two right now. How are you?"

I regained my equilibrium and asked him to sit with me briefly on the nearby bench. "I sort of decided last minute that I needed a change. I guess Kari filled you in. We're getting to know the South African branch of Leila's family. Fascinating group. I'm doing some volunteer work at Onderskeid, the big public hospital here in Cape Town. Kari probably told you Tess joined us. She's doing infectious disease and several other rotations at Onderskeid. I'm not certain of everything she's got her hands in, but she's spending a lot of time with Harrison Sherako. He's spearheading the Ebola work. Primarily she's supposed to be doing ward and clinic consults. The reality is she's knee-deep in treating Ebola patients.

"I know you haven't met either my wife or new-found daughter yet. It's a shame you're so tied up. This would be the perfect opportunity to see them. Sure you can't spare an hour or two? They're both really special."

"Sorry, Erik, I'd love to, but I just can't make it."

I detected tension in Mark's voice. It was also strange to hear my given name. Then, after a pause, he continued, "I'm here for my company. I've actually been here quite a bit more recently. We're expanding our pharmaceutical footprint here. Erik, sometimes my work leads me to information that isn't public knowledge. This is one of those times. It would be best to get Tess out of the Infectious Disease Department. I can't tell you anything more right now. I shouldn't have even told you that."

That part of the conversation was clearly over. The warning was enough. I needed to persuade Tess to make a quick exit. She'd have to listen this time. Trying to hide the tremendous anxiety I was suddenly experiencing, I said, "Thanks for the heads-up. I got you. Maybe a year from now you can explain. So, Mark, I guess you really can't join us this evening?"

He looked out at the surf. "Wish I could. I'm leaving soon, and there are several matters I have to clear up. I just needed a short break to clear my head. I'm just about done with the project I'm working on. We'll do it next time I'm here, or even at home. Kari wants to see you all badly."

"There is nothing I would like more," I said immediately. "A detour when we have to go back to the States is already on the books. Hey, let's take a picture and send it to my sister. She'll love it." I whipped out my phone, but before I had the chance to unlock it, Mark had deftly maneuvered it out of my grasp.

"Erik, let's hold off on that. I'll explain when the time is right. And don't worry, it has nothing to do with another woman. Gotta go. Shalom, Erik, keep your eyes open here and stay well."

I watched him walk away casually but also purposefully. It was clear he had an agenda I wasn't part of. The entire interaction was bizarre. Not for the first time, I wondered about my brother-in-law's job. It was a stretch to think that the information Mark imparted was derived from his pharma work. I was completely stuck on his warning and how to handle it. Tess would not be happy, particularly since I didn't have any solid data to convince her with. Whatever Mark was referencing seemed to have significant implications. But the idea of hospital intrigue was not exactly foreign, or welcome, to any of us.

BACK AT THE RANCH

CAPE TOWN, SOUTH AFRICA

ONCE I GOT HOME THAT EVENING, I again raised the issue of Tess's Ebola work with Leila.

"Sweetheart, today I had the craziest experience. I was walking, tripped, fell, and was helped up by none other than Mark, Kari's husband. He was in town on pharma business. He's on his way back to Tel Aviv, otherwise he'd be here right now.

"Oddly enough, Mark told me that something isn't right at the Infectious Disease Department at the hospital. He couldn't tell me what the actual problem is, but he was very serious. I think it must be tied in with the data Phuti's cousin stole—the gift that keeps giving. I need to find Tess a way out of there. I just want to make sure you're okay with not saying anything to anyone about it until we're officially back in the States. It's not a problem we need."

Leila stared at me, started to say something, thought better of it, and said simply, "I agree. Been there, done that."

I was glad we were on the same page. Now, the task of speaking to Tess. It was time to use, then bury, the insider information Mark had provided.

TESS LIVES TO HACK AGAIN

CAPE TOWN, SOUTH AFRICA

I WALKED INTO TESS'S ROOM. She was busy on the computer, looking very serious. I said hi but got no response. I elected to leave her alone and wait to talk until dinner.

Per usual, Leila had made an amazing feast. Once we sat down to eat, I said, "Tess, you're pretty quiet tonight. Were you working on your book?"

She looked pensive and unhappy. "I wasn't going to say anything, but I think I have to. I overheard a conversation earlier today. I was in one of the Infectious Disease side offices on the computer, crunching some data. Everyone else had gone for the day, and clearly no one knew I was there. The director, Mashaba, came in with a visitor. They were discussing payments to Red Mountain Pharmaceuticals, and they were talking about increasing the reimbursement for the Ebola drugs to the Foundation. Who wants to pay more for drugs? That wasn't even the most concerning part. One of the voices sounded like Noah's, and I got a short glance, but I'm not one hundred percent sure it was him.

"In Boston I took a look at those documents you mistakenly took from your dead friend, Slobodan. The data he had made it seem like this was a great drug. Obviously, that's why we're using it. But there were those preliminary studies from the DRC site that showed incredibly high toxicity. When that information got out, the big drug merger failed. A couple billion were riding on the announcement. I didn't even think about it until we got here. Yonaker-Wood tanked, and Red Mountain stepped in and purchased it for almost nothing. When I started working with Dr. Sherako, I read all about what had happened."

Leila looked mortified. "What if Noah is in the middle of something illegal? VJ, when we talked about this, I didn't think it would hit this close to home. It's hard to imagine him involved with criminal activity. He seems so extraordinary."

Tess interjected, "What do you mean, 'When we talked about this'?"

I answered, "Tess, about that—we also have some concerns about what may be happening with the Foundation. Someone I know tipped me off. It was very indirect, but he suggested that all of us keep our distance.

"Let's face it, things here, or anywhere, for that matter, may not be what they seem or should be. If somehow Noah is involved, and I certainly hope he's not, that's not good, but best to keep it to ourselves. This is not our home field."

With a distinct edge in her voice, Tess asked, "VJ, what do you know? And who told you?"

I was conflicted but settled on the best response I felt comfortable with. "I can only tell you this. I was warned that what is happening with the Foundation *is* corrupt. The source is rock solid. And no, it is not someone you've ever met. For personal reasons, he asked me to keep this information very quiet. I have to respect that."

Tess cleared her throat. "VJ, wait, you didn't let me finish. I stuck around after Mashaba left. Axel helped me hack the director's computer. I got a lot more information about the Foundation. Your source is correct. It looks like they're some type of money-laundering conduit. Red Mountain Pharmaceuticals is at the center of whatever the Foundation's doing. There's more."

I swore to myself in Swedish, then said, "For God's sake, Tess! We've already been down this road. Are you out of your mind?! Do you think this is some game? They play for keeps. What's your plan now? Do you think the people involved in this scheme are any less cutthroat than Petra? If anything, they're probably worse. Time to back off. Nobody is threatening us, and this isn't our battle to fight. I haven't told you—the man that was killed on the game reserve? It was no accident. Remember Phuti, our tracker? The man was his relative. He'd stolen some documents. Guess where he worked—the ID Department at the hospital. The same place you're at right now."

Tess was undeterred. "VJ, you think I don't understand what's at stake? I decided to be done already. I had to try to find out if there was any threat to Dr. Sherako, and to see if I could find any confirmation regarding Noah. The bad news is that I did find references to payments to an N.A. It's not definitive evidence, but it really worries me."

Leila's anguish was written on her face. "Let's talk about this for a second. It's just so hard to believe that Noah really is involved with something like this. But it's a big leap between thinking he may be dirty and knowing it. Should I talk to Ayanda?"

I shook my head. "I know how you feel. It's the possible moral course of action. Think it through, though—on what basis would we say we have suspicions? If there is even a hint that information could have come from Tess, then we have big problems. I still have no idea if what happened to Slobodan was anything other than an accident, but none of us needs to find out for sure. The same players are probably involved. Agreed?" Leila acquiesced.

Tess spoke again, calmly. "Remember I told you I found more? The money that's being laundered is from heroin."

"Well," I said, "you've been a busy bee. Anything else you want to tell us?"

Tess looked uncomfortable, but didn't say anything other than "No, not really. *No.*"

I took several deep breaths. This story was getting worse by the second and far more dangerous. I was glad Tess and I were going to one of the rural health clinics the next day. I didn't want either of us to be anywhere near the hospital.

We had planned to be in South Africa for at least four more months. Leila, Tess, and I all wanted to stay. Every day the essence of the country was becoming a greater part of us. The people were warm and exuberant, the landscape was nothing short of amazing, and the medical world was utterly intriguing. The country offered all the things we'd hoped for and so much more. Now I was getting a severe reality check. As with many places, there was a corrupt underbelly.

I was trying to decide if my decision to turn a blind eye to obvious criminal activity was morally reprehensible or savvy, but there was no choice to be made. I could not jeopardize my family by getting in the middle of this mess. I would contact law enforcement once we left, but not a minute before.

WATCHFUL EYES

CAPE TOWN, SOUTH AFRICA

THE SUPERVISOR OBSERVED Salome as she finished her cleaning shift at the hospital. He noticed her slowly put the cleaning tools away. It was obvious she was beat. She had asked him for double shifts six days a week. Her husband was out of work, and it was either take on extra work or not feed her family. She was one of many of the hospital support staff from Nyanga township, the murder capital of the Western Cape.

Actually, multiple smaller townships constituted Nayanga. These were the places that Blacks and those of mixed race were permitted to live during the tyranny of apartheid. Unfortunately, Nyanga remained a very dangerous place, not just because of the rampant gangs. Sewer service, water, and electricity were daily uncertainties. The most economically disadvantaged in Cape Town populated this area. The enclave stood near the international airport. Salome's dwelling consisted of pieces of corrugated tin sitting practically on top of her neighbor's collection of corrugated tin. The supervisor knew this all too well. He had escaped Nyanga when he got his current job. He never wanted to return. He also wanted to do anything he could to help Salome, an incredibly dedicated woman with a tremendous spirit. She, and people like her, were the backbone of the city.

He approached her just as she was about to depart. "Salome, how did your night go?"

With a tired voice she answered, "Sir, just fine." After considering for a second, she added, "There was a woman in the director's office. I have been waiting to see you to tell you. She was doing something on the computer in the room. I have not seen her before."

His attention sharpened. "What did this woman look like?"

Salome tried to focus. "She was young, short, white, long dark curly hair. Attractive girl."

The supervisor had a strong suspicion who it was. He had watched the visiting medical student since she had arrived. That was his job.

"Wait a moment, Salome." He went to his office and retrieved photos of the Caucasians working in the ID Department. When he returned, he showed her the pictures. Within seconds she picked out the photograph of Tess Ryssdal.

The supervisor said, "Good work, Salome, you will find extra in your next paycheck." She smiled broadly, very pleased with her boss's obvious approval and the prospect of more rands coming her way.

The supervisor stepped back into his office and immediately contacted his real boss. "The young woman from Boston. The one you had me keep an eye on. She was in Mashaba's office. Shall I secure her for you today?"

The measured, stern voice on the other end of the call said, "No need for that. We will address the issue."

The supervisor thought, *This will be a problem for Ms. Ryssdal.* How severe the price, he wasn't sure. He felt genuinely bad.

There was no choice but to pass along the information he had gleaned. To do less would have only come back to hurt him. The rewards with this group were substantial, the penalties for poor performance steep. If someone crossed his employers, being killed and eaten in a game park was not out of the question.

SITTING BACK TO CONSIDER what the supervisor had just reported to him, the man with the beautiful smile turned off his phone and sat back in his chair. Tess had been on his radar from the moment she arrived. He knew what she was going to do almost before she did. An idea came to mind that he thought would work perfectly. After all, weren't carjackings an everyday event in parts of South Africa?

ROAD RAGE

WESTERN CAPE PROVINCE, SOUTH AFRICA

TESS AND I WERE TRAVELING a distance to get to the rural clinic. The trip had been planned for weeks and was independent of what we'd been doing at the hospital. Both of us looked at it as a way to contribute. Solomon had offered to escort us, but we had been in the country long enough that I felt secure with the journey and the rules of the road as they were. Thankfully, as we drove, we weren't talking about Noah or Ebola. We were having a merry little chat about HIV in pregnant women when I caught sight of a disabled vehicle ahead. A clearly distraught woman was frantically waving.

My instincts to help overwhelmed any sense of reasonable caution. Solomon's earlier warning forgotten, I pulled over on the gravel behind the broken automobile and opened my door. By the time I got out to assist and walked past the hood of our vehicle, the woman had mysteriously disappeared. Somewhat dismayed,

I stood there for a minute looking around, just in front of Tess's window. I heard her shout, "VJ, get back in the car now!"

Suddenly, a man came from the bush and ran directly toward me wielding a large knife. I was stunned and didn't react as quickly as I should have. Tess did. She'd already grabbed the Vektor from the glove box when she saw the woman vanish. Using the training she'd received in Boston, she fired the entire ten-round magazine at the attacker. The multiple holes in his chest quickly halted his advance. She screamed at me, "Get in and drive!" I did as I was told and slammed on the gas.

The crazy event was behind us in an instant. It was almost as if it hadn't happened. I still didn't understand what *had* happened. I stammered, "Tess, what just . . . Are you okay?"

Tess responded flatly, without hesitation. "I'm fine. I eliminated a threat. And guess what? We're not going to say a word about this to anyone but Leila for the time being, maybe forever. Who knows who this guy is working for? I don't intend to let this get complicated by involving the police. They'll ask about the gun, which we both know is totally illegal. They probably won't like it that I killed him. My guess is that the woman won't say anything to anyone. She will just haul him away and get another accomplice to carjack someone else."

I didn't know what to say. I was obviously upset by the attempted carjacking, and kicking myself for my own foolishness in being so easily deceived. But I was also disconcerted by Tess's matter-of-fact response. Yet she was right. She had acted decisively, accurately assessing the situation and firing the gun with authority and confidence. It was as if she had rehearsed the scene in her head in anticipation.

Our appearance at the health clinic would have to wait. Neither of us was in the frame of mind to carry on as if our lives hadn't just been threatened. We called ahead and explained that we had been victimized by food poisoning. Ironically, it was not us but the man with the knife who had been the poisoning victim. It just happened to be the high-velocity lead variety.

The ride home was quiet. I was contemplating the fact that now both my daughter and I had willingly killed people who were a threat, not the kind of shared experience most fathers and daughters have, and quite different from a focused afternoon together in the operating room or providing primary care in a South African village. I decided to broach the subject delicately.

"Tess, if you want to talk about putting ten rounds into that guy, let me know. I'm here for you."

"K" was all she said in response, clearly deep in her own thoughts.

Leila was surprised to see us back so early. Our faces betrayed that all was not well. Tess explained, "VJ stopped the car to try to give some help to a woman who looked like she really needed it. A man with a knife came after him. It was obvious he meant to kill VJ and steal the car. Either they didn't see me or they saw me and didn't care. I shot and killed him, and we left. There isn't much more to tell."

She stared at both of us in disbelief. "What did you just say? You killed someone and drove away? What?!"

I tried to calm her down. "We really didn't have a choice. It all happened so fast. Reporting this will just create problems."

Leila wasn't convinced. "I can think of a hundred ways this can come back to be a problem."

I sat down. "Leila, you're right. Maybe I should speak to Solomon."

Tess defiantly interjected, "No! There was no one else on the road. No one passed. That woman isn't telling anyone. We need to just put this away. There's no point in involving Solomon. It puts him in an untenable position no matter what he recommends. This is something I can easily live with. Getting carjacked and dying today in South Africa was not on my bucket list. Having to explain myself to the police in this country isn't either."

Leila calmed her. "Okay, Tess, for now we'll do that. Still, we do need a clear story if anyone comes asking questions. You were obviously acting in self-defense." Tess agreed, and the deal was struck, though it ended up being a story we never had to tell.

Later that night, when we were getting ready to go to bed, Leila said, "Tess is not exactly your run-of-the-mill person, is she?"

I stroked her hand. "No, she's not. And neither are you. I think you would have done the same thing without hesitation. You both have certain wonderful but savage tendencies. Birds of a feather . . ." The look Leila gave me was not entirely loving.

As Tess predicted, we never saw any news reports about the dead man, nor did we have any unwelcome visits from the police. What occurred would remain a secret among the three of us. I harbored a sense of guilt for pushing us to come. Leila felt a similar guilt for agreeing so readily. I reminded her that the Cooperative was born and bred in the good old U.S. of A. The world can be an unsafe place whether you are sitting in a schoolroom, attending a movie, or worshipping in a mosque, a church, or a synagogue.

ACTION/REACTION

CAPE TOWN, SOUTH AFRICA

AT HIS PLUSH Cape Town office, the man with the beautiful smile was most unhappy. Tawanda had been shot and killed in the process of the carjacking. How could he have known that the intended victim would be armed? They were supposed to be easy targets. The support team rolled in too late to do anything, though it was probably better that way. A gun battle would have drawn attention and solved nothing.

He should have guessed Tess would be a difficult mark. Taking her was no less important; he just had to be more imaginative. Even though she and VJ could not have thought what occurred was anything but a random event, he had to assume their guard would be up.

A new idea formed. He glanced at his computer screen at the plane reservations that were recently made to take the Akekawanze-Brio group to Tsitsikamma National Park.

WEEKEND SOJOURN

EASTERN CAPE PROVINCE, SOUTH AFRICA

NOAH AND AYANDA were over at our house for the afternoon. We had invited them the previous week. None of us were comfortable with their presence given what we suspected.

Eliza had joined us too. The girl was truly a spitfire. She kept us all entertained and lightened the tense atmosphere. As the day progressed, I couldn't help but feel that whatever suspicions we had were wrong. Noah's words only reinforced my prior belief that he seemed to have tremendous character and a strong moral core. As I questioned myself, the conversation turned to adventure. Apparently, Noah's family had extensively explored the country during his childhood and teens.

"You must join us for a trip to Storms River Gorge in Tsitsikamma National Park," he said. "We will kayak, hike, ride ATVs, bungee jump. The views of the canyons and ocean are breathtaking. So many wonderful things to see and do. It is not close—five hundred eighty-five kilometers. But it is quite a special place.

The flight takes only fifty minutes. You need a break from all this hospital seriousness. A few extra days away will harm no one. We would be pleased to take you. How can you say no?"

Eliza virtually exploded with excitement. "Oh, we're definitely in!"

With alcohol on board, the stress of the shooting behind us, and a renewed sense of well-being, I consented. "It sounds like fun. The benefit of having few obligations is having few obligations."

Leila and Tess simultaneously glared at me. Eliza caught Leila's look of disapproval. "Come on, Auntie, be spontaneous! You always complain that VJ is too serious." I turned to my wife and gave her an "Is that so?" raising of my eyebrows.

Ayanda added her two cents. "It would be so wonderful if you could join us, Leila. Tsitsikamma National Park is truly worth it."

Noah said, "No need to worry about this at all. I took the liberty of booking the trip for this weekend. All the details are already addressed. And yes, Eliza, I assumed you would be coming." With a big smile she gave him a fist bump. I managed to ask some pointed questions about security. He assured all of us that no problems would arise.

When Leila's cousins and Eliza left, I received the anticipated double-barrel onslaught. My wife started first. "VJ, is it my imagination or did we not have a conversation about Noah possibly being part of a massive crime syndicate?"

Tess followed. "Is your brain working at all?"

I considered various responses. I settled for a weak apology. "I know I shouldn't have committed us. Eliza seemed so enthusiastic. Lord knows I have my doubts, but Noah just seems like such a good person. There has to be a better explanation for all of this. No matter what, we should have a good time."

Tess started back up on me. "Fun for who? Do you have any idea how uncomfortable this makes me? I can say the typical things about moving into a relationship too fast, et cetera, et cetera, et cetera—all the usual bullshit. Noah is a smart man. He will see right through it. The last thing I want is for him to have the slightest suspicion about what we think might be true."

I didn't really have a good response. The best I could do was say, "Let me think about it." Ultimately, I came up empty. Absent a convincing way to back out that wouldn't raise question marks, the long-weekend sojourn remained a go.

PART IV

GONE, BABY, GONE

EASTERN CAPE PROVINCE, SOUTH AFRICA

THE LOGISTICS OF THE TRIP proved to be easy. Staying at the Storms River Gorge camp was anything but camping. "Glamping" was more accurate. Noah had arranged for all six of us to reside in elegant lodging. It was as he described—like so much of the country, stunningly beautiful.

Tess settled on the "I need to take it slower" approach. Noah acted the gentleman, she reported. Neither Leila nor I noticed any difference in his demeanor whatsoever. Eliza helped run interference, with her puppy-like energy and constant injection of chatter. They were by no means empty words; there were just a lot of them. Noah took particular care to listen and respond to her in an adult, sensitive way. I couldn't reconcile his behavior with what I had been contemplating.

On the first day of hiking, we took in the Dolphin Trail. It carried that name for good reason. From the shore we watched schools of dolphins playing in the ocean. They didn't seem to be worried about anything. We tried to relax in this seeming mini-paradise and forget the issues brewing at Onderskeid. Though I didn't realize it fully, Tess was navigating the eye of the hurricane. I was hanging on the periphery. Then we were all sucked into the vortex.

Just before dusk on our second night, sounds outside drew everyone's attention. In the middle of the river outside our cabins, a truck seemed to be stuck and in danger of washing away downriver. What it was doing there in the first place, I had no idea. A woman was standing on top of the cab screaming her bloody head off. Jaded by the recent roadside event, I wasn't fast to respond. I just stood outside, transfixed by the unfolding drama. Leila started to move toward the water, but I held her back. It was reflexive. Out of the corner of my eye I saw Tess walking around the side of the building. Something else had gotten her attention. Distracted, I didn't think anything of it.

Over the next half hour someone managed to get a winch and haul out the truck. The woman on the roof jumped onto the back seat of a friend's motorcycle, and they sped away. At face value the fiasco appeared to be an absurd clusterfuck. None of it made sense. Until it did.

The second I confirmed Tess was gone, I knew what had happened was anything but random; in reality, it was a well-orchestrated distraction. Her hacking episode had obviously not gone unnoticed. Eliza had been transfixed by the outrageous water display and hadn't seen Tess at all. The first person I sought out was Noah. I hadn't seen him at all during the entire river event. I found Ayanda. "Where is Noah? Tess is missing!"

She looked horrified. "Noah got called away earlier today. He had to go to the veld urgently. He left several hours ago. Can you not reach her on her phone?"

I shook my head. "She left it behind. It's sitting on the floor inside. I found that out after trying to call her fifteen times." I dialed Noah's cell. No response. I planned to track him down wherever he was, but I needed immediate information. I called my brother-in-law, Mark. I had to know whatever he knew.

I was lucky; he answered my call. Trying to stay calm, I said, "Mark, the people I think you're keeping tabs on just kidnapped Tess. I guarantee it. She hacked into one of their computers, and they must have found out. Please tell me anything you can."

There was a deep breath on the other end of the line. "Erik, I have no idea what you're talking about or how you think I can help. Perhaps you can come to the house tomorrow morning. I'm sure we can work all this out. Kari would love to see you. Let me call her and tell her you will be over for brunch." Then he hung up. Breaking bread the next day in Israel was of course absurd. I got the message. Kari would be the contact point.

SITTING IN A CHAIR at a Mossad safe house, now wide awake, Wildstein considered how to assist his brother-in-law's daughter without compromising the operation, assuming she was still alive. The game could already be over. Still, he thought the people who'd taken her would want to know what she'd discovered and who she'd shared the information with. Additional bugs had been successfully planted in the offices of the men they were monitoring. These were the same men who'd discussed the Ebola Foundation at Onderskeid. If it was true this group had her, there was potential intel he and Pinchas could acquire. Wildstein contemplated the implications of this new wrinkle on their own operation.

I WAITED TWENTY MINUTES before contacting my sister. Kari beat me to the punch. I saw her name pop up on my cell. "Erik, what happened? Mark just called and told me you need his help. Where are you now, and when can he connect with you?"

I related the details of the event and coordinated a meeting site back in Cape Town the next day. I was trying to figure out who would know we were in Tsitsikamma and where we were staying. The answer kept returning to the same person. In fact, it was Noah's idea that we take the trip. Now, very conveniently, he was out doing *official* work.

I was kicking myself yet again for falling for the trap, and desperately hoping that whoever took Tess was only trying to send a message. My experience told me differently. I was in a state of controlled panic. Any chance of getting her back relied on my acting thoughtfully. One of my many failings is the intrinsic need to manage people and situations. In this case I had to subvert my own impulses and follow every instruction Mark provided.

That night was the worst of my life. I rented a car, and Leila and I drove back to the city with Eliza. The explanation to persuade her to join us was complicated, but we prevailed. There was very little to say in the car.

After Eliza fell asleep, we tried to run through different scenarios. If Mark was who I was now beginning to think he was, I had a lot more confidence that he could help, rather than official law enforcement. What could they do? Fortunately, Leila shared my opinion.

Before we left, we asked Ayanda not to say anything to anyone. She decided to stay for the rest of the weekend and fly back as originally planned, and promised to advise us the very second Noah contacted her. She realized the gravity of the situation. Knowing we had some prior experience with problems of this type, she also promised to stay mum. Our suspicions regarding her son were not shared. If he did surface, I didn't want him to be spooked before I could interrogate him.

Late in the drive, Eliza poked her head forward between Leila and me. "I heard what you two were talking about. I'm scared, but I know you will get Tess back. I'm not going to say a word to anyone, particularly not my dad. I know him; he'll try to help. But I know that's not what you need now. We're leaving next week. You have to tell me when Tess is safe. If you think there is the slightest thing I can do, just tell me. I'll do it."

Leila spoke first. "Eliza, this is a very difficult situation for all of us. I appreciate that you seem to understand how important it is to keep all of it quiet. You're right—if your dad finds out, he'll do everything he can. Unfortunately, there's nothing he can do, and at this moment, nothing you can do. We'll let you know the second we have her back. I think you know: We are definitely getting her."

I had nothing to add, so I just stayed quiet. I thought to myself, *Eliza is definitely cut from the same cloth as Leila. This is someone we can rely on.*

By the time we reached Cape Town, I was spent. Mark and I were set to meet at Sea Point Promenade in two hours. It was the same place I had tripped. It seemed appropriate. I closed my eyes for a moment, and an hour evaporated. The ping on my phone alerted me to a text. I breathed an immediate sigh of relief when I saw it was a picture of Tess, with the time and date verified. She didn't look hurt. The message was nonetheless chilling: **Meeting soon. Will discuss Tess return. We will cut off her arm if you are not there. Pick up contact phone from your locker at Onderskeid.**

When I connected with Mark, his words were somewhat reassuring. "VJ, obviously the fact that she is alive means a lot. We have assets that should help us get her back. Let's talk about what needs to be done." He and Pinchas, his partner, were resolute about helping.

A NIGHT AND A DAY PASSED. Tess suspected they were waiting to break her down. She was determined that it wouldn't work. Another man had come, joining the two holding her captive. He was tall with thick blond hair. He smelled like he had just left an animal reserve. He looked the part as well. The man pulled up a chair in the barren room. With a characteristic Afrikaner accent, he said, "Tess, you know why you are here. You need to tell me what you saw, why you did it, and who you told. You mean nothing to us. We will release you unharmed if you give us the information we need. Otherwise, you and your family have much to fear."

Tess considered her response. She knew that the man was lying. There was no way they would just let her go. She still had leverage, though. They weren't sure how much she'd downloaded or what she'd passed along. There was no way for them to know. If they decided to kill her, their operation would still be at risk. In the back of her mind she considered the idea that the harming part might include rape. The idea terrified her, but she resolved to fight to the death before allowing it to happen.

She'd devised a compelling story that would play into their idea of what would motivate a young woman. With as much emotion as she could muster, she said, "While I was working in the Infectious Disease office, I heard part of a conversation between the director and a man I thought was my boyfriend, Noah. I care about him a great deal! I wanted to find out what he was doing with the director. There had been many rumors about the director taking money earmarked for patients. So I took a look at the director's computer. It was just sitting there, open. Thankfully, I didn't see anything with Noah's name on it. Believe me, that would have been a deal-breaker for our relationship. I was waiting for the right time to talk to him about it all. Then, you assholes kidnapped me. That's where we stand. I have nothing to tell you because I don't know a damn thing."

The blond man rose and took out a sleek Beretta. "Young woman, I am not stupid. You seemed to easily kill my colleague on the road. You have a choice now. I want the full story. Tell me everything you saw on that computer."

Tess regarded him carefully. She did not take her adversary lightly. Emphatically she lied, "I barely saw anything. Frankly, I have no interest in whatever you and your wonderful little gang are into. I will never change what happens here. To quote my relatives, 'TIA—This Is Africa.' You must know that my family has connections in the government. They're not just going to let you keep me here."

The man holstered the gun. Before he walked out, he turned, and said, "Here is our message, Tess—leave the country and say nothing to anyone, *ever*. Take that path or die. Straightforward choice."

Tess didn't like being told what to do by anyone, particularly people threatening her. She didn't really buy that they'd truly let her go. It was abundantly clear that this group had the will and the manpower to do terrible things. She would forever be an obstacle that they'd be all too happy to eliminate. With those facts in mind, Tess continued to plot strategy.

She remained locked in the colorless room. She had no means to help her escape. Inside there was a cot, a chair, and nothing else. They'd traveled a substantial distance but didn't seem to be close to any major city. She tried practicing meditation, to no avail. Outside there was a din. Grunts and howls penetrated the quiet of the night. Even if she'd wanted to sleep, it would have been impossible. She was kicking herself for being so stupid. How had she allowed herself to get into this situation? Her adrenaline had gotten the better of her. She came back to the same question: How did Noah find out? It had to be the custodian.

While the incident with the truck in the river was unfolding, she'd looked over to the cabin where Noah was standing, and he'd beckoned her to join him. Distracted by what was going on, she'd started in his direction. An odd thought was tugging at her. His face had looked slightly different. Also, his eyes. She remembered being curious about that as she walked his way. She finally decided the lighting had created odd shadows. Moments later she felt a hand over her face. Before she could scream, there was a sting in her arm. In a very short time the lights went out. Now here she was, stuck in this room.

Noah was not her immediate problem. She needed to escape. Her interrogator had suggested her release was impending. But hours went by and nothing happened. She speculated that the blond man had to check with a boss or bosses.

A large, silent man gave her food and led her to the bathroom when the need arose. He remained mute, no matter how she prodded him. There was another man, Raffy. He had identified himself at the outset. He wasn't in charge, but was directly responsible for her care. The man was an absolute pig. He made no secret about ogling her. She would have worried more, but apparently she had been declared off-limits, at least for the present.

MARK AND PINCHAS monitored the conversation remotely. One voice said, "We use the girl to draw him out. We find out what he knows and who he told. Then we kill them both. Very clean. A man and his daughter disappear in South Africa—so what. Nothing unusual about that."

The second, heavily accented voice responded, "Raffy, you stupid man. Wife here. Very connected. They not stop looking for VJ and girl. Very bad for business. Must give girl back. Persuade them to leave, say nothing. Kill both when get back to Boston.

Make look like accident. Happen every day there too. Kill wife at same time. She smart lady. Trouble for us."

The voice that they now knew was Raffy relented. "Boss, I'll do whatever you want. Keeping either of them breathing makes me nervous."

A third voice was heard. "What did she find out on Mashaba's computer?"

A man with a distinct Afrikaner voice spoke up. "I questioned her closely. She was looking at the computer for two reasons: First, she heard a voice that sounded like her boyfriend and wanted to know if he was involved in something nefarious. The good news is that she still doesn't know the truth. Secondly, the word on the street is that Mashaba has been skimming money, taking resources away from the sick Ebola patients. She got the answer to the second question, but not the first. Beyond that, she doesn't seem to give two fucks what we are doing. I don't think she found anything about the guns, diamonds, or heroin."

The voice with the thick accent was heard again. "She may, she may not. Poor choice to snoop. Cost her life. Her father life. The wife life. No choice for us. Cannot take chance. Money too big. We just not do it now. Kidnapping good message. We rough her up. Then they leave soon. This doctor Sherako, he infectious disease doctor. Too bad he get in way. We eliminate him too. Except we wait until he done at Whitefire. I know other infectious disease doctor. Smart man. Make him disappear." Marjanovic had spoken. There was no further discussion.

Mark and Pinchas looked at each other. Pinchas spoke first. "The question is not *if* we shut them down, just when we do it, my friend."

Mark agreed. There was a clear path forward. The entire operation had to be stopped. It was crucial to coordinate the mission to prevent Marjanovic's move against his brother-in-law's family with the action already planned near the Afghani-Pakistan border. Wildstein took what he had learned to his second scheduled meeting.

IN CAPE TOWN, another drama was playing out. Mashaba was having a quiet dinner at his favorite restaurant. This girl, Tess, had become a major thorn in his side. The computer theft episode with Queenie had been bad enough. Now he'd had to explain himself again to Marjanovic. That conversation had been singularly one-sided. Fortunately for him, there seemed to be no changes in the flow of money, and no one from SAP had come knocking on his door. His job as the Foundation director was safe for now.

In fact, he took great satisfaction in his position. Through his life, he had always wanted to do good. Here he was, in charge of an organization that was saving lives. The criminal side of his role was just a necessary evil. He had come to terms with that reality long ago. He took some solace in knowing he had information about Red Mountain and their dealings with heroin, arms, and diamonds. These outsiders always underestimated him and his reach in his native land. He was ready to use the information *if* and *when* it was needed. He worried that the time was coming soon, but resolved to put it aside for the moment.

Tonight was going to be exquisite. First a wonderful meal. Then, he was scheduled to indulge in the talents of a new fifteen-year-old the pimp had promised him. He was excited by this one in particular. She was a fresh import from the Middle East. Mashaba preferred the young ones. They always let him do what he wanted.

The restaurant staff knew him well. His status guaranteed rapid service, the tastiest cuisine, and marvelous wines. Normally the Merlot he'd ordered was particularly special. Tonight, it tasted rather pedestrian. He called for the sommelier, who apologized profusely. Rather than get a new glass, Mashaba chose to focus on the dessert. The elegant mousse didn't taste right either. His stomach became upset, and he soon became confused. He couldn't remember what he'd eaten.

Mashaba wasn't aware of it, but at that very moment the little engines in his cells called mitochondria were no longer able to do the essential job of oxidative phosphorylation. That small task is mission-critical for living. He stumbled outside, but was quickly overcome. Simultaneous to the seizures starting, his cardiovascular system collapsed entirely. As Mashaba lay dying in the empty street, his last thoughts were those of regret—he'd so miss his latest planned sexual conquest. The pathetic life of the director was now a thing of the past. Cyanide tended to do that.

MOSSAD EXTENDS WARM GREETINGS

TEL AVIV, ISRAEL

MOSSAD, ORIGINALLY ESTABLISHED in 1949 by Israeli prime minister David Ben-Gurion as the Central Institute for Coordination, was now known as the Institute for Intelligence and Special Operations, or simply the Institute. It was widely renowned for its superior intervention skills. Countless world-threatening terrorists were effectively targeted and eliminated. But, as had been proven in Dubai years earlier, overconfidence could lead to disasters. The Mossad operation had become a huge black eye for the agency.

In an obscure white prison-like building just outside Tel Aviv, the director, Talia Lozowick, contemplated this history. She and the prime minister were staring at the feed from the forbidding Hindu Kush mountain range on the Afghani-Pakistan border. Intel from South Africa was being converted to direct action. This operation's success was critical.

The unknowing targets were attempting to cross at the Dorah

Pass in Badakshan Province. They had been traveling day and night through the bone-dry, rugged terrain. Several internal squabbles had made the journey even more tense. Their bosses seemed to ignore the hardships these men were enduring to drag the weapons to Pakistan. A huge payoff was promised. Now they were close.

The point of interception came into view courtesy of a patrolling section of lethal U.S. Marine AH-1Z Viper attack helicopters. Each pair of twenty-foot blades on the main rotors propelled the battle group forward. Helmet-mounted sight and display systems cued the gunners ready to engage their payload.

The road-weary smuggling team was surprised. The director and prime minister could almost see the looks of despair on their faces. The original Special Operations group of AH/MH-6 Little Birds had been diverted at the last minute to a different, equally important engagement, but the Marine contingent proved more than capable of handling the assigned task. A hailstorm of death unleashed by the nose-mounted 20mm three-barrel auto cannon, side-mounted Hellfire missiles, and 70mm hydro rockets decimated the group of terrorists in short order. The Americans were doing exactly as suggested: reclaiming their stolen armaments. Payback is a bitch. Wazeer would have a hard time recovering from this huge loss. The arms were gone, and now he had many fewer reliable men.

A wide smile formed on Lozowick's face. She turned and looked at the prime minister. The two leaders shared a triumphant toast.

Lozowick also took pleasure in knowing her delivery of this piece of quality intel would help her a great deal in future interactions with the U.S. She had only recently been elevated to the role of director. Continuing the positive relationship between Mossad and the CIA was necessary for her success. Mostly she was happy because this was a win for the Israeli population. Someone wouldn't lose their brother, father, wife, mother, daughter, or grandparent from a terrorist incursion. That was her raison d'être.

Mark Wildstein and Pinchas Saperstein had done well. In addition to obtaining the intel to sabotage Wazeer's arms deal, they had identified another asset that might help destroy one active branch of the South African organized crime syndicate. If there was the potential to shut down players in the illegal arms and heroin trade from Afghanistan for at least a year or two, Lozowick was interested. Pinchas had spoken to her about the options. At first she'd vetoed the idea, considering it far too risky. The two field operatives were very insistent and highly persuasive. Eventually Lozowick gave a green light to the second phase of the operation. The mission objectives were in sight and ready to be actioned

WHEN I HAD OPENED my locker and recovered the burner phone, there was a note attached: "Reconsidered. Do this the way we say or we return her to you in not one, but many pieces." Subtle.

The meeting with the Foundation's stooge took place in an industrial section of the Cape Town docks. Mark and I had established very specific parameters to govern what would be said and when. I glanced at my own burner phone. It wasn't yet telling me what I wanted and needed to know. Feeling like a caged animal, I glared at the goon sent by the crime group to convey their terms.

"Dr. Brio, in order to get Tess back, you must agree to leave the country immediately and stop any further investigation into our group. Also, and very importantly, the Akekawanzie clan must not use their government positions to do anything unwise. In Mozambique, you will find your daughter. Directions will follow. Any deviation from the plan and we will take care of both of you. Am I clear?"

"Crystal clear," I said with the disdain the lowlife operative warranted.

RAFFY STARED AT TESS. There was something different about this woman. Her eyes grew cold and menacing, almost as if she was casting an evil spell on him. She gave him the creeps. He couldn't do anything to intimidate her. The woman they'd used as bait in the failed carjacking reported that Tess had quickly and efficiently gunned down their man on the road. That fact told him everything he needed to know. He didn't really enjoy beating up the fairer sex, but this was necessary. The brass knuckles in his hand would do the job. Vanderweiss had come to talk to her again and apparently was satisfied with the answers she had provided.

The boss had decided that it was safe to leave one small woman in the care of two big men. Raffy was still shocked their prisoner was being permitted to live. He felt about her as he would a scorpion. What he was about to do was the message to stay out of their way.

He drew back to strike, but just as Raffy's fist began to move forward, a bullet changed the contour of his head. Brain splattered on the wall, *Pulp Fiction* style. Tess was startled. So was Raffy's compatriot who'd been restraining her. He released his grasp just enough for her to move. As he did, he experienced a vicious blow to his groin, followed by one to his face. All of Tess's pent-up anger was spent attacking the man. Nothing improved for him when he finally struggled to his feet. Simple breathing became the issue as the garrote tightened around his neck. The end was quick.

With the task completed, the masked stranger spoke quickly as he pocketed his weapon, as did his companion. "Shalom, Tess. Erik sent my partner and I here for you. Please come." Tess had to think for a second to remember that Erik must be VJ. Whoever this was knew him from some other world.

Together, Tess and her rescuers left the isolated compound. For the first time, the former prisoner caught a glance of where she'd been held. The noises she'd heard at night were baboons, who stood dispassionately watching her departure. She spotted one baboon sitting on top of a tree trunk calmly downing a can of soda. Where he got it, she had no idea. It was oddly characteristic of the strangeness of the day. There were also penguins wandering around, busily engaged in daily penguin business, oblivious to the human presence. Charming little guys. She thought of asking the lot of them to gather their friends and help. Nothing like a troop of baboons and a waddle of penguins to create a getaway-masking ruckus.

After pressing a button to send a text, the first man quickly guided his charge into the waiting van. He was obviously relying on neither the baboons nor the penguins to help. When they got in, he took off his mask and said, "A pleasure to officially meet you, Tess. That was quite a job you did on that man just now. I'm impressed. By the way, I'm your uncle Mark."

She looked at him with utter disbelief. "Did you just say you're my uncle?"

Calmly he clarified the statement. "Yes, I am. I am your father's sister's husband. You know, Kari, the sister that lives in Israel. I'm Mossad."

Tess put the pieces together. "Jesus, Mark. I knew about you, but I didn't know you're Mossad! VJ never told me that."

The man smiled. "That is because he never knew it. I suspect he does now. By the way, this is my associate, Pinchas Saperstein. We were able to convince our boss to sign off on this operation because we suggested you have critical intel about this guns, money, heroin, diamonds exchange."

Tess lit up. "Well, *Uncle Mark*, that information I can give you—*in detail.*"

FOR THE THIRD TIME I looked down at my cell. Finally, I saw the message I was hoping for: All clear. A broad smile crossed my face. The rodent looked at me with questioning eyes. "Brio, is there something funny about this conversation? I assure you our group is very serious about this transaction." He was not aware that the numbers in his own army had just been reduced and that in a relatively short time, he would say hello to his own god or gods.

I found that fact highly entertaining and after a pause responded, "Yes, I understand what you told me. But what is it people say? 'Truth is just the perception of reality.' My perception and your perception of the same situation may be entirely different. You believe you are in control of this conversation because you have my daughter. The reality is that isn't true." The man's face betrayed sudden uncertainty. I continued, "I assume one of your colleagues is nearby watching us. You think you are safe. You probably don't appreciate that I have my own protection. Look to your right, my friend. See that woman sitting on the bench? Do you appreciate the Beretta she's got trained on you? She's an excellent marksman. I suggest you leave now and take whatever other scumbag you brought with you."

After considering his options, the bewildered Foundation acolyte said, "Brio, I hope you understand who you are dealing with. Your life isn't going to be worth five rands." He then beat a hasty retreat. Once he and his associate departed, I walked over to the menacing armed woman with the wild jet-black curly hair and gave her a kiss. Both of us were relieved with the outcome of this skirmish. Our experience with the Cooperative had prepared us for the looming battle.

Mark had already briefed us about the Foundation's real plan to exterminate the Brio contingency. Mossad's surveillance proved to be rich with information, including the data pertinent to us. When my wife heard the words, she wasn't threatened, she was incensed. Her resolve to destroy the Foundation was absolute. They didn't realize she would be every bit the dangerous adversary they'd already created in Tess. I was glad these two women were part of my tribe.

Leila and I stealthily made our way to the Mossad safe house in Fresnaye, a quiet, predominantly Jewish section west of Cape Town, where Tess would be delivered. While we waited, I called Ayanda, hoping she would know something about Noah. She said that his "emergency field assignment" was finished and he was returning to Cape Town soon. We planned our own reception.

When Tess was finally dropped off, the reunion was sweet. She gave me a hug I'll never forget. Although she was obviously tired, her focus remained sharp. She said, "I need to get home to get Mark my USB drive. They need what I have. They were pros. In and out in seconds. Made it seem like they had done it a hundred times before."

I reassured her. "We cleared out everything from the old place. Your bags, computer, and all our stuff are safe right here. We've got work to do. The Foundation is going to come back at all of us now."

They started the war, but we were now on the offensive. We had no real choice. Just as the Cooperative had underestimated us, so too did this group. Mark, Pinchas, Leila, Tess, and I sat together for a brief strategy session. What we planned would demand more manpower. Fortunately Mark had already received permission to add several additional personnel. They were en route.

We took time to breathe and get some well-deserved rest. Once we regained our footing, Tess said, "VJ, I believe Noah engineered the kidnapping. I still don't have any absolute proof, though. Just before they grabbed me, Noah was standing next to the porch. He asked me to join him. What did he tell you?"

I answered, "I reached the same conclusion. And I never got a chance to speak with him. That day, his mother told us Noah got called out for an emergency problem in the veld *before* that commotion in the river. She said he had no satellite coverage and could be gone for days. I've been trying to track him down. Ayanda says he's headed back to Cape Town as we speak. Getting you returned was all we cared about. If we ever see him again, and I'll be very surprised if we do, the group is going to have an interesting conversation."

Tess flatly said, "I'd like to connect with him and Ayanda."

All of us understood both the specific and existential threat the Foundation posed. Now more than ever, Tess wanted to strike back.

She continued, "I was very lucky you had that meeting with Mark, which by the way wasn't an accident. Mark gave me the straight story on the way here. He was trying to warn us off before something like what just happened actually happened. The Foundation was slightly less fortunate. I'm going to take them down." The steely glint in her eyes was the same as on the day she eliminated the carjacker. The cobra tattoo adorning her ankle should have been a warning to anyone thinking about crossing her.

I looked at Tess and Leila. "Tess, I understand how you feel. Believe me. But we need to stay level-headed. For now, no one can know where we are. I'm afraid we're going to be quarantined here for a short time. Leila, you have to tell your brother that Eliza can't come by because we're all sick with some aggressive flu variant. And be sure to mention that you mean all three of us. That will let Eliza know that Tess is safe. They're leaving soon anyway, so it shouldn't be a tough sell. Tell him we'll catch up when we get back to the States."

I decided there was no better time to try to gain as much of an advantage as possible. Pulling out the card I'd saved, I made a call to my old adversary who'd helped mastermind the fraud at MRMC. I figured that of all the people I knew, Rick could provide the best insight into the psyche of our formidable opponents. After all, black market dealings were his specialty. He didn't seem surprised to hear from me. It was as if he could see the future that day on the beach in Grand Cayman. I guess he knew me better than I did, because here I was, tapping him for advice. The man provided information and insight that was tremendously useful. I had long since stopped caring about Rick's illicit activities. I also knew somewhere down the road there would be a price to be paid for his help. Given my needs, that fact was irrelevant as well.

Hanging up the phone, I examined the reconnaissance photos Mark and Pinchas had taken outside the Red Mountain Pharmaceuticals offices. Everyone coming and going wore hats and sunglasses. It was difficult to see details clearly, but there was one picture that appeared to show Noah. The evidence continued to pile up. Laying a trap for him became the first order of business.

Leila contacted Ayanda and told her we wanted to surprise Noah with a small outdoor party—recognition for the hard work he'd been doing. She had no idea what we suspected and loved the idea. Leila begged her not to mention a word about any of us to him, to enhance the surprise. She agreed.

She did ask about Tess's abrupt departure from the camp and our worry. We had made up a cover story that suggested she'd left to help with a flash Ebola outbreak, and that my worrying was the result of a terrible miscommunication snafu. She apparently bought it, and the arrangements were made.

The hardest part was Ayanda. She would be devastated to learn of Noah's treachery. But she would want to know. We all earnestly believed that Ayanda was not involved with the Foundation, though there was still a chance we'd been fooled. Of course, if she was in league with Noah, then she would warn him straight away about our "surprise." We had a backup plan just in case.

Suspicion was eating at Leila, making our conversations unusually terse. I was sad for all of us. What was unfolding was not part of any scenario we had envisioned for the sabbatical.

When Noah finally returned two days later, Leila got the call from Ayanda. The sting was in play. Mark and Pinchas had staked out the perfect site, intentionally chosen to give us maximum protection. If Noah had anything planned, we would be ready.

The family of two arrived. When our eyes met, there was not the slightest hint of shock in Noah's. A beautiful smile erupted on his face. "VJ, so nice to see you! My mother did not tell me we were having a surprise get-together. I am so glad you can join us. I hope you have brought Tess."

I corralled Noah and escorted him out of range of his mother, whom Leila had engaged. Doing my best not to smash his head into the nearby retaining wall, I snarled, "Noah, Tess isn't here yet. It's time for a conversation. I think you know what it will be about. Let's start with everything you know about the Ebola Foundation, Red Mountain Pharmaceuticals, and the money laundering that's happening there. We're aware you're in the middle of it. How you could endanger Tess, I have no idea.

"Before you grabbed her, she downloaded everything from the director's computer. We also know about the diamonds, the heroin, and the guns. By the way, about those guns. The CIA has them now. Poor planning on your employer's part. We are more than happy to have the SAP interview you about all of this. Why don't you take this opportunity to explain to me *just what the fuck* you've been doing!" While I was having my say, I watched his hands carefully. I was fingering the Vektor in my pocket.

Noah looked at me with wide, innocent eyes. "VJ, I don't understand at all why you are yelling at me. I also do not have the slightest idea what you are talking about. I know only that the Ebola Foundation funds research and that Red Mountain Pharmaceuticals supplies their medication. They took over from Yonaker-Wood. These matters are not my area of expertise."

I continued to boil. "Do not for a minute stand there and deny what you've done! Tess heard you talking to the director. You set her up to be kidnapped! You're just lucky we got her back safely."

He still looked like a deer in the headlights. "Please explain further. What is this time that you say Tess heard me speaking to someone I do not know? And when is it you say I helped kidnap someone I care so much for?"

I was in no mood for the lies coming from his mouth. "On Tuesday the eighteenth, you were in the office with the director of the Foundation. In Tsitsikamma, you lured Tess to be taken by your boss at nine thirty."

He shook his head, "VJ, neither of these things are true. On the date you quote, I was at a dinner meeting with the health minister in Durban. I remember specifically because it was difficult to get there. And look here at my plane ticket." He showed me the boarding pass on his cell. "I left one and a half hours before you say this event at Tsitsikamma happened. I think, VJ, you have temporarily lost your mind."

For the first time I felt a tinge of doubt. I thought, *Tess never saw Noah full face during that meeting and did not identify any reference to him in the computer files other than the initials N.A. There was glare from the lights on the cabin on the evening of the kidnapping. What if the person who beckoned to her just happened to look like Noah?* "Okay, Noah, let's suppose for a moment that you are telling me the truth. Why the sudden departure?"

He pulled out his phone again. "VJ, look at the pictures of this flood in this village. As I have told you before, I work for the section of the health department that deals with natural disasters. There was worry of cholera and typhoid. See me in this video? See when it is dated? We just returned, and now you accuse me of this absurd nonsense! Now *you* tell *me*. What is going on, and how is Tess?"

I was completely disarmed. Noah seemed to be telling me the truth and had substantiating evidence. While it was certainly possible all of it was manufactured, his protests and responses to my questions sounded sincere. I pulled out the Red Mountain photograph and said, "Look at this picture. This was taken outside Red Mountain Pharmaceuticals. What were you doing there?"

He protested again. "VJ, I have never been there—ever!" He took the photograph and examined it closely. "VJ, look carefully at the man you say is me. Do you see this scar on his right cheek? Do I have a scar on my face? I can tell you I do not. It is not as if I am wearing makeup!"

"Noah, do you wear contact lenses?"

"No, I have perfect vision," he answered sharply. "What kind of question is that?" I told him that Tess had also mentioned that his eyes looked different.

I made a call to Mark to see if he had more surveillance footage taken at the Foundation meeting site where Noah theoretically was. Several minutes later a short video arrived on my phone. Together we studied it. The similarities were overwhelming, but the differences distinctive enough.

Noah pondered what he'd seen and learned, sighed deeply, and finally said, "It seems, VJ, that I have a twin brother. I swear I knew nothing about him. That's shocking enough, but to find out that he's mixed up in such terrible business is truly sad."

Though completely flabbergasted, I concurred with his logic. What I had thought was impossible earlier suddenly became not only possible but entirely reasonable. It also occurred to me that now there was a new problem. This man clearly knew Noah existed and had used that information against Tess.

Another portion of the video, less distinct, had caught my eye. But I wasn't yet sure if what I was seeing was what I thought I was seeing.

Tess made her appearance while we were deep in discussion. Though she had promised she would practice restraint, she instantly flew toward Noah in a rage. Like her mother, Tess could go from zero to absolute banshee in seconds.

"Tess!" I yelled. "He didn't do it! It wasn't him!" She stopped in her tracks, but still kept her distance. I whipped out the photos. "Is this the man you saw at Tsitsikamma? Focus on the scar on his right cheek."

She settled down and studied the pictures. She looked at Noah and looked back at the photos. The eyes were also a different color. Noah had brilliant green eyes. The ones she had seen at Tsitsikamma were mud brown. That night she had not focused on the scar, but in hindsight remembered puzzling over what looked different about Noah. Now she saw it clearly, as she did the truth. She rushed to hug him, anger dissipating into affection. The long embrace was followed by a passionate kiss.

Relief washed over me. Tess as well, I could tell, but Noah remained uncertain. He'd navigated a crisis in the veld, returned to stand accused of horrible deeds, and now was faced with the reality of a malevolent, previously unknown twin. Before diving into that topic, we signaled to Leila and Ayanda and asked them to join us. We explained to Ayanda in broad strokes what had happened, leaving out the carjacking and specific details of Tess's rescue. Director Mashaba's death was public knowledge. We all understood it was anything but accidental.

Naturally, Leila's cousins wanted to go public and involve SAP. Without divulging our sources, we were able to convince them otherwise. They offered to provide the assistance of the extended family and their government connections, but we demurred. The option was certainly appealing, but it seemed likely to add complications without guaranteeing anyone's safety. The last thing we wanted was to put more people at risk.

The discussion turned to the startling revelation about Noah. No one had an explanation for the one-sided secrecy about his twin's existence. We agreed that everything we discovered would be kept under wraps until the three of us were safe. The Akekawanzies would carry on as if they knew nothing.

Before they left, we figured out how we would contact them if needed. Tess handed Noah a copy of the USB drive with all the incriminating data for safekeeping in the event it was needed. After hugs were shared and they left, Leila's words captured what all of us were thinking: "I'm angry and I'm ready."

PRESSING THE ADVANTAGE

CAPE TOWN, SOUTH AFRICA

WHILE WE AWAITED the arrival of the additional Mossad agents, Mark and Pinchas briefed us on the information they were cleared to divulge. Bhaduri was named as the wizard behind the curtain. After Tess was rescued, Bhaduri had dropped off the radar. The bug Pinchas had placed on him was no longer functioning. Locating him again would help us and Mossad.

With little else to do while we were waiting, I voraciously devoured online newspapers. I came across an article about the recovery of the Kashmiri chief minister from a protracted illness. It was Asiya's husband, Nithan. Only then did I remember speaking to her about his crusade in Kashmir against Bhaduri.

I contacted Asiya to inquire about her husband, and also to find out what I could about Bhaduri. I obliquely suggested that Bhaduri had entered our sphere and wondered if she could give me any helpful information about the man. After a series of e-mails and texts, we finally connected by phone, and she immediately issued warnings. "VJ, I believe there is a lot more to the story than you are telling me, and I assume that there are very good reasons for your inquiry. I probably don't have to remind you that this man Bhaduri is evil. Nithan, in fact, has just recently left the intensive care unit. Bhaduri's man poisoned him with ricin. We were fortunate. Most would not have survived. You must protect yourself in any way possible. He has an extensive network."

I pushed the conversation a bit. "Asiya, I think he is still here in Cape Town. Is there anything you know that could help us find him?"

"Well, perhaps. He has a taste for young girls," she answered acidly. "He runs a prostitution ring here and imports them from all around the world. We see them at our hospital when they get abused. It's horrible. Nithan mentioned that Cape Town is a way station for many of the African women. It seems Bhaduri's half sister manages the operation there. Her name is Kundu. Find this woman and you might find Bhaduri." This was vital information that I thought it likely Mossad did not have.

I hung up after getting more details about Bhaduri and her husband's condition. It was indeed a miracle Nithan was alive. Asiya had used virtually every medical fact in her considerable armamentarium to help support his care and recovery. Had he been married to anyone else, his obituary would've already been on the internet. Fortunately for Asiya and Nithan, Mossad had no intention of allowing Bhaduri to ever return to Kashmir—leaving Cape Town was not an option. Of course, tracks would be covered, and the event would be recorded as an unfortunate circumstance. There wouldn't be the slightest suggestion that a foreign government had taken down an Indian national abroad—even a very bad one.

THE REINFORCEMENTS

CAPE TOWN, SOUTH AFRICA

LIRAN AND GALIT, the two new Mossad agents tasked to help us, walked through the safe house door. Introductions were made, and pleasantries exchanged. Liran was a large man, an obvious battle-tested warrior. Galit, though smaller, was no less impressive. The short-sleeved shirt she wore revealed firmly toned musculature. Her piercing green eyes only reinforced the sense that this was not someone to cross. Both instantly communicated incredible competence and intelligence.

They had done their homework. Gesturing to Tess, Liran said, "It seems your daughter has a career that involves more than medicine. Mark gave us a detailed list of her accomplishments. I know some people who could use her talents. She seems to be *very* cunning and *very* shrewd."

I chewed on that reality for a minute. After a quick snack, the pair took their leave and grabbed a few hours of well-earned rest.

While they were recharging their batteries, I got some positive news from Mark. As suspected, Bhaduri was still in the city. Asiya's knowledge, along with several South African connections, had led them to Kundu and Bhaduri himself.

"VJ," Mark reported, "we found him with a fifteen-year-old. She's now on her way out of the country to safety, and he's with us." Old habits die hard. The man was a monumental dirtbag. He didn't know it yet, but he was about to provide us help and the pathway to his own demise. A coup for the world.

Now refreshed, Liran and Galit sat in the kitchen drinking coffee. Mark and Pinchas joined them and the three of us. It was time to put together a coherent plan. Since a truce was not on the table, we either had to cripple the Foundation leadership so severely that they couldn't fight again or entirely remove them from the equation. The latter scenario seemed more likely.

Pinchas handed Tess, Leila, and me state-of-the-art GPS trackers. "We need to know where each of you are at all times. It is strange for us to be working with civilians, even ones with as much experience as you three have. But the Foundation is after you, and we can use that information to our collective advantage."

I spoke up. "A person I know suggested that the best way to get their attention is to pinch their next heroin shipment. Nothing like taking product to start a conversation. They won't be expecting us to make that kind of move." There was a certain Robin Hood appeal to the idea of taking from rich criminals. "Mark, can Bhaduri tell you anything about how and where it comes in?"

"Yes, I think we can still get that information."

Galit smiled. "I like it. Since we got Tess back, they have to be on edge. As we speak, they're probably searching for all of you. At least throw them off the scent and make them work hard. Take my word for it: The effort strains resources. Here's the story you tell your doctor friend, Solomon. You and Tess had an experience going out to the veld that you don't want to talk about, but it threw you. You've decided you can't come back, and you've decided to take an extended vacation in Europe and then return to Boston. You'll supposedly fly Swiss Air through Zurich and have a vehicle rented in your name. That should create some confusion. We will also make sure your names appear on the passenger manifests. The Foundation and Red Mountain are probably the same entity. We know they have eyes and ears in the hospital, so the message will get to the right person. There's no way they'll be able to track you. We'll have some time to plan and make this happen. Mark and Pinchas, it's time to make your little bird sing."

With awe, I sat listening to the four operatives hash out options. Ultimately a plan was hatched that was brilliant in its audacity. I added more of the advice that my friend, Rick, had provided. Why his smuggling operations were so successful was immediately clear. He was a logistics genius.

THE RED MOUNTAIN WAR ROOM

CAPE TOWN, SOUTH AFRICA

DAYS LATER at the Cape Town International Airport, a curious thing happened. Two men from the Foundation wearing airport security uniforms spied their target. Their connection had informed them that a man and a woman under the name Akekawanzie were booked on a Swiss Air flight to Zurich. They lay in wait, determining that taking the woman first would be easiest. Leila was easy to pick out. The flowing mane of black curly hair and the tall athletic figure were distinctive. She was engaged in deep conversation with an unknown man. The men figured Brio was likely in the bathroom and moved in, converging on the woman. The first said, "Leila Akekawanzie, we need you to return to our office. We found something in your luggage that we'd like to discuss with you."

The woman turned defiantly. Except it wasn't a woman, it was a teenaged girl. "My name is Eliza, and you didn't find anything in my luggage because I don't have any. Dad, these men are criminals, I guarantee you." The two uniformed men shared a moment of uncertainty. It was long enough for Eliza's father to clock the first man in the head with his steel-edged briefcase and grab his daughter, but not before she slammed her open palm into the second assailant's nose. Blood gushing from the open wound on the forehead of one of them and the nose of the other, the injured men ran through an emergency exit. Alarms were now sounding loudly at each gate, shutting down all boarding and departures. It was a disaster for everyone in the terminal.

When an actual airport security team arrived, they escorted Eliza and her dad to a small room. They asked her about what had just happened. She told them her version of the truth: "The man came up behind me and tried to put his hand in my crotch. I think he thought I was traveling alone. Pervert. Fortunately, my dad was there." They bought the story and released the pair.

After Eliza and her father were alone, he questioned her gently. Eliza provided the explanation. "Aunt Leila, VJ, and Tess are dealing with some new trouble. I'll explain it all to you, Dad, but right now I have to call Leila and tell her what just happened."

IN A SEPARATE PART of the city, a different conversation was occurring. "Boss, our representatives in Boston say they haven't seen any evidence that Brio and the two women have come back. The people at Onderskeid heard him talking about how much he liked Switzerland. We thought we tracked them down to a flight to Zurich. That didn't pan out. We're checking other flights. We think they might have gone to Geneva. We're scouring the hotels and Air B&Bs in the area. Nothing so far." The man purposely left out the debacle at the airport. The number of mistakes was mounting, and that conversation could only end badly.

Marjanovic remained displeased. "I not like this. Brio, he

crafty man. He got someone else on side. That how he get girl back. Deal in Afghanistan get blown up. Wazeer very upset. Rebels too. They get diamonds, but lose many men. Things not right here. I change mind. You find Brio, Tess, Leila, wherever they are. You bring to me. I kill them myself. What happen Sherako, Ebola doctor? He still doing job?"

Basil, the man with the beautiful smile who also happened to be Noah's twin, spoke up. "Yes, he is minding the flock and doing a damn good job. No one else there has gotten sick. They should be working again soon. I found a replacement for Jaars."

"That good. Next heroin shipment due soon. We must have no problems. We need double security. Bring in heavy artillery. We get American weapons we divert from Wazeer?"

The beautiful smile returned. "Boss, come here and see." Basil led the boss to the storage area. The arms cache the rebels had taken included the new short-barreled M4 carbine assault rifles, Mossberg 590 tactical shotguns, M16s with M203 grenade launchers, and M249 SAW machine guns. The gleam of the weapons restored Marjanovic's sense of well-being.

He was mad at himself for underestimating his opponents. The question was, who was helping them? The hit on Raffy and his compatriot was extremely professional. They had known where to find Tess. None of it made sense. The possibility occurred to him that Brio was CIA and that his "sabbatical" to South Africa was nothing more than a cover for spying on his operation. It didn't seem likely, but everything that was happening was highly unusual. Yes, the security around this next shipment would definitely be stepped up. No one was going to interfere with him again.

THE HEIST

CAPE TOWN, SOUTH AFRICA

WHEN BHADURI WAS INTERROGATED, he divulged the details of the heroin load. He was under the misunderstanding that his words might save him. Our contingent now had a time and a place. The collision course with the Foundation was inexorably moving forward.

The call from Eliza only confirmed what we already knew. I was hoping they'd continue to waste resources looking for us in Europe. Leila had to spend considerable time on the phone convincing her brother, Peyton, before he left for Atlanta that she was adequately protected. He wanted to stay in South Africa, but fortunately she was able to prevail in her argument. She was right, and he grudgingly accepted reality; particularly in light of the incident that had occurred with the fake security men, it was far safer for Eliza for the two of them to exit the country.

Mark leveraged one of his connections to gain access to military-grade ordnance courtesy of the South African military. The cost for the well-trained mercenaries to take the weapons was steep, but worth every Israeli shekel and American cent. The requisite arms were obtained.

The day after we received delivery, I noticed the page-three article in the *Cape Times*, "Armory Break-in Yields Thieves Major Haul." There were few specifics, but the author speculated that the weapons would likely end up in the hands of drug dealers, rebels to the north, or both. I had to suppress the urge to call the woman myself and tell her the truth.

The treasure trove of equipment impressed even Mark and Pinchas. Included in the arsenal were South African Vektor R4/R5 carbines, Sig Sauer P226 pistols, M26 fragmentation grenades, smoke grenades, Belgian FN MAG machine guns, a Thales Squire battlefield surveillance radar system, and my personal favorite, old Russian RPG-7s. Apparently, the new rocket-propelled grenades were not available yet. Oh well, we'd have to make do. I didn't have access to anything like this when I was a lowly Swedish soldier.

Tess seemed enamored with the Sig Sauers. Pinchas eyed the American Mk13M7 Marine sniper rifle with the Nightforce Optics scope. It was the latest Marine upgrade. Word on the street was that someone had used it for a successful kill at over two thousand meters. The nano body armor was also new and improved. I believed this haul would give us a huge advantage. No one said anything about fair.

The seven of us ventured out to get acquainted with our ill-gotten matériel. We'd purchased a large used van, changed the plates, and filled it with all of us and our equipment. The three-hour drive to the expansive South African veld was consumed with discussion about the impending action. The wilderness provided ample space for war games. Mark and his partners schooled us on planned tactics and strategy. Tess was a quick study, and I watched her transforming into a warrior.

Back in Cape Town, the Mossad quartet continued to be extremely professional—no bullshit, no bravado, just focus. They carefully inspected the docks where the heroin shipment was due to arrive. Every detail of the physical terrain was accounted for. Mapped out were the positions each of us would take and what our jobs would be. If one of us got functionally removed from our individual station, the zone would be cross-covered. As little as possible would be left to chance. Latest-issue coms would provide for instantaneous tactical adjustment. We rehearsed the operation multiple times at a sister pier in the Duncan Dock area. Finally, the logistics were wired to the point Mark and Pinchas felt comfortable. They were in charge. Leila, Tess, and I were there to provide support.

Twenty-four hours before the shipment due date, I took Leila's hand in mine gently. "You still good with this? We can report everything to the police and count on them to do their job."

She didn't hesitate. "VJ, I've considered all the options. We are can-do people. Mark, Pinchas, Liran, and Galit are can-do people. We are also ready. This plan is going to work, we're going to get their heroin, we're going to draw out their leadership, and we're going to chop off their fucking heads."

I raised both eyebrows. Whereas curse words were a part of my minute-to-minute conversation, Leila rarely swore. "Okay," I said. "Guess that settles that."

Tess had been withdrawn. I'd tried to talk to her about it a few times during the lead-up, but she'd brushed me off. I was sitting on the couch, finally reading the conclusion to a book I'd started months earlier about the genesis of the Magnitsky Act in the States. Congress's bold move clamping down on the Russian oligarchs was a blow for good in the world. Despite the gravity of what we were about to do, I needed to occupy my brain with something else. Tess sat down next to me.

"VJ, I'm ready to talk. I'm not sure what to do with this person

I've become. I take chances, get us into a life-threatening mess, kill people, and plan to potentially kill more people. Have I become Petra? Have I always been her and not really known it? I don't want to be that person. But, honestly, the whole thing is giving me an adrenaline rush. I am a hundred percent ready for tomorrow. I will not hesitate to blow them all to hell with the RPG and those frag grenades if I have to. I feel like I'm in some alternate universe. There's the part of me that wants to be a dedicated physician helping people, and there's obviously this other part of me."

I gave her what I hoped was a reassuring pat on the shoulder. "Tess, you're definitely not Petra. She had no regard for anyone but herself. You truly have a heart of gold. But you're definitely no longer the Tess you thought you were, either. We all evolve over the course of our lives. You've just taken the fast track. I have an idea about what you might want to do when all this is over that I think will satisfy this new you. In the meantime, try not to be so hard on yourself. Introspection is important, but don't let it cripple you. We're going to work through this challenge and go back to a reasonable existence. Trust me."

My words seemed to help. Tess rose from the couch and picked up one of the pistols. She handled it carefully, as she'd been instructed, then replaced it in its holster. What Tess *had* become was a person for our opponents to fear. Her resolve was clear. She hadn't hesitated when she was protecting me, and I knew she never would when the stakes were high. Special she was.

During daylight hours we made small talk. Liran and Galit were masters at crossword puzzles. They conquered page after page of an Israeli crossword puzzle book with fiendish intensity. Leila read the latest in a series of World War II historical fiction novels. She'd immersed herself in this genre. She said it gave her perspective on our own challenges. Tess focused on a medical paper. I finally finished my book, and did a lot of nothing, contemplating the next moves.

Around noon on the chosen day, Pinchas and Mark held a final briefing session. We were ready.

We rode wordlessly in the van. I felt strangely calm. Preparation does that. Pinchas flipped on music, Creedence Clearwater Revival. I felt like a character in *Apocalypse Now* or *Platoon*. Except it wasn't a movie. This was the real deal.

At the designated location, the arms and ammo were unloaded and ferried to our positions. We afforded ourselves ample time to set up and ready ourselves. Extra eyes had been hired to patrol the area to verify that none of the Foundation's soldiers made an unexpected appearance. My new ally, Rick, had helped us find the underground information we needed along the way. His worldwide network was staggering in breadth. Mossad's connections in the city were not nearly as extensive so they had to sign off. We needed in-the-know criminals, and Rick was the necessary conduit. The sweeps were clean.

Their connections in the city were not nearly as extensive. We needed able-bodied criminals. Rick was the necessary conduit. The sweeps were clean.

Night fell; it was starless. That was a major bonus for our team. Each of us wore a black bodysuit and full face mask. Our Invisio M4 wireless communication system permitted us to whisper and still hear each other, even in the face of gunfire.

Pinchas was perched high above the pier with the Mk13. He'd done this before in Lebanon and Gaza with the Israeli Defense Forces. Efficiently, he'd mapped out the planned kill zone, marking the distance, and picked markers that would help with last-second adjustments. His laser sight indicated the targets would be approximately two hundred meters downrange. With little wind to contend with, there would be negligible alteration in the trajectory of the rounds—another plus for us.

He didn't like killing people at all. The goal was to secure the heroin and leave. Enemy kills would be dictated by unfolding events. Leading up to the engagement, he and I had shared notes. Ironically, some of our experiences were not that different. One in the war theater, the other in the operating room theater. Rarely did every outcome unfold as anticipated. The key was to successfully follow the credo of the Israel Defense Forces and United States Marine Corps: Improvise, adapt, overcome.

Pinchas scanned the activity below through his scope. The craft arrived on schedule. Bhaduri had told us the truth. Persuasion, applied correctly, is a strong driver. The delivery people launched into action with impressive focus. No wasted movements. Almost a thousand keys of heroin were off-loaded from the dhows—traditional wooden sailing craft—to the waiting trucks. The traffickers preferred this type of boat because it could carry large enough loads but sneak in and out of ports while keeping a low profile. Security was greater than expected. Lots of men. Mark issued several commands to adapt to the increased force assessment.

With the shipment loaded into the waiting vehicles and no indication of a threat, their security appeared to let down its guard just slightly. The diesel trucks revved their engines, sounding like caged wild animals, eager for release. The convoy started down the road.

We snapped into action. At the predetermined choke point, C-4 charges created two mountains of rubble on the already narrow road. The lead and tail vehicles were stopped with no chance of forward or backward escape. Gunmen poured out of the trucks, guns blazing at nothing specific. Without warning several stray bullets struck the position Liran and I occupied. I looked over to see if my fellow combatant was okay. Blood was pouring out from around one elbow. I applied a battlefield compressive dressing. This was not going to be quite the one-sided battle I'd envisioned. The Foundation was ready and armed to the teeth. Quickly, though, it became apparent that their counterattack lacked leadership and structure. Score one for us.

As the tactical surveillance monitor called out targets to Pinchas, Leila and Tess held their own weapons in reserve. After a lengthy argument the morning before, they'd consented to be support. In case of impending disaster, they would engage with the RPGs and frag grenades. We'd rehearsed several scenarios, including complete failure and retreat. Winning remained the primary focus, however.

Pinchas employed his sniper rifle with deadly precision, smoothly moving from one well-aimed target to the next, never pausing, never missing. He emptied two magazines of five rounds in one minute. The hostiles shooting at us fell rapidly. From their own protected nests, Galit and Mark fired with the FN MAGs on the targets Pinchas couldn't see. A renegade with a grenade launcher was one of them. He was silenced the instant he revealed his position. A round to the head made shooting part of his immediate past. With Liran stabilized, I was able to contribute from my slightly compromised position with an R5.

The firefight rapidly dissipated. Seeing what was happening around them, the drivers jumped outside their vehicles with hands raised. The shooting stopped. It was over in minutes. The tactical surveillance system confirmed that all threats were eliminated or captured. Nobody died that didn't have to.

I immediately turned to check on Liran, who seemed to be doing okay. We were on a very strict timeline. Once the police arrived, they would assume the battle was a turf war between competing organized crime organizations, which in essence it was. We needed to be gone before they reached the scene. A small bulldozer that was pre-positioned made short work of the rubble. Mark had recruited his own set of drivers, who took over the trucks as soon as it was safe. They were all locals in the event any of the vehicles were stopped, since none of us fit the profile of someone innocently transporting goods through Cape Town. One of our recruits grabbed the prisoners and led them to a waiting refurbished army transport.

The seconds were ticking away. Truck three wasn't starting. It seemed that the engine block had been struck with several rounds. Mark put all of us to work to redistribute the load of our newly acquired heroin. Pinchas remained topside to scan for visual or audio indicators of SAP activity. He caught chatter on the police scanner and announced, "Ladies and gentleman. Time to go. Leave what isn't loaded and exit as planned." About half the truckload remained. That would be a negotiating problem for us but would allow SAP to claim a small win.

Our haul was deposited in a nearby isolated warehouse, protected from prying eyes. A number of local addicts were not going to get their normal fixes. Once we had a moment to settle, I had a better chance to examine Liran. What I saw when I cut away the sleeve wasn't ideal. There were multiple shrapnel wounds, one in the bend of his elbow adjacent to critical nerves and arteries—tiger country, in the lingo of surgeons.

"Liran, you're one tough guy," I told him. The injury had to be killing him, but the man was stoic. "We've got to get you to the OR right now."

Mark spoke up. "Erik, is that really necessary? Can't you just keep on some pressure and dress it? I don't think it's smart to have that kind of exposure."

I considered the sagacity of my brother-in-law's words. "Mark, you're absolutely correct about exposure. But Liran could lose this arm if the problem isn't addressed quickly and by the right person. I can't exactly ask Solomon or one of his colleagues. That leaves me to be the right person to take care of this, and I'm damn well going to do it. We'll get it fixed as quietly as possible and bypass the Emergency Department." Leila gave me a confirmatory nod.

"I'll give you a heads-up the second I'm finished. Come on, Liran. We'll take the car we parked. The rest of you can go to the warehouse and get transport from there. Liran, you should also change clothes. Right now, you might draw a little attention. I guess I'll have to do the same. There are scrubs in the trunk. There are lots of extras."

The weapons were hauled away, and we parted expeditiously.

LATE NIGHT AT ONDERSKEID

CAPE TOWN, SOUTH AFRICA

LIRAN AND I snuck in the back entrance, and I placed the call to the OR supervisor, quickly identifying myself.

"Mr. Dlamini, sir, I have a friend visiting from the States who accidently hurt himself. I'm worried he lacerated his brachial artery and both his median and ulnar nerves. I need to explore him. Can you get the microscope, the vascular set, and the C arm? This might take a while. Don't worry, he hasn't had anything to eat or drink for more than six hours. Are there any open rooms? I'd like to get him in as soon as I can." One benefit of working at a public hospital is the lack of need to get pre-approval from the insurance company. I was the pre-approval.

With surprising ease I got Liran into the holding area. Our anesthesiologist asked him all the standard questions: *When was the last time you had anything to eat or drink? Have you or any family members had any prior problems with anesthesia? Do you have any heart or lung problems?* When he came to the question about how Liran hurt himself, it was quashed with a death glare that unnerved even me. "Shop accident." Case closed.

We rolled in with minimal delay. The gun and knife crowd, mercifully, was resting tonight. Once Liran was under, I removed the pressure bandage. One of the pieces of shrapnel had dislodged. The squirt of blood almost hit me in the face. Quickly I applied pressure above the artery and requested help getting the tourniquet on.

After a stat prep, I set about the business of identifying what was and was not lacerated. It took every bit of self-control for me to dampen my own adrenaline and successfully navigate the case. Liran ceased to be Liran. He became an arm with an injury that needed to be fixed. As expected, there was a jagged piece of shrapnel embedded in the antecubital fossa. The brachial artery was a full casualty and needed to be fixed. There was just enough collateral blood flow to prevent the forearm tendon compartments from being damaged in the short term. I wouldn't have to release them. That was a huge plus.

I placed bulldog clamps at the two ends of the artery and started the process of excising the injured tissue and repairing it. I debated fixing the large vessel directly versus harvesting and using a vein graft. Finally, I decided I could get away with a direct repair. There wouldn't be too much tension. The graft would take longer, and I wasn't sure how much time we had before we were discovered and something bad might happen. But if my fix didn't look good, I'd take the chance, take it down, and use the graft. No way I was going to leave the OR with something that wasn't perfect.

Luckily for Liran, there was just a partial laceration of the median nerve. A big nerve repair would also challenge the ticking clock. I wasn't saying much while I was working, so nobody else did either. Although the hospital wasn't rich, the equipment was outstanding. Everything I needed was right there, including the

6-0, 7-0, 8-0, and 9-0 sutures, and an excellent microscope. In the operating room, the small things make the big things work out.

When the repair was complete and the blood freely flowing through the artery without leaks, the tension in the room diminished. I still was pretty quiet, something the team definitely wasn't used to.

The OR supervisor walked in. "VJ, it looks like everything went well. Should I call the floor and tell them he's coming their way?" I glanced at him and shook my head no.

He looked at me with questioning eyes but said nothing further. The event that brought Liran to the OR could never be discussed or even hinted at. No one in the OR bought the bullshit cover story about him having a shop accident, but they were savvy enough not to inquire further. I loved this team.

Once I finished closing, I bundled up the Mossad agent and babysat him in the post-anesthesia care unit until I could escort him out of the hospital. It was far from ideal, but entirely necessary that I whisk him away as soon as possible. It would only be a matter of hours, if not minutes, before the wrong people would find out I was in the hospital.

One of my anesthesiologist friends saw me sitting by Liran in the PACU. "Hey, VJ, what are you doing here? I heard you were in Switzerland—something spooked you and you took off. We figured it was the Ebola outbreak we heard about at the Whitefire mine. Hey, that worries us too. Problem is, we live here all the time. Good thing Sherako's up there. If anyone can get it settled, he can. By the way, you look like you've been in a boxing match."

"Yeah, I've been doing this Krav Maga class. It got a little out of hand." I wanted to end the discussion without drawing unnecessary attention to my presence. "The time I've spent here has been great. Unfortunately, we have some issues at home that I have to address. Tonight was a favor for a friend. We'll be back as soon as we can."

He clapped me on the back. "Good luck, man." I went into the bathroom and looked in the mirror. My face was cut in multiple places. I hadn't even realized it. I'd had my surgical cap and mask on, so no one else had noticed. It was definitely time to leave.

Despite being so big, Liran roused from the anesthesia relatively quickly—the arm block helped enormously. I threw some new scrubs on him and found an XXL white lab coat for him to wear. He was extremely compliant with everything I asked him to do.

"VJ, thanks for fixing me up," he said sincerely.

"Liran, are you kidding? You just risked your life to help us! I'm already indebted to you guys for saving Tess. I'll do anything for you any time, any place."

He looked uncomfortable. "I still appreciate it."

I guided him to the side lobby door. Just before we exited, Liran stopped me.

"Hey, VJ, I have to piss like a racehorse. Let me hit the can before we go."

I laughed. "Yeah, they loaded you up with IV fluids. You're going to be going a lot. Do you need me to go in with you?"

Liran shook his head. "I'm good. You're not getting near that part of me."

"Okay, I'll just wait outside then."

I walked through the doors. The cool air felt good, and I took a deep breath. All of a sudden, I was exhausted. The stress of the entire day was taking its toll.

My sense of well-being evaporated the instant I felt the barrel of a gun against my temple. The voice said, "Brio, the boss would like to talk to you. He thinks you have something of his. He's not happy at all." The man motioned toward a waiting car, suggesting that I join him.

At the same moment Liran walked through the doorway. The gunman must have mistaken him for one of the staff. White coats throw people off. Gesturing with his weapon, he said, "Move on, this is a personal issue."

With his good side, Liran disarmed the man with a crushing forearm shiver. Now completely disoriented, the man was unable to fend off the ensuing blow that snapped his neck. I had time to pull out the pistol I was carrying in my bag as an insurance policy. This time I didn't hesitate and directed fire at the car. I'm not certain what the driver was thinking, but he must have assessed the situation and decided to live to fight another day. He was gone in seconds. We also left post-haste. Someone at the hospital would have to determine what to do with the dead body adorning the side entrance.

LAIR OF THE WOLF

CAPE TOWN, SOUTH AFRICA

"LET ME GET STRAIGHT," Marjanovic fumed. "You go get Brio. Another doctor come out of hospital. He beat your partner to death. Brio shoot at you. You run. Is this correct?" The poor man had no time to answer before the swift blow to his head knocked him unconscious.

Basil watched passively. The heroin was gone but was already paid for in diamonds and cash, which would make for a very uncomfortable confrontation with the crime syndicate waiting to distribute it. Marjanovic would now be under a great deal of pressure. He'd have to take some chances to get the product back.

Rash decision-making in this business was never good. The wheels were falling off the wagon. Basil was also worried his twin brother might now be aware he existed. That would lead to uncomfortable inquiries. *This may be the best time to make a deal and get out,* Basil thought. *The partnership will find me full-time work in the States.* Though the idea of being under Mikalyn de

Grom's thumb was distasteful, he would do it. Brio seemed to have gained the upper hand. Indeed, whoever was backing him wasn't playing games. The onslaught against a well-armed, experienced security team was impressive in both its audacity and efficiency. Never in a thousand years had Basil envisioned a scenario like this when he originally snatched the girl. No one would have.

Marjanovic barked an order, and Basil snapped out of his trance. His private plans would have to wait, at least for a few hours. "Get every piece data about Brio. Any person he ever know, ever meet, ever fuck. All people he related to. I need information now!"

THE HEROIN KINGS

CAPE TOWN, SOUTH AFRICA

GALIT WAS SIPPING a cup of coffee when Liran and I arrived. It was clear she'd been worried. They had a very tight bond. "Well, it's certainly good to see you both. How'd everything go?"

I went over to the kitchen and poured steaming cups of java for myself and Liran. Before I responded, I felt a hand on my shoulder and the presence of others. Leila, Tess, Liran, Galit, and I all sat down at the table. Quite the motley crew. Now criminals, four of us killers, hiding a massive shipment of heroin.

I finally answered Galit's question as I set the pistol on the table. "The surgery went fine. The bullet shrapnel lacerated the main artery to Liran's forearm and hand, but he had good enough collateral flow to hold out until I fixed it. The post-op care went smoothly up until the point that some of the men from the Foundation tried to kidnap me. Clearly, they put two and two together and decided I was part of the heist. Someone in the hospital tipped them that I was there. They had to have had people posted at all the exits. We used one that I *thought* no one knew about, and they were still there. Unfortunately for them, they didn't know Liran was coming through the door too. The man holding the gun on me had his career permanently ended when Liran destroyed his spinal cord. I put two rounds in their escape vehicle, but it got away. That's the long and short of it."

Leila sat silently, as did the others, digesting the most recent part of the saga. Eventually she spoke up. "This keeps getting better and better, doesn't it? Obviously we have no choice but to finish it. I think it'd be wise for us to get some sleep. Liran, you look pretty good for someone who just underwent a major procedure, not to mention saving another member of the Brio family. I'm going to keep an eye on you, though, just to make sure there aren't any complications. I want you to work on deep breathing and take this aspirin. It will help keep that artery from clotting." I watched with appreciation as Leila went into professional nurse mode.

Tess nudged me while I was washing the coffee cups. "Can we pull this off? I mean finish this thing permanently. Suddenly, I'm tired of all of it. I take responsibility. I know what I told you just yesterday. It may surprise you, but I wouldn't be upset if the merry-go-round stopped soon. I feel schizophrenic."

I took her in my arms while she cried silently. I genuinely felt that we were in a strong position and tried to reassure her. What I couldn't say was that the danger was over. She knew I couldn't say that. We were negotiating a narrow tightrope. It was all surreal. But now, we were ready for next steps.

The team reconvened around the table the next morning, at least vaguely rested. All of us were still amped from the events of the previous night. Liran was recovering with no signs of a complication, which was the best news.

Mark spoke first. "We took this junk to draw out the Foundation, and now we have it and they *know* we have it. That was step one. They still don't know who *we* are. Except for VJ, of course. That's our major advantage."

He looked around at each of us, nodding his head approvingly, before continuing. "We're now ready for step two. When we find Marjanovic and take him down, this ends. We get what we want. Leila and Tess, with all due respect, we'll tackle that job. You've both done enough. I intend to have one of my associates handle the negotiation. I spoke with him this morning. Sorry, guys, but he gets a cut of the heroin to distribute before the deal goes down. That's the price we have to pay for his help. That's not up for discussion."

Leila and I glanced at each other. This made sense, but it didn't make either of us feel better. We'd treated plenty of heroin overdose patients in our time, and were loath to be part of a plan where any of the heroin we'd captured would see the light of day again and put more people's lives at risk. Again, fuzzy shades of gray. Necessary compromises for the quintessential "greater good." There was no choice.

Mark provided more details. "Part of the agreement for the return of their shipment will include a simple demand. Marjanovic himself has to be present. He's going to refuse to do that at first. The reality is that he's in a terrible bargaining position and will have to comply. We'll make it very clear up front that we have his voice signature. He's going to be covered heavily by his own security team and will never expose himself outside. He'll expect a blunt-force trap, but we'll get to him a different way. We should have just the right weapon to finish his career once and for all. The question is, how will he try to get to us? We're going to make it as hard as possible. None of us will ever show our face—most definitely not you, VJ."

We waited for the special delivery from Tel Aviv. Once Mark

had it in his hands, we were ready to move forward. Our intermediary worked through channels at Red Mountain and, as anticipated, the meet was set. I allowed myself to feel optimistic. We had the smarts, the technology, and in my mind the upper hand.

THE AGENT

CAPE TOWN, SOUTH AFRICA

OUR MAN CASUALLY extracted a cigarette, put the pack down on the table, and began smoking. If Marjanovic didn't smoke and refused the offer, our man was ready to employ the backup plan. The poison agent was embedded in the marked cigarettes. A tiny applied dose would take care of business.

We watched from the remote monitor. The camera system was lodged in our representative's clothing. A man with a beautiful smile sat down in the embroidered chair. He said nothing. I almost fell off my chair as I stared directly at Noah's twin.

Then another figure strode across the room. I recognized him instantly even though the room was unusually dark. Our camera zoomed in on that all-too-familiar, angular, intense face. It could be no one else. Those were the same eyes that virtually burned through me when we were exchanging briefcases in Boston not that long ago. I snapped out of my distracted state. There was something wrong! It was his pupils. Our operation was blown!

I yelled to Mark even though he was sitting next to me, "It's Slobodan! He knows! Call him back, call him back now. He knows!"

It was already too late. Slobodan took out a cigarette from his own pack. Instead of attempting to smoke it, he squeezed from the end a slight mist that went directly into the face of Mark's operative. Noah's twin looked on placidly until Slobodan circled behind him, suddenly grasped his arms, and sprayed him with the same mist. The smile vanished—he looked confused and horrified. Coughing, Mark's man and the man I now realized must be Slobodan's chief lieutenant began showing severe respiratory distress, and fell to the ground with their muscles twitching. Both began to seize uncontrollably. The effects were truly terrible to witness.

Slobodan peered down at the fallen bodies. He frisked our representative and found what he was searching for. Holding the camera and microphone, he addressed me directly. "Hello, VJ, you smart, very smart. Not smart as me. Always make good differential diagnosis—infectious disease doctor like me best at that. I do my research. I figure out plan you might use. I know you not on your own. You think I not have friends too? Friend from Russia get me poison I need. Interesting we both choose same method. You give me idea. You still not understand I better than you. My brother, Matija, not understand that either till I kill him."

Gesturing to his fallen comrade, he continued, smiling wolfishly. "This man not reliable. Now we get to business of getting me my heroin. We make deal. I contact you this time." Adding emphasis to his words, he took out a sidearm and emptied the bullets into the two men, who until that moment appeared barely alive. The picture rotated wildly, then the video ceased functioning.

Mark turned to me. "What just happened there?! How does

he know you?" I looked gravely at my partner and explained what I could as clinically as possible.

"That man goes by Slobodan. Who knows what his real name is? I thought he was dead, though it's now obvious that he staged his own death." I didn't mention that I'd had to do the same thing in order to defeat the Cooperative. What a strange, or perhaps not-so-strange coincidence. Maybe he'd gotten the idea from me. He really had done his research.

"He is actually a doctor from Serbia, but trained in Russia," I went on. "I worked with him in Boston. Obviously, I had no idea he was running Red Mountain and the Foundation. He did a good job keeping that information under wraps. He's extremely smart. The other man he just poisoned and shot was the one who lured Tess when she was kidnapped. If nothing else, it's helpful to know who the adversary is."

Inside I was going crazy. I understood that any further conversations about heroin were just part of Slobodan's agenda. What he told me moments earlier on the video feed suggested this was also about more than business. It was about conquest. We'd be racing again to the bottom of the mountain, but one of us wasn't going to make it to the end.

"Slobodan's weakness is his ego. We can use that against him. We'd better make damn sure to move that heroin to a secure location immediately. If he doesn't know where it is yet, it sounds like he'll find out."

Mark acknowledged that reality. "I'm on it. How did you figure out that he knew what we were going to do?"

I explained, "When I saw that his pupils were dilated, I knew he had taken something to counteract one of the Russians' favorite poisons—modified Novichok number five. It causes all the ugly things to happen that you just saw. Atropine helps counteract its effects. It also makes your pupils dilate.

"He must have combined it with something else, likely pralidoxime. That drug comes in autoinjectors. Many hospitals stockpile them for mass casualty situations from nerve agents. I'm sure he has access to it. The amount of atropine necessary to prevent Novichok, VX, or anything similar from working is huge. When I saw his eyes, I realized he either knew or guessed what direction we were going. The comment he made about differential diagnosis—in medicine, it is the first thing we're taught. Collect the data, then make a list of disease processes that fit. Never settle on just one possible explanation for a problem.

"Slobodan probably had several options if he deduced incorrectly what our plan was. Without saying it, I'm sure he believed that agents of the CIA or Mossad could be helping us. He knows you've used poison agents in close quarters in the past. He knows I have family in Israel. Did you see the news about the Foundation director being found dead in the street? No chance that was an accident. If Slobodan used poison on him, then it would be on the forefront of his mind. So here we are. Your man is dead, and our adversary is still on the loose." This chess game was still being played out. The problem was Slobodan had just taken our rook. I stewed about the next move.

Mark said, "This is a huge problem! This *cannot* come back to Mossad. That happened in Jordan and became a massive black eye for us!"

I'd never seen Mark so visibly upset. Taking Slobodan out of circulation had to happen quickly. Mark left our outpost and corralled Galit, Liran, and Pinchas. Together they launched into getting the heroin location moved, easier said than done. This wasn't home turf for them, and we were no longer strictly on the offensive.

I left the monitoring bunker to take the short walk to the car, consumed with thoughts of Slobodan. I was duped in Sierra Lakes. Why he'd tried to kill me there and fake his own death still wasn't clear, but obviously what we saw in his briefcase had set the wheels in motion.

My phone rang. Leila was calling to see what had happened. The adrenaline rush from the past few days' events was gone. Clearly I wasn't thinking as I should, or exercising caution appropriate for the circumstances. I didn't notice the SAP officer approach, but my accent must have gotten his attention.

I sat down on a bench, briefly explaining how our plan had unraveled. Several minutes later, I looked up and saw rotating blue lights in front of me. I held my breath. "Leila, the SAP is here. Stay on the phone and just listen."

Two officers got out of the car. "Are you Dr. Erik Brio?" the tall blond one asked. "We have some questions to ask you about an incident at Onderskeid." Relieved that I wasn't being asked about heroin, I said, "I'm Brio. How can I help you?"

The larger of the two men said, "Dr. Brio, a man was found dead outside one of the hospital entrances. A witness told us that gunshots were fired, and he placed you there. We were wondering if you could join us at the station. The commander would like to ask you about all of this. This is voluntary, of course, but we think it would be good if you came nonetheless."

Cops investigating dead people around the hospital isn't good for anyone. I considered the options. The absolute last thing I wanted was the SAP sniffing around. I definitely didn't want them talking to anyone else. I would suggest that Liran had already left the country if they brought him up. I would be happy to explain that he had foiled the attempted robbery, that I had grabbed the gun off the man trying to attack me, and in my rage, I had fired at him. That I was so upset that I had thrown the gun in the ocean afterward. I scrutinized the name badge of the one in charge. It looked legitimate. I decided that complying with their wishes would create the least amount of difficulty. So, I went with them.

"Just a moment, Officer Vanderweiss," I said. "Can I call my wife and tell her where I'm going?"

Stiffly he answered, "Dr. Brio, no need to worry about that. We'll be done with this quickly." The hair on my neck bristled, but I really had no choice now but to go. Satisfied Leila had heard the conversation, I shut off the phone. I didn't need the SAP going through my contact list.

I entered the back of the SAP vehicle and strapped on my seat belt. What choice did I have? I was locked in. No way to get out from the inside. As we sped away, the officer riding shotgun offered me a cigarette.

Vanderweiss chastised him, "You idiot, the man is a doctor. He doesn't smoke. Of course, hijacking a load of heroin—well now, that is another story entirely. By the way, Dr. Brio, we are glad to have finally found you. You have been quite elusive, much like the game I usually track. Our intelligence wasn't perfect. Lucky for us, that SAP officer standing near you had the picture we distributed. We're part of a special task force. Having friends inside the SAP is very helpful for most of what we do. Small things like moving heroin around the city. Getting your name on the persons of interest list was extremely easy. By the way, we'll take that phone now."

What else could I do but hand it over? The thug in the passenger seat took the device, smashed it with the butt of his gun, and tossed it out the window. As the reality of what was happening struck me full force, the two men laughed. I spoke quietly: "So when do I meet with Slobodan?"

There was sadistic laughter again. "Man, that will be some time from now. You should relax. We have to drive up to the Whitefire Diamond Mine."

The day was not shaping up as I'd hoped. Several times I tried to engage the men in conversation, digging for anything that might help. The effort was in vain. Whatever Slobodan planned for me was going to be a complete surprise. I could hardly wait. He knew we had the heroin but hopefully not where. Although he wanted me, he wanted the heroin too. No doubt there would be negotiations to try to make the deal work. This time I would be the bait.

LEILA REACTS

CAPE TOWN, SOUTH AFRICA

THE SECOND THE PHONE went dead, Leila ran to Tess. "Gather up everything you can as quickly as you can! We have to leave now. I'm not sure, but I think Slobodan might know where we are. VJ just got picked up by the SAP, or at least someone pretending to be the SAP."

Leila and Tess frantically scanned the house for any clues that would lead the Foundation to Liran, Galit, Pinchas, Mark, or the heroin if they were truly burned. They rapidly loaded suitcases, crammed them in the car, and left, Leila driving.

Tess kept a hand on the pistol in her lap. She was ready if any immediate action was needed. Simultaneously she dialed Mark to let him know what was happening and to warn the others away from the house. They arranged a meeting. Before Mark hung up, Tess asked, "What if this really is the police and not Slobodan?"

Mark replied clinically, "Nothing changes—we will still find him and kill him."

SHERAKO SAT IN THE CHAIR, staring at the man now directing the show at the Whitefire mine. In turn, Slobodan sized up the man who was simultaneously his ally and adversary.

"Dr. Sherako, I sincerely thank you for all you do to clean up camp. Ebola very bad actor. You not know this about me. I infectious disease specialist too."

Sherako's face demonstrated genuine surprise. Slobodan continued, "I most recently attend at Massachusetts Regional Medical Center. I work there with Tribolsi. He die unfortunate death. Work on Ebola drug continue in Cape Town. I come here to see progress you make with our drug. Do much better than trial in DRC. What happen there? Poor outcome kill Yonaker-Wood deal. Allow Red Mountain step in."

Sherako experienced a moment of sudden clarity. Slobodan was the man he had seen administering to patients in the DRC tent months earlier. It couldn't be anyone else.

"Dr. Marjanovic, in fact we have met before. I think I can explain the problems with the DRC arm of the study. You gave those study patients a little something extra. You knew it would kill them and sabotage the merger deal. That wasn't very nice, was it?"

Slobodan brushed off the rhetorical question. "Business different than medicine. Those people sacrifice for our business. DRC not good place to live. We pay off family of dead ones. They do well now. Everybody win."

The circuitous, pathologic nature of Slobodan's words boggled Sherako's mind. "So what is it you have in mind now, Dr. Marjanovic?"

Slobodan grinned. "That easy—you keep working for Foundation. No one know I the one who kill those people in DRC.

They think it you. You the one there. No one who work there left to tell different story. They too have bad outcome already."

Sherako processed this further revelation. He knew he would find a path forward to navigate through the mess. However, for the time being, he also understood he was stuck. The thought infuriated him.

I CLOSED MY EYES for a minute. Like Tess, I'd grown weary of the game. We passed areas thick with greenery. Now we were on the old N1 approaching Rawsonville, a section of the road that defined nothingness. Suddenly there were several loud bangs as the tires blew out. The car swerved violently, skidded, then came to a stop. Vanderweiss yelled, "What the hell?!"

Two men in full battle gear, holding military-grade weapons, stood in front of the police vehicle. They motioned for Vanderweiss and his partner to exit the cruiser. Obviously seeing no clear alternative, they did as directed, leaving me inside. For reasons I will never understand, the shotgun rider made a move for his pistol. Then, just as quickly, he was dead. He had ignored the first rule of engagement: It's easy to be hard, it's hard to be smart. Do not attack someone if you are outgunned. He also broke the second rule: If a Mossad agent has the drop on you, do not threaten that person. It won't end well. In more colloquial terms, everyone knows, or should know, they will fuck your shit up—like immediately.

Once Mark had disarmed and cuffed Vanderweiss, Pinchas liberated me from the backseat. I was exhilarated and relieved. "Happy to see you guys, more than you can possibly know. Thank God for that GPS tracker you tagged us with. You keep bailing out the Brio family. I don't know what to say."

Two more figures walked out from the bushes with large smiles. Galit spoke first. "They're not the only ones you owe. How do you plan to settle this debt?" I actually had an idea about that.

Mark drove a truck from its hiding place and opened the door. "Okay, VJ, time to get you back to Leila and Tess. They're pretty worried. This kidnapping thing is getting old."

"How'd you get to me so quickly? I thought it'd be at least another hour or two, best case."

Liran, even with one arm incapacitated, was still there to provide support. "As soon as they took you," he said, "Leila called. She knew you had your GPS tracker. We locked on immediately. Since you were headed out of town, it was clear the police story was bogus. This truck allowed us to use some secondary roads. No speed limits, either. It was easy to beat you to this spot. We're fortunate it's so deserted out here. Any more traffic and we might have had some explaining to do."

I borrowed Mark's phone and called Leila. She and Tess were safe and quite happy to hear that I was as well. There was a short debate about how best to handle Vanderweiss. At some point he'd be expected to check in. It was important to try to buy as much time as possible. With a gun to his temple, he made the call, indicating that everything had gone smoothly and he and his partner were well underway. He'd witnessed the penalty for lack of cooperation.

Before getting in the truck he said, "You know, Brio, it was nothing personal. I do whatever Slobodan tells me to do. But after this business today, my life is worth nothing. For my own sake, I hope your friends here find him and finish him off."

"That makes two of us." Despite my sense that he wouldn't present a problem, Galit hog-tied Vanderweiss for the return trip. After checking him carefully to make sure he, like me, wasn't wearing a GPS device, we decided to stash him in the warehouse with the heroin when we got back to Cape Town. He would no doubt be a good source of information about Slobodan's criminal operations. The stolen police vehicle was driven well off the side of the road and torched, along with the thoughtless accomplice.

On the return route, the explanation for Mossad's rapid appearance became clear. The drive back was substantially truncated by the off-road path. Home was no longer either of the places where we'd been. There was no direct evidence we were compromised, but Mark and Pinchas both felt extreme caution was necessary. The new haunt was closer in town and presumably safe. In this cat-and-mouse game, certainty was impossible.

ALL THAT HAD TRANSPIRED had pushed Slobodan to shift his center of operations to the Whitefire mine. He struggled to maintain internal control. At first, he was ecstatic when Brio was in his grasp. After the initial conversation, new attempts to contact Vanderweiss yielded no response. He knew his nemesis had escaped. He was utterly furious, again.

This battle over the heroin had become a personal contest. He and Brio, mano a mano. He wouldn't stop until one of them was dead. If he could get the girl and the wife, all the better. He would have time to deal with them once Brio was eliminated. Slobodan was content with the dollars he had stashed in the Caymans. The Ebola Foundation transactions had been good to him.

Still, his backers in the Russian Bratva remained in the background, paying attention. They had checked off on the elimination of his brother, Matija, but they would be unhappy if the heroin trade wasn't restarted. They too were profiting enormously from the venture. This load was a large one. The Bratva was not a forgiving group. Everyone has to answer to someone, and they remained his master. The problem *had* to be fixed. The question was how to return the fight to his home turf.

Slobodan was in deep trouble but still held an ace. He had the chemical design structures of the new Ebola drug. Matija had eliminated the people who did the original work. However, now more than ever, Slobodan needed to come up with the heroin. His police ruse to grab Brio had been a spectacular failure.

WHITEFIRE DIAMOND MINE ADVENTURE

NORTHERN CAPE PROVINCE, SOUTH AFRICA

ONCE WE RECONVENED in our latest shelter, Leila and Tess greeted me with the same emotion I had felt when Tess was rescued. I wasn't gone long, but long enough. Twice in a month for one family was overwhelming.

Hours later, Noah contacted Tess, telling her he had to meet her to give her a package. She returned with a burner phone that had been dropped off at his office with explicit instructions for delivery.

The call was made at the designated time. Once again I had the pleasure of speaking with Slobodan.

"VJ, my friend, you still have my heroin. Why you want this? I quite sure you not going into my business. I also quite sure you in business with someone else, though—CIA? Mossad? What they want?"

I didn't answer his question, of course, but did present the demands of the group I said I was representing, and settled on meeting logistics. The deal we'd brokered was a façade for both parties. He wanted us, and we wanted him. Now the time and place were determined.

We saw no choice but to attack. Slobodan was at the Whitefire mine, so that's where we had to go. If we didn't, he would just move his base of operations, and the heroin-diamonds-cash-guns exchanges would continue. And he would continue hunting down me and my family until he found us. Neither outcome was an option.

Mossad remained fully committed to completely removing the man as a threat. After the fiasco in Cape Town, they were watching carefully. Mark and Pinchas obtained the satellite intelligence we needed. We were mentally ready to fight this next battle. As a seven-person team, we focused on our tactical approach. Liran's battle wound would prevent him from engaging directly, but as he'd done on the trip to rescue me, he was ready to assist in any way possible.

Not long afterward, Tess looked at her phone and saw an odd message from a number she didn't know: **Friend at Whitefire mine. Understand you may want data about Ebola situation here.**

She texted, **How do I know you are a friend?** A moment later the answer came back: **Maybe medical students should love Ebola**, something she'd said to Sherako the first day she met him. She decided to engage. **What can you share with me, friend?** The next text said, **What do you need?** Tess responded, **A map of the camp would be helpful.**

The next morning we got something even better—pictures of the blueprints of the Whitefire Diamond Mine. These items were followed by a simple statement: **Happy hunting.** Tess sent back multiple smile emojis along with several skull-and-crossbones images.

We surveyed the flat landscape of the mine for the most favorable breach point. The satellite photos we got from our Israeli allies were extremely helpful. Each of us carried a small map with the layout of the buildings and security measures based on the intel from Tess's inside source. Going in blind would have been a disaster. Without question, Slobodan and his men would also be on alert and ready for us to show up. The diamond mine was a hard target. That would make our job particularly difficult, if not close to impossible. If there was another choice, we would have made it, but there wasn't. Our big advantage was the Ebola quarantine, which had significantly diminished the Whitefire mine security forces.

Tess was able to forward the computer data she'd hacked about the Foundation's shell corporation bank transfers to her classmate, Axel, who then worked a bit more Syndergaard magic. In a New York minute, Slobodan's fortunes were ghosts of their former selves. What had been there was now hiding elsewhere. Slobodan wouldn't know how it happened, but he'd have to think my fingerprints were on the cyberattack.

The heroin exchange was arranged to occur at an open space Slobodan had specified outside the mine. There was literally no place for a sniper or anyone else to hide. The approach had no cover. I didn't like any part of it. The deal was that he would cease all interface with Wazeer and the Afghanis, and we would give back the product. Our mine incursion was set to occur before the agreed exchange. While we hoped for surprise, we didn't expect it.

The Whitefire mine was huge. Aerial photos showed the original massive open pit occupying more than a quarter of the compound area. Production from the huge hole had ceased decades earlier, but it remained as a testament to what once was. It was like a ghost town in the middle of New York City. The diamond processing areas, infirmary, barracks, maintenance shacks, and administrative offices were scattered around the remaining encampment. We were also aware of two primary underground shafts with miles of offshoots. An entry point near the pit seemed to be the most vulnerable, so that was our target.

We were able to drive close to Whitefire undetected with the aid of new Troya Ninox night vision goggles. Vehicle lights in this open expanse would have immediately compromised us. Outside the mine, Liran set up the Thales Squire battlefield radar surveillance unit that had been invaluable during the drug heist. It was also a major asset to help identify hostile drones. Tess had yet again prevailed in the participation discussion. She was tasked with helping Liran while maintaining a heavily fortified fallback position. With our coms, we would know when and where to look for threats. Using the maps, Pinchas found a location to set up a sniper's nest that wasn't perfect, but good enough. Armed to the teeth, all of us were ready.

ENDGAME

NORTHERN CAPE PROVINCE, SOUTH AFRICA

FROM HIS REMOTE DEVICE, Slobodan monitored the security camera feeds that were standard, and particularly the ones that weren't. There was a part of him that hoped the deal would proceed as agreed, but his inner voice told him that wouldn't happen. Nothing had gone as planned. What should have been a routine transaction had become a debacle. He pulled out a pack of American cigarettes and lit one. After taking a long draw, he created a series of perfect smoke rings. He was now fully in control and ready to dominate. The mine was ringed with groupings of improvised explosive devices. This late addition to security was a nice touch. Getting into the compound would be problematic. He continued to watch with great anticipation.

THE TIME HAD COME to make the push. Mark launched a small multi-camera drone, another marvel of Israeli technology, to scan for barriers to entry. The armaments were even more extensive than we had thought. Slobodan was clearly expecting our incursion. With the combined data from the Thales and the drone, we found a path. Mark, Pinchas, Galit, and I advanced into the mine area with extreme caution, then fanned out. Leila had agreed to take up a position separate from Liran and Tess in the event we needed a retreat covered. Staying on coms, we assumed positions in the preselected locations. Pinchas successfully reached his perch and readied himself to engage.

Through her night vision goggles, Galit spotted the location where Slobodan was supposed to be. She and Mark moved toward the target. I held my ground. Pinchas covered their approach.

Off-site, the Thales lit up. Liran calmly passed on the critical information. Rapid-succession rounds from Pinchas liquidated two of Slobodan's men. The path was clear to finally corral Slobodan. Mark and Galit readied themselves for the attack. With great stealth they disappeared into the building. There was a live body occupying the boss's office. A short firefight ensued. Galit took the man down. I heard Mark swear. "Not him. We have to keep searching."

Without warning, several explosions simultaneously erupted in my sector. I was completely isolated. A shot rang out, and the bullet grazed my arm. There wasn't any significant damage, but it definitely hurt. I dove for cover by a nearby wall and found myself leaning against one of the large conveyor belts where raw materials were processed. Multiple catwalks were in my line of vision and possibly accessible. I couldn't see where the firing was coming from. About twenty meters from my position was the massive sheer wall of the open pit. Our report said it was 450 meters across by 175 meters deep. It was one of the ten largest in the world, I knew. There were some scrub brushes for cover but nothing great. That was not the place for me to go. A person would be lost forever after a misplaced step. There was a small machine housing unit about three meters above the ground. I was surrounded by a metal-and-concrete jungle. There were multiple small sheds, houses, towers, holding tanks, and assorted structures designed to do the daily job of mining diamonds.

Another shot ricocheted off the railing next to me. With no better alternative, I entered the closest refuge, the main shaft of the underground portion of the mine. At that moment, I didn't realize I was being herded there.

The large bore tube looked like the entrance to another world. There was an electric transport vehicle that I jumped in and gunned down the path to nowhere. I came to a series of doors that automatically opened when the car arrived. There were intermittent points of divergence. I took a random path. I had no idea where I was going, but it seemed to be safer than what was behind me.

After a few minutes, I found myself in what was clearly a large maintenance area. Huge machines in moderate states of disrepair sat unattended. Electric cables lined the ceilings and the walls. It was damp. Pooled water was everywhere. The Ebola quarantine had suspended all work. I felt like I was alone in an abandoned space station and being hunted by an alien. I scouted for a defensible position and any additional handy weapons.

ABOVE GROUND in the mining camp, Galit and Mark were confronting their own problems. The counterattack was even better coordinated than expected. Fire was being exchanged, and they were both pinned down. Galit had gotten hit in the leg, but the shot missed everything important. She was able to continue. The enemies they were now engaging were protected from Pinchas's sniper perch. The scope of the fight demanded their absolute, complete attention. Neither one was in a position to help VJ. It wouldn't have mattered if they could. They had no idea where he was. The coms and GPS tracker ceased to function deep in the mine.

SLOBODAN AND VJ KISS AND MAKE UP—NOT

NORTHERN CAPE PROVINCE, SOUTH AFRICA

AS I WAS SCANNING the area, I heard a voice call out my name. It was not coming from the headset. "VJ, you brave man to come for me here. Somehow you take money. I not happy about that. You need tell me how get it back."

I turned around and stood face-to-face with my tormentor. I had no idea how, but he'd gotten the drop on me. Seeing the surprise on my face, he just laughed.

"VJ, I watch everything you do since you get inside camp. Latest camera technology." Slobodan showed me the live feed he was monitoring on his mobile device. "I want you down here alone. Better way to talk in private. Your friends hard people. Make it challenge for me say what I need say."

I contemplated the best path out and decided on delay. Slobodan regarded me carefully. I asked, "So what are we doing in this Ebola swamp?"

Slobodan was coy. "VJ, you know I not take chance. Our drug

a wonderful thing. We take care people here. They healthy now. Sherako do fine work. I decide to keep him now, kill later.

"VJ, you good man. You always try do right thing. You think I not know you. I do. I used to be good man, good doctor. Too greedy. I like money. I like nice thing. Sometime bad decision made. Underestimate you. This bad decision. Not know Mossad your ally. Would never have fuck with you or daughter. She tough, very tough. Like father, I now see. Yes, you very tough, but not have makeup of pure killer."

I glared at him. "What makes you think I'm working with Mossad?" I was just talking, hoping someone might come to the rescue.

Slobodan simply smiled and became downright loquacious. "I told you. I smart man. When daughter get rescued I try to think how you do this. I know you not able to do by self. I check up more on you. I remember from talk we have in Sierra Lake. You have sister in Israel. Brother-in-law who work for drug company. Light go on. He really work for different kind company. Sometime two plus two equal four. That how I figure you might try poison me. I have my finger coated with superglue so none get on me by accident. Effective tool. I use cyanide for Mashaba, also man at that wedding you go to. He get in my way. Try shake me down. Cyanide easier.

"VJ, funny thing. I find out about you before you know me. Working at MRMC always part of my plan. Need Tribolsi for Ebola research data. I perfect person to fill role. I work in lab for year. Not see many people. I get tired of that. That why I start attending, for fun. But I meet Petra before you kill her. We like friend with benefit. She not understand my real agenda. Funny thing person reveal after few drink and good sex. She have animal appetite. She tell me she frustrated by hand surgeon she work with. Not tell me why. I not listen clear enough."

While I continued to scan for avenues of escape, Slobodan explained what had happened. It was as if I was his confessor.

He proceeded to describe the details of his foiled plan to kill me, his need to kill or be killed by his own brother, Matija, with only a few bits I hadn't already guessed. He had turned to someone named Gwinevere to help him, and apparently there was a very large menace by the name of Miro out there. The most disturbing thing he intimated was that there was someone tracking Noah. Why, he didn't divulge.

Then, forcefully, Slobodan demanded, "I want we get heroin back. I want money back. Important to me. Bratva want their payment. I owe them now. They not nice guy like me. Cut off your ball and stuff in mouth. You sharp guy. You know I kill you soon. I not shoot you yet, unless forced. Ebola do good job enough. Bad way to die. You not want that. Avoid mess; I make easy. Shoot you in head. First you need give me information."

Slobodan then feigned to wax poetic. "It funny, VJ, in United State all conversation about doing right thing, saying right thing, paying careful attention to everyone feeling. I say bullshit. In Africa I realize that we and wild beasts are same. There are hunted and hunters. Nature cruel. No political correct lions. Like them, I am hunter. You, most always yes, not today. Today not be your day. Sort of like worthless slob Miro pick up. We quickly needed man to solve problem. To solve problem, Miro need cut off his head. Bad for him, good for us. Same thing identical brother your wife cousin. Cousin not know about my man. We use for advantage."

A CHANGE IN CIRCUMSTANCES

NORTHERN CAPE PROVINCE, SOUTH AFRICA

THE MAN HAD IDENTIFIED his target and single-mindedly pursued it. Chaos had overtaken Whitefire, but it was just a small distraction for him. The marksman carried the prized Hoyt Powermax Bow with the sixty-three-pound draw. Set in its rest was a Rage trypan broadhead arrow. The razor-sharp blades on the business end were designed to blow through an elk. This intended prey was considerably smaller. Hunting in the veld with the bow was far more sporting than using a rifle. He felt extremely comfortable with both the weapon and his own ability to employ its killing capacity. The job at hand demanded both patience and precision. He followed the uniquely distinctive prints, giving no hint of his own presence.

After a lengthy pursuit, the hunter saw his victim finally move into a comfortable maximum effective forty-meter range. Slowly the man drew back, ready to release the arrow. Silently he cursed. The prey had shifted position again, eliminating the solid kill shot. He debated his choices. A decision was made. The arrow took flight.

The victim's body turned violently, and he cried out with agonizing pain. The large arrow had sliced through his shoulder, creating a two-inch posterior gash with a larger hole in the front from the expansion of the broadhead. It was similar to the effect of a hollow-point bullet. The gun was in his hand no longer. His flailing right upper extremity became useless to him.

The hunter watched with satisfaction but kept a slight distance. He knew the man was done, but readied another arrow in case his instincts were wrong. Though he had strong suspensions, he wasn't completely certain about the identity of the other man in view. He advanced slowly, watching carefully as the two opponents continued to engage.

I DIDN'T KNOW where the arrow came from, but was happily stunned by my change in fortune. I called out hopefully, "My name is Erik Brio. I am a doctor. I am a friend."

No one responded.

Slobodan's face contorted in pain, while his body was listing badly. The airborne torpedo had done its work, and the gun he'd been holding was now far from reach. I picked it up to protect myself from Slobodan and whoever had shot the arrow. My injured nemesis continued to negotiate. Anticipation of impending reality can sometimes make a big difference in one's life perspective.

"VJ, I stop my business. Go back to medicine. You get help for me. You think once I die, this business all over. Nyet! You in for big surprise. Miro look for you if I not call him off. Miro bad man. You not want mess with him. This enterprise much bigger than me." The blood welling on his shirt looked like a problem. There was a substantial chance his subclavian artery was lacerated. If this was the case, he was in serious trouble.

A lecture I once viewed suggested utilizing intellectual humility in any debate and opening one's mind. This discussion merited an alternative approach. There was no middle ground of agreement. I decided to do the humane thing. I snarled at Slobodan, *"Do svidaniya, ya ubyu tebya, ublyudok."* He looked at me with questioning eyes.

As I pulled the trigger, Slobodan realized once again he was wrong about me. I knew he would never completely leave me alone. I had absolutely no problem finishing the job that the unknown assailant had initiated when he shot the arrow. When Slobodan fell backward, I took a cell phone shot of his lifeless body. I didn't really know why I did that. Somehow I thought it would be necessary for something. If this Miro character surfaced, which I doubted he would want to do after all this carnage, that would be a fight for another day.

I wondered about the decisions we make each day that culminate in our lives. The error I made in mistakenly picking up a briefcase resulted in being dragged into an international drama. I was tired. I hadn't asked for any of this, yet it had occurred. Slobodan was gone from the world. Good riddance.

I sat on a nearby machine and thought about the chaos of the last few weeks, ending in the sudden termination of threat. An arrow arriving in the darkness, felling my opponent, was too bizarre to contemplate. It was somehow apropos considering all else that had transpired.

Maybe the best thing going forward was to hide in plain sight from whoever else was supporting Slobodan's criminal syndicate. I needed to think about it. Perhaps Washington, D.C. It was a nice place—lots going on. Leila never was really thrilled about being in Boston, and I could still do volunteer work. I decided to talk to her about the change. Solomon's friend was right—better ten years too early than a minute too late.

From the shadows, the archer finally surfaced. His bow was drawn. I held the gun ready to fire. He called out, "My name is Ethan Smitheman, but my father is Harrison Sherako. I came here to protect him."

I smiled and laid down my weapon. "Then we are on the same team."

He still looked very concerned. "Do you have any idea if my father is safe?" he asked as he deftly removed and cleaned the arrow from the lifeless body. He also snatched a second 9mm Beretta hiding in Slobodan's jacket. My decision to kill him had been a good one. The bullets in that gun were probably meant for me.

I offered my hand to shake. "Such a pleasure to formally meet you. I imagine you're the 'friend' who contacted Tess. The intel you provided was a huge benefit. If we were successful topside, he's okay, and one of my colleagues should have him now. You're pretty handy with that bow. Nice work. You certainly helped save my sorry ass."

He shook his head. "Actually, I'm pretty upset with myself. I didn't take the kill shot when I thought I had it. I waited too long. I had to settle. He still could have gotten you. I was banking on disarming him."

I laughed, while shaking my head. "That may be the worst pun I've heard, but that's alright. Let's see what we can do about finding your dad. By the way, from what I've heard he's quite a guy. Doesn't give a damn about himself, just his patients. As you are aware, Tess got a chance to work with him. I'm counting on the fact that you know the way out of here."

Ethan nodded in agreement and said, "Yes, I do know the way out. And yes, that's why I contacted Tess. I overheard Slobodan yelling at one of his men about losing VJ again. He said, and I quote, 'You watch, that man try get me here now. He relentless like me.' I told my dad about it. He knew exactly who VJ was. That's also when he told me about Tess and the importance of reaching out to her. My father is special in a lot of ways. My mom will tell you that. This won't surprise you—he thinks the world of Tess.

"Just curious," Ethan continued. "I heard you say something in a different language to Slobodan before you shot him. It sounded Eastern European. What did you say?

"It's just an expression I picked up from a Russian friend. Roughly translated, it means 'Goodbye, I will kill you now, motherfucker.' "

Ethan was duly impressed. "You get an *A* for subtlety. Why did you speak to him in Russian? I thought he was Serbian."

"He is," I confirmed, "but he did part of his training in Moscow. In the dark ages, when I thought we were friends, we had a funny discussion about Russian slang. I knew he'd understand me. Not that it really matters now."

Ethan and I carefully emerged from the bowels of the mine, neither of us knowing what to expect. We were armed and battle ready. Besides his bow, Ethan was carrying Slobodan's other gun. All was still. I scanned the buildings and saw no signs of life, and quietly worried that everyone was dead. Then, out of the corner of my eye, I saw a shadow move. Over my now-functioning coms, I was relieved to hear Mark's voice: "VJ, we see you. Tell the man you're with that we have eyes on him and he needs to disarm."

Briefly I protested, "But he's a friendly."

Mark did not look on our conversation as a debate. "Tell him to drop his weapons immediately."

I turned to Ethan. "Hey, my guys want you to drop the gun and the bow. Please humor them. They want to make certain you mean us no harm." Fortunately, Ethan didn't balk. He placed his weapons on the ground and assumed a nonconfrontational position. Galit, who was limping, Pinchas, Mark, and another man emerged. It was Harrison Sherako. He ran forward and gave Ethan a bear hug.

Their reunion was genuinely heartwarming. It reminded me why I enjoyed life as a surgeon. It was about helping people. Sherako was now going to be able to do that, unencumbered, on a grand scale. Slobodan was absolutely correct about the vagaries of life. I didn't know where I was on the grayscale.

Galit, Pinchas, Liran, Mark, Tess, Leila and I made the most unlikely team, yet we had accomplished a major goal.

"It was a little touch and go there for a few minutes. Slobodan made a tactical error going so far down after you," Pinchas informed me. "As you predicted, his ego was his Achilles heel—it got the better of his judgment. There wasn't that big a security team here, and Slobodan was the command and control center. With him gone, eliminating the guards took some work, but we got through it mostly unscathed. Drones are a wonderful advantage. Galit picked up a scratch or two, but we can confirm that the mission parameters were satisfied. My presumption is that Slobodan is a confirmed kill. We won't have to deal with him again, right?"

I showed him the cell phone shot. Mark studied the picture. "Center head shot. Good work."

I asked, "What about Sherako? Was he being kept where we thought he'd be?"

Mark said, "Not at all. That part was a near disaster. The man watching him left when the shooting started. Guess he didn't view Sherako as a threat. Sherako left the security building and was working his way toward Slobodan's office, determined to take him himself. I don't know what to say about you bloodthirsty doctors. Pinchas thought he was one of theirs and almost shot him. Fortunately, my partner is a thoughtful, controlled man. He double-checked that set of pictures Tess gave him. The extra second he took to verify his target was critical to Sherako staying on this side of a coffin."

When Tess and Liran joined us, the infectious disease wizard gave her a hearty embrace and said, "Despite my best efforts, you made it here. You did a good job of hiding this part of your skill set. Are you going to keep helping me in Cape Town? There's a lot of work to do, superwoman."

Tess regarded him circumspectly while deciding on her response. "Dr. Sherako, I admire who you are and what you do immensely. I'm no longer certain what the future holds for me. Can I take a rain check on the invitation?"

Sherako smiled widely. "Tess, that you can. Just tell me if there's anything I can do for you, ever. I'll be there."

I remembered my mistake in Sierra Lakes and discussed it with Mark. With help from Ethan, he and the team prepared for the final step. Once we were certain all the remaining Whitefire personnel were accounted for, I nodded to Ethan. He'd found the ordnance and with some help placed it appropriately. Then, he pressed the detonator. There would be no potentially incriminating evidence left behind this time. The mine shaft with Slobodan's corpse was obliterated. No more diamonds for heroin or guns or anything else. Tons of dirt solved that problem.

PAYING THE BILLS

NORTHERN CAPE PROVINCE, SOUTH AFRICA

WE SCOURED SLOBODAN'S OFFICE, eyeing multiple large stacks of packaged hundred-dollar bills. When we appeared in the compound, Slobodan must have rushed. The door of the safe was, conveniently, left slightly ajar. Inside was a small box and several large sacks. I picked one up to confirm my suspicions. I handed Sherako the bags of diamonds and several stacks of money.

"I don't know what we're supposed to do with all this. I do know a certain hospital that could benefit. Otherwise it will all go to some government agency that would lose it, abuse it, or have it stolen. I have complete confidence in your ability to distribute these funds to those who need them most. The SAP is going to get the heroin. They'll love the positive publicity of a major drug bust."

I did hold back a large handful of diamonds, as payment to

Rick for his help. His advice was instrumental in our success. I liked the idea of keeping that account open. One never knew what the future held. The other treasure I found was a stray USB drive. I could only imagine what files it contained.

START AGAIN

CAPE TOWN, SOUTH AFRICA

WHEN THERE WAS TIME to do mundane things like check my e-mail, I opened the one from Asiya. Nithan continued his unprecedented recovery and was almost ready to again assume his political responsibilities. Life was getting better by the second.

She attached a picture of a headline in the local English language newspaper: "Crime Boss Bhaduri Perishes in South Africa: Heart Fails Him." Life in the fast lane. Sometimes it catches up.

ANOTHER REVELATION

CAPE TOWN, SOUTH AFRICA

NOAH AND AYANDA met us for a cleansing hike up to the top of Table Mountain. Leila and Tess were impressed with my push to take the harder, steeper route. During the climb we focused only what was in front of us and what we could see by looking around, but once we reached the top we laid out the picnic gear and absorbed the spectacular vistas.

Ayanda asked, "Are we ever going to be privy to anything that has happened to you all in the past few weeks?"

I responded truthfully, "I'll tell you more about the who and the why when I can. Suffice it to say that we were able to resolve things in our favor. However, there's a fantastical story to tell you both. I have information on a recovered flash drive that explains Noah's background.

"Noah, you were part of an experiment. Your biological parents had no idea. In the 1970s a group in New York pulled this off with multiple sets of twins. The people behind the scheme intentionally placed twins in different families with different educational and economic circumstances to see what would happen. There's even an American documentary about it called *Three Identical Strangers*."

Noah stared at me wide-eyed. "What?"

Ayanda exclaimed, "So that was why they cared so much about what we did and what we made."

I nodded affirmation and continued the explanation. "The study done here in Cape Town was designed to replicate the New York group's work that was never published. It was terminated, though, about three months before Noah and the brother we know about were born. A government official caught wind of the study and cracked down. Before any of the families could be notified, yours included, the government official mysteriously disappeared. All the records disappeared as well.

"Fast-forward twenty-eight years. Noah's twin brother did not take the righteous path. Now he's dead. There's something else, though. The information references a third brother."

Everyone looked at me incredulously. "Yes—triplets. The three boys featured in the documentary knew nothing of each other's existence until two of them happened to meet serendipitously. The pair chose the same college to attend. The publicity from their reunion reached the attention of the third boy. It's a story too incredible to believe, but actually true. Noah, the South African adoption group who brought you to your parents must've been thrilled beyond belief when they were given the same opportunity the New York crew had."

Noah murmured, "I have another brother, I have another brother."

After the shock of the revelation sunk in, I pressed on. "Your third brother got placed with a well-to-do family in Pretoria. That's where the story goes cold. I've done everything I can to find out anything else about him. Even Axel, our hacking wizard, wasn't able to locate any more information, at least not yet. He's still working on it. But, and that's a big but . . . The person who provided this information would not be counted among the righteous. He suggested your other brother might also be part of a worldwide crime syndicate. Perhaps the two had found each other and were in league.

"Noah, I'm going to make an impossible request. For right now, do not act on what I've told you. Any effort you make could end up harming you or your family. Your dead brother knew about you and used it against you. We have to assume this third brother may be in the same position. The further this inquiry is from you, the better off you are."

The shock of what I had revealed and the nature of my warning made for an interesting day, to say the least. Fortunately, Leila's family understood the magnitude of the potential danger, and my request. They promised that any future discussion about the topic would remain entirely private. I also promised to keep them in the loop.

LEAVING

CAPE TOWN, SOUTH AFRICA

SOLOMON, KARINA, LEILA, TESS, AND I sat on our friends' luxurious back porch, holding glasses of Stellenbosch's finest wine. The course of events had prevented our planned trip to their vaunted wineries. That thwarted indulgence was top on the list when we returned. The going-away event they hosted had been a blowout. All of us were still recovering with a "hair of the dog."

Solomon didn't know details about what had happened, but he had a general idea. The OR adventure with Liran and the temporal link to the dead man outside the hospital had not escaped his attention. Slyly I asked him, "Last night was amazing. Is it okay that we stayed until the end of the party?"

Solomon said seriously, "No, VJ, that is where you are wrong. It is just the beginning. You never really escape South Africa. It's like dating the most beautiful, enchanting, psychotic woman. It's a constant challenge, but you can't completely walk away. You'll be back."

The analogy hit me in the face. I shuddered as I thought again about Petra. Absent that infatuation, though, there would be no Tess. Now I couldn't imagine a life that my daughter wasn't a part of. So there it was—risk and reward, South Africa in a nutshell.

Tess spoke up. "South Africa is such a rich place, so many textures. I love the people here, at least most of them. Dr. Sherako and I have been talking about how much work needs to be done. There's no question I'll be here again. Sooner rather than later. It'll at least be somewhat easier to get back to Cape Town from Israel."

Leila and I both looked at her quizzically. She had a Cheshire cat grin. "I've been talking to some people. No one there takes existence for granted. I understand that better. I'd like to explore the country. Fascinating cultures, history, lots of things to see and do that aren't necessarily medical. It works for me."

She and her new Mossad friends had clearly engaged in some serious conversations. With or without a slight nudge from them, I was certain Hadassah School of Medicine at Hebrew University in Jerusalem would permit her to finish her rotations. I suspected Tess would fare rather well in Israel. Her perspective on the world had morphed. Too much had happened to fall back into the day-to-day at Harvard Medical School. If the Israel Defense Forces or Mossad came knocking on her door, I wouldn't be surprised. With her intelligence and four newly acquired champions, it would be hard for her to fail. An additional plus was that having Tess in Israel would provide a good excuse for me to see my sister. That said, I was already missing the daughter I'd discovered and come to love so much.

THREE'S A CROWD

WASHINGTON, DISTRICT OF COLUMBIA

BACK IN THE UNITED STATES CAPITAL, the beautiful young man with the amazing smile glanced at himself in the mirror. Too bad there were only two of them now.

Josiah felt the loss of his brother Basil like the change in the Force in *Star Wars* when Obi-Wan Kenobi died. The brother he had never shared a day or even a word with. His mentors had made sure of it.

The Cape Town adoption agency thought it would be oh so curious to place him in an environment with well-placed U.S. diplomats desperate for an African child. They never knew his destiny was to be an actual Trojan horse. His family also never knew that he was one of three. He knew it; they couldn't. His mentors, forever in the background, made certain of every detail of his ascent.

Glovertown Prep, near the Washington National Cathedral, was the perfect place to connect with all the right families, partying notwithstanding. It was also a direct ticket to Yale for college and law school. There were a few indiscretions along the way. A girl or two left in his wake. Just speed bumps. Privilege had definite advantages.

Now, here he was, in his new job, clerking for a flawed Supreme Court justice. This one was married and had two darling children, but the judge was also a man with a penchant for forbidden fruit. The type that gets your ticket punched from the Garden of Eden into a place where so many want to make you their own girlfriend. He was a pillar of the community, and had been particularly skilled at keeping his secrets from everyone—everyone except Josiah's mentors.

Mikalyn de Grom, Josiah and the Russian Bratva controlled this pathetic creature. The list of players on the world stage with a desire to influence U.S. Supreme Court decisions was quite long. Josiah had the virtual keys to the throne and an agenda. He was going to be very difficult to stop. And he had definite plans for the innocent third brother in this odd set of Cape Town triplets.

RETURN TO SIERRA LAKES

SIERRA LAKES, CALIFORNIA

THE PLANE LANDED. I stepped out, took in the fresh mountain air, gazed at the majestic snow-glazed Sierras, and felt instant comfort. I was back, and absolutely no one seemed to be after me.

I was "baching" it again. Leila was visiting her parents in Atlanta. She owed them that. Eliza was back there as well. Leila and her niece were peas in a pod. Her brother had a load of impending international business travel. The three of them had come up with the plan for Eliza to stay with us for a time when we moved to Washington, D.C. With Tess in the Middle East, I thought Eliza would be a nice addition to the family. I passed it by Vika and Cat, and they gave it the paws-up.

Yet again, I was forced to take the always unpredictable flight to Sierra Lakes from Los Angeles. There was no choice. My LA-based truck had returned to the motor intensive care unit. One of my buddy's kids had been T-boned by some dimwit sexting his girlfriend instead of stopping at the red light. The fact that he had his manhood exposed during the accident turned out to be problematic. Replants in that area are more challenging than in the hand. Fortunately, the microsurgeons at USC are talented.

I opened the front door to the house, glanced at the newest water damage to the ceiling, hiked up the stairs, and promptly collapsed on the couch. About an hour later I woke up and decided to head over to the Rib Rattler for a drink and some food. I had no intention of going farther. Two minutes after I sat down, I spotted my buddy, Johan, the police chief. His cop spidey sense must have divined that I'd be there.

Johan sidled up beside me at the bar. "VJ, here you are. I just got back from a nice fishing trip with a friend who's an ex-cop from LA. He's a pretty sharp guy, not much to look at, but good people. I trust his instincts. We got to talking. He has his doubts about you. Lately when you show up, people disappear. I need to hear you speak the words. Say 'I, Erik Brio, had nothing to do with my friend going over the railing by the Conway Summit."

I wearily shook my head. "Johan, you don't know the half of it. I'm going to create a new problem for you. It wasn't Slobodan after all. By the way, Slobodan's not my friend, and currently he is extremely dead."

Johan interrupted, "Of course it was someone else, and of course Slobodan is apparently dead again; why would I expect anything different?"

"Johan, you're a funny man. Anyway, some innocent guy found himself in the wrong car with *definitely* the wrong person, got murdered, had his head cut off, and was substituted in that vehicle. Slobodan told me he was a transient the hit man picked up from I'm not sure where. I'll have to leave it to you and the new sheriff to figure out how to pursue that lead. I don't have a twenty on the hit man. For the record, his name is Miro. In the meantime, let me tell you about the little adventure we just had in South Africa."

He pulled out his cell. "I'm going to call Lorraine. It sounds like we're going to be here a while."

I nodded. "Tell her to join us for breakfast."

When I finished, Johan sat in silence for some time. Finally, he offered one word of advice. "Plastics."

I laughed out loud. "Funny you should say that. I just saw *The Graduate* again last night. I've watched it seven times. Brilliant film. I never have figured out how things were supposed to go for Benjamin and Elaine. My guess is that it was complicated."

Johan took a long pull on his lager. "You mean sort of like everything you find yourself in the middle of?" He took something out of his pocket and put it on the table. It was a deformed bullet from my .17 HMR. One of several I'd used to kill the two assassins an eternity ago.

"Johnny over at the incinerator found it and hung on to it. For some reason he finally decided to give it to me. But I have no use for it. I thought you'd want it, though. It might have some sentimental value." Johan gave me a sly wink and got up to walk away. He turned and said, "Dinner tomorrow?"

I just sat there for a few minutes and contemplated what a life this had become.

A COMPANY OFFER

BOSTON, MASSACHUSETTS

WALKING BACK to our town house after my return to Boston, I felt strange being on the streets of the city again. It felt too normal. Two familiar faces came around the corner. They stopped as if they were waiting for me. Initially, I couldn't place them. Then the light went on. Our friends from the customs line at the Johannesburg airport and the fabulous restaurant, Javier and Amanda.

"Dr. Brio, how are you?" Amanda exclaimed. "So wonderful to see you again! Did you enjoy your stay in South Africa? Do you have a minute to talk?"

My antennae immediately went up. I studied each of them. Their demeanor was not that of the newlyweds we had met, set for an adventure in the wild. They were serious in a way that told me it would be a good idea to indulge them. I couldn't imagine that they were Russian agents or part of the Foundation or whomever Slobodan said was backing them, but there was always that possibility, and I stayed on guard.

I said, "Funny to see you here in Boston. I'm getting the feeling that you weren't in South Africa on your honeymoon, and our meeting wasn't entirely an accident. Now, if you need a hand consultation, it would be better if we did it in my office. You have to do all the paperwork first. I'm not even allowed to think about your medical problems unless you do that. Never let good medical care get in the way of the almighty efficiency-killing electronic medical record system. Sorry, I had to get that out. So what *can* I do for you two?"

Amanda said, "Dr. Brio, you are entertaining. The crazy thing is that I do have this finger that sticks in the morning after I play a round of golf. I suppose we'll have to get to that later. No, we want to talk to about something entirely different. That was quite a show you put on in Cape Town."

I looked at her, trying to mask my genuine surprise. She went on. "What, did you think all that was going to go unnoticed? We've had our eyes on Slobodan, his brother, Matija, and the Foundation for some time. He was a pretty slick operator. When you got to be chums and took him to Sierra Lakes, we wondered if you'd crossed to the dark side. When he *died* there, we were even more curious. Figured maybe you had just won an internal power struggle. This was all speculation, of course, but as you know, not every lead is always a good one. When you left your computer on the plane in Zurich, it gave us a chance to see what you were up to. Some of those pictures of mangled limbs are pretty disgusting. As you might have guessed, there wasn't anything incriminating. If we were looking for a mass murderer, though, we might have had a problem.

"Our associate, Samuel Benjamin, was already in place at Onderskeid to monitor what the Foundation director was up to. Then you and Tess happened on the scene. That certainly made the job of tagging you easier."

Javier continued the story. "The diamonds for arms/cash/heroin deal was a new expansion of Slobodan's interests. You and your team put everything together. What you did was pretty ballsy. I was extremely curious how you brought in Mossad. That was an amazing feat. Then we did a little more digging. Mark Wildstein is a good man. I hope he treats your sister well. At the Agency we admire that type of careful planning and execution. You and Mossad took care of a couple of major headaches for us. It was not unnoticed by our own director. She wants to have a chat with you when you're ready."

I flinched. He just smiled and continued, "I see that look of concern on your face. Not to worry, she's an admirer. No one is going to say anything about you, your family, and friends knocking off a drug lord and most of his gang, or that you made off with millions in cash and diamonds that you turned over to the hospital. Who would we tell? Certainly no one here. What do you say, VJ—that's what they call you, right? Viking Jew, crazy nickname. I like it, though. It suits you."

Javier handed me a card. "Here's the contact information. We are interested in Leila and Tess too, but for the moment, let's keep this conversation between us kids, at least until you meet the director. Perhaps then we can all share a nice reunion. There's a health policy fellowship there for the taking if you'd like it. It would be a pleasure to have you closer to Langley."

I heard what they said and contemplated my response. I decided to keep it simple. "By the way, do you two have real names?"

Amanda spoke up. "Well, I've always liked the name Amanda. You can still call me that." Pointing to her colleague, she added, "And to me, he looks like a Javier. Let's stick with that too."

I just shook my head. Why should I expect anything but obfuscation from the CIA? After we turned to go our separate ways, Amanda started to laugh. "VJ, there is another small detail I forgot to mention. That movie about your experience at MRMC that your Swedish friend was planning—not going to happen.

Sorry, maybe thirty years from now. Depending what happens with all of us, maybe not even then. Agency policy."

I answered, "I guess I would have assumed as much. You two have a wonderful day."

It would have been too much to hope that no one in the intelligence community outside of Israel had keyed in to what had transpired. While we were in South Africa doing what we were doing, it was an alternate universe for me. The gangs and corruption in the country kept the harsh glare of sunlight off our enterprise. I thought again about the Swedish movie pitch. This latest adventure would make a great sequel. Too bad it was a story that could never be told.

I realized what we perceive as everyday "reality" is only a rough facsimile of what is actually happening. We are being observed or judged by any number of people at any given time, contingent on whom we interface with. As soon as I crossed paths with Slobodan, there was a radar lock on me. The intelligence world plays games and fights battles that few are privy to understand. Depending on the whims of the individual puppet masters, the globe bends one way or another. We are not quite the tiny marble world balanced in the hands of the aliens suggested by the conclusion of *Men in Black*. But not so far from that, either. Navigation of the orthopaedic milieu, where people do incomprehensible things to themselves every day, is far more straightforward.

My experiences with Petra and then with Slobodan were painfully illuminating. I had engaged in struggles on a micro level. I knew I could now easily get sucked into something on a much grander scale. The question was, what exactly was going to follow? I didn't know how Leila would react. Necessity had dictated my life. Now here I was, being courted by the spooks. I tried to think of myself as they saw me. The two portraits were incongruent. Like Tess, I was conflicted with who I thought I was and who I actually was. To find the answer, we would both have to continue to search within ourselves.

EXTRA INNINGS

BOSTON, MASSACHUSETTS

MIKALYN DE GROM continued to check her phone for a response. The Bratva was none too pleased with the loss of heroin and diamonds in Cape Town.

Fortunately for her, the fallout was limited to those most closely associated with Red Mountain Pharmaceuticals. She narrowly escaped the pogrom that followed. Now more than ever, she wanted to maintain a low profile. Gwinevere was a casualty of the deck reshuffling. What had happened to her was not pretty. De Grom had heard the word "dismemberment" bandied about. As expected, Miro was not part of the purge. Individuals with his talents were harder to replace.

There was no direct evidence, but de Grom strongly believed that Brio had yet again managed to cripple if not destroy a powerful syndicate. The man was an absolute menace. Her desire to crush him was visceral, almost overwhelming. The woman she had tailing him reported back the unwelcome news. Now, sud-

denly, she was forced to call off Miro. Her text to him was simple:
Brio CIA. Stop now!

She muttered to herself, "We're not done yet, my friend." High heels clicking as she crossed her office on the hardwood floors, she opened the door for her waiting confederate. It was a man with a beautiful smile. "Hello, Josiah, we have much to discuss . . ."

THE BEAT GOES ON

BUTEMBO, DRC

ON THE OUTSKIRTS OF BUTEMBO, a city of nearly a million about thirty-five miles from Beni in the eastern DRC, Victor Kalenga peered through the curtains at those annoying health workers. They seemed to be everywhere.

His friend had mentioned they would be coming. Something about a ring vaccination for Ebola virus. Victor knew this was just another ruse. There was no way he was going to let any of those people near him. Who knew what lies they were peddling? It didn't matter. He was traveling to Uganda the next day to see his connection. Then, in less than seventy-two hours he would be on his way to Washington, D.C. There, a huge party was planned for his arrival.

As he walked into the bathroom he glanced at the mirror. He realized he'd have to go to the store to get some medicine. He was coughing and needed drops for his red eyes. He said to himself, "Probably just a bad cold."

THE END—FOR NOW

ACKNOWLEDGMENTS

Once again I would like to thank the love of my life, Ellen, for encouraging me to complete this novel and allowing me to move to the next. Fortunately, I still have a day job to pay the bills. Our children, Erika, Jess, and Ben, continued to provide fresh insight about plot twists and human behavior for those under thirty-five. Jessica's marketing ideas should also put many dollars in the hands of the fine people at Doctors Without Borders.

I would like to recognize my siblings Linda, Beth, and Andy for who they are and what they do every day to make the world a better place. My father, Leonard Brown, authority on all things, was a great sounding board during our weekly breakfasts. I particularly appreciated the ideas provided by Caroline Morse.

Linda Brown, Nancy Glaser, Sharon Reich, and Len Gregory, along with Drs. Gina Magit and Diego Mirales, spent countless hours reviewing the manuscript, contributing ideas, and lending moral support. They are each magnificent people. If I ask them to do it again, I worry for my life. Then again, who knows, that may be the plot line for *Scalpel's Mark: No Secrets*. Thank you!

ACKNOWLEDGMENTS

Erika Brown, Ben Brown, David Sherako, and Jan Hudson examined the earlier "finished" book and provided numerous, valuable ideas, then it was back to the drawing board for me. I know the book is vastly improved now. Each of you are wonderful!

Dan Lingman and Ron Mattson have both served their country with great distinction and provided significant insight and assistance with this book. You two are the best!

Two specific scientists added to my understanding of the Ebola virus and treatment protocols. They preferred anonymity. Thank you both!

I would like to extend my sincere appreciation to the physical/occupational therapy and office staff at Torrey Pines Orthopaedics. Office flow was constantly interrupted with plot or sentence questions that they enthusiastically tackled for me. They are great!

The OR/PACU and office staff at Mammoth Hospital are truly amazing. I described just a few of their exploits in the pages you read. Jason Lakey, Sandra Bowman, Bart White, Jim Barnes, and Dr. Peter Clark are the real deal. Were it only true that I could match even a small percentage of what they accomplish every day. They do the things that we watch on YouTube and ask how anyone can do that. Their contributions to this book cannot be underestimated.

Thank you again to Walter Bode, Phyllis DeBlanche, and Anna Knighton for their Herculean editing skills. They, like my friends, have to brace themselves for round three.

The exercise of writing a book, particularly a self-published one, is a vanity endeavor. I took several liberties on the back cover. The nickname in Russian for Nikolai is Kolya. *Y* is the initial for Yossarian, the protagonist from my favorite book, *Catch-22*. Sobaka means "dog" in Russian. Nikolai Yossarian Sobaka is the complete name of our eleven-year-old Australian shepherd. Muzz is the nickname we gave to our Australian shepherd puppy, Vika. She wiggles her butt constantly when she is excited, hence the moniker W. B. Muzz. Rachel L. Carson was a pioneering environmental activist, and Rachel P. (Pickles) Carson is our epidemiologist daughter's cat. Through my interactions with this trio of devoted animals, I divined what they thought about *Scalpel's Plunge: End of the Party* and documented it for them. Hopefully you the reader will share their positive opinions.

Early in this book I referenced a quotation from Admiral Hyman Rickover. The words were taken from a chapter in the extremely compelling *Sailing True North: Ten Admirals and the Voyage of Character* by James G. Stavridis. I recommend this work to one and all.

Thank you to those of you who made it this far. The ride will start again in a few years.

Best to all!

Richard A. Brown

Made in the USA
Columbia, SC
01 June 2022